I0600935

Rajani Chronicles II
Resistance

Brian S. Converse

Copyright 2018 by Brian S. Converse

This is a work of fiction. All characters in this publication
are ficticious and any resemblence to real persons, living
or dead, is purely coincidental.

ISBN: 978-0-9987964-5-1

Cover Art by
Lawrence Mann
www.lawrencemann.co/uk

For LAZDE
Always

Thank you to all who contributed in some way to the
publication of this book, including
my excellent editor, Melissa.

I'm eternally grateful.

Thanks, mom.

Recap

James Dempsey was a Detroit Police Lieutenant until he inexplicably awoke aboard an alien spacecraft. He and four other humans, Yvette, Gianni, Rick, and Kieren, learned they had been kidnapped by a group of Rajani who were fleeing their home planet. Rajan had been invaded by intergalactic pirates known as the Krahn Hoard. The Rajani pleaded for assistance in ridding their world of the Krahn invaders, offering in return a gift beyond measure: objects that, when implanted into their hosts, gave them incredible powers.

In dire need of training in the use of these powers, the Rajani ship, the Tukuli, stopped at a space station in search of someone who could build a training area aboard the ship. The station offered its own dangers, though, in the form of the Alliance Society for Peace, the police force of the Galactic Alliance. Led on the station by Ries an na Van, the ASPs would immediately jail the Rajani if they were discovered.

Amidst the new experiences and dangers, James and Yvette allowed their attraction for each other to become a fierce romance. Loners by choice and chance, the two humans were surprised and happy to find someone while so far from home.

With a daring escape from the station and the ASPs,

the Tukuli made its way toward Rajan, only to be shot down over the planet's surface by the Krahn Hoard's enormous mothership. The humans abandoned ship, separated into escape pods, while the Rajani crew stayed aboard in hopes of steering the ship away from the capital city of Melaanse.

Now they must hope they can find their friends on the surface of planet, as well as any type of Resistance from the Rajani population...

Prologue

Bhakat raced down the corridor, hoping for enough time to reach the bridge and persuade Rauphangelaa to run to an escape pod. Or carry him, if that's what it took to get him off the dying *Tukuli*.

He came to the door and pushed the open button as the ship shuddered violently. It felt like one of the engines had either stopped or dropped off, and the floor began to tilt slightly as the door opened and he pulled himself through.

Rauph was sitting in Janan's usual seat, pulling the steering yoke, and under incredible strain, from the looks of things. He didn't turn when Bhakat screamed his name.

"Rauphangelaa, we need to get off the ship!"

"We can't let it crash into the city!" Rauph yelled back, still fighting with the controls.

Bhakat carefully made his way to where his Master sat, walking clumsily across the tilted floor.

"Help me keep her up," Rauph grunted.

Bhakat reached for the controls, working along with Rauph to pull it back. The viewscreen showed them moving lower over the city, and then the wide expanse of the ocean beyond. It was going to be close.

The two Rajani pulled as one, keeping the nose of the ship

as straight as they could. Within seconds, the last building was past the viewscreen, and they had an uninterrupted view of the vast ocean.

"Strap into a chair," Rauph shouted. "Let go!"

Reluctantly, Bhakat let go of the yoke and crawled toward the captain's chair behind them. His arms felt like dead weight at his sides. He made it to the chair and climbed up into it, fastening the crash belts.

"Hold on!" was the last thing Bhakat heard before the jarring impact told him that they had hit something.

Chapter 1

Alliance Society for Peace Commander Ries an na Van, Chief Protector of Sector 7, Subsector 2, which included the Mandakan Solar System, could not have found himself in more trouble if he tried. Not only had his own ship, the *Interceptor,* been disabled by a fugitive Rajani starship named the *Tukuli,* but the *Waverider,* the ship he had dispatched to Sector 9, Subsector 3, otherwise known as the Rajani System, had also been disabled and set adrift in space by the same fugitive starship.

Now Commander Thydosh Complin of the *Waverider* was attempting to pass off his failure onto Ries, claiming Ries hadn't properly informed him of the *Tukuli's* weapons' capabilities. In response, the Alliance Society for Peace Central Command had recalled the *Interceptor* and all of its crew to the seat of the Alliance and were planning a full investigation into the events that led up to the *Waverider's* disablement.

This meant Ries would be under close scrutiny from his superiors. It was attention he couldn't afford. He needed to generate a defense for his failure with the Rajani ship, or he could be looking at a loss of his command. He could possibly even face jail time, if the High Command discovered some of his less-than-legal activities aboard the Mandakan Space Port, where he was currently stationed. He oversaw all commerce on the port, both legal and illegal, and had allowed both, as long as he received his proper cut of the profits.

He didn't know anything about the Rajani, outside of the usual stories every child in the Alliance was told while growing up. The Rajani were supposed to be hulking monsters; ruthless killing machines who showed no mercy, whether their victims were male, female, offspring, or eggs. Their bloodlust and despicable deeds were told to frighten children into behaving from one end of the Alliance to the other. His mother had been more practical in her tactics when it came to punishing misbehaving young ones. You behaved or you were eaten. It was simple, but a very effective deterrent.

Ries wanted to know more about the Rajani. He wanted to know the truth about them, and about how they could have disabled his ship without using any known weapons. This was why he found himself sitting at the large desk in his quarters aboard the *Interceptor* and logged into his ship's central computer via his cranial implant. He'd been ordered to dock the *Interceptor* at the Gorplash Space Station, orbiting the planet Asnuria, seat of the Alliance Society for Peace Central Command. He and his crew were to be confined to the ship until his superiors finished their investigation and decided whether or not to levy any punishment.

Ries closed his eyes and cleared his mind, seeing the Galactic Alliance shield before his eyes. He opened his eyes once more, still seeing the shield in front of him, as if it were projected on the bare wall instead of only in his mind. His cranial implant was networked into the vision and hearing centers of his brain.

"Begin search," he said in Talondarian Standard, though

if he wanted, he could have thought the command. He was still a bit old-fashioned when it came to technology, and liked to feel as if he were having a quiet conversation with the central computer. It gave him a sense of autonomy, at least, instead of feeling like he was only a small hardware component in the central computer's network.

"Command acknowledged," the *Interceptor's* central computer said, though there was actually no sound heard in the room. This query was private. "Awaiting search parameters," the computer continued.

"Rajani species overview," he said, after thinking about where to begin. Best to start at the beginning if he really wanted a thorough understanding of the subject.

Everything Ries did was thorough. After a brief instant, a scroll of files began to appear on the wall in front of him. When it stopped, he picked one that looked promising and told the computer to read it aloud.

"The Rajani species was discovered in the Talondarian Standard year 10563," the computer began. "The Rajani were admitted to the Galactic Alliance in Talondarian Standard year 10574. In 10591, began interstellar offensive against Planet A472, a planet in Sector 9, Subsector 4. Completed offensive in 10592. In 10594, began offensive against Planet A463, a planet in—"

"Stop," Ries said. He had a feeling that he'd be there all day if he let the computer list the complete history of Rajani aggression toward other planets. "Refine search. No need to list all of their conquests. Tell me about their civilization."

"Rajan. See Planet A490."

"Proceed," Ries said, taking a drink of kolan, a beverage he had received as a gift from the King of Mandaka himself, for his service to the planet. It was one of the main exports of Mandaka, and in high demand around the Alliance. His personal stores were worth a considerable amount.

"Classified, Level 7K4. Access denied. Inquiry logged," the computer responded.

Strange, Ries thought. Why would information about the planet Rajan be classified at the highest level of Alliance security? "Computer, tell me of Rajani history."

"Rajan was discovered in the year—" the computer began.

"I told you to skip that part," Ries said, beginning to get angry. If he didn't know any better, he'd think the central computer was being deliberately obtuse. But for what purpose?

"Input parameters of search request," the computer said.

"Tell me about the current Rajani society," he said, trying to stay calm.

"Rajan. See Planet A2242," the computer said.

"What?" Ries asked, confused. Why did the planet have two Alliance Designation Numbers? Was it even possible, or had some administrative underling input a wrong number?

"Rajan. See Planet A2242," the computer responded again, thinking he hadn't heard its initial response.

"Be quiet while I think for a moment," he told the computer, irritably. He took a large mouthful of kolan and swallowed it, feeling a tingle pass up his antennae. Finally, it occurred to him. There were two Designation Numbers, because there were two different planets. It was the only answer that made sense. The Alliance was an enormous bureaucracy, and any administrative clerk had two or three other admin personnel checking their work. Something as important as an Alliance Designation Number wouldn't stay incorrect for long.

"Computer, access files for Planet A2242. Specifically the history of the planet as it concerns the Rajani."

"See Ruvedalin Initiative," the computer answered.

"Proceed," Ries said. He was starting to regret even taking an interest in the Rajani. They could all dry up and die as far as he was concerned. Sometimes he hated his own curious nature; it had gotten him in trouble many times.

"Classified to Level 7K4. Access denied. Inquiry logged. Warning, security violation detected. Authorities have been notified, per Directive 9WQ2."

"Blast!" Ries yelled, pounding three of his fists on his desktop and shutting off his cranial link with his other hand. He stood up and paced for a minute, his antennae twitching in disgust and frustration.

The ship's central computer spoke over his room's communication system. "Security breach reported. Violation of Alliance Code T567. Commander Ries an na Van, you are hereby placed under house arrest and relieved of your duties until further notice. Please comply."

"What?" he asked, incredulously. "I didn't do anything wrong. Computer? Computer, acknowledge." There was no answer. He sat at his desk and touched the button below his earhole that activated his cranial implant.

Lines of text appeared on the wall before him, in front of the Alliance Society for Peace crest. It was the same text as the proclamation just made by the *Interceptor's* central computer. "Computer? Computer!" He gave up and turned off the implant in disgust, knowing he had been disconnected on purpose. He'd been wrong in his earlier assessment of his situation. He could be in more trouble.

◊

Tumaani tuc Afraati was enjoying a late dinner with three of his mates when the Krahn attacked. His oldest offspring were no longer younglings, having left his estate and started families of their own. His youngest were now

Pledged to other Elders' Houses, as was the tradition, so only he and his mates and a few servants were now living on his large estate.

The sound of explosions and weapons being fired suddenly sounded throughout his house. Tumaani stood and looked out the window, seeing small ships firing at the buildings of his estate from the air. Many of the buildings were already burning, with thick, black smoke billowing up from their windows.

"Tumaani, what is it?" asked his third mate, Narven, wide-eyed. She was the youngest of his mates, and prone to excitability.

"I don't know who they are," Tumaani said. "Rulina," he yelled at his second mate, as he saw a building explode just next to his house through one of the windows. "Get everyone downstairs to the basement. Quickly!" He ducked as another nearby explosion shook the house. "Zanth," he yelled at a Sekani servant, "make sure all of the doors are locked, and then join them in the shelter."

He headed down a short hallway to his estate's computer system and quickly began implementing security protocols to the central computer located in downtown Melaanse. As Keeper of the Past, it was his duty to both keep his species' history chronicled completely, and also to ensure any sensitive information didn't fall into the possession of outsiders. Especially when those outsiders were currently attacking his planet.

He didn't know at the time who was attacking, only that they weren't from Rajan. Rajan had no weapons, so they must have come from off-planet. He had just locked down the last file when he saw a broad-sent message notification flashing on his computer screen. He pushed the button, opening the message, and saw it was from the Keeper of the

Stones, Rauphangelaa. The message stated Rauphangelaa had escaped on his ship, the *Tukuli,* and would do what he could to bring back help.

He heard another explosion just outside his front door and saw black smoke billowing down the hallway toward him. His house was on fire. He needed to make sure everyone had escaped safely to the basement shelter. There was the sound of running feet, and dark, armored figures approached through the smoke. Tumaani turned to run away from the hissing monsters but was hit on the head and knocked unconscious by the force of the blow.

◊

When Tumaani woke up, he found himself lying on the ground, covered by a blanket, and looking up at a torn and dirty canvas, some eight feet over him. He was in a tent. By the quality of the light, he could tell it was either late afternoon or early morning.

His head ached, and he thought he was going to be physically ill if he moved, so he lay there for a moment, until it occurred to him his head was cold. It was a sensation he had not felt in many years; not since the time he had become an Elder. He sat up slowly, reaching a tentative hand up to his head, afraid of what he'd find. It was bare. Shaved. His Ralik was gone. All that was left were a few wisps of hair missed by whatever had been used to shave his scalp. He leaned over, his eyes filling with tears.

He cried silently, afraid to make a sound, not wanting to alert his captors to the fact he was awake. The flap of his tent opened suddenly, and he backed away quickly, wiping away tears as he did so, unable to see more than a dark silhouette filling the doorway.

"Tumaani?" a voice asked softly. "Tumaani, it's me."

Tumaani sobbed in relief at the sound of his second

mate's voice. It was Rulina. She had made it out of his house alive. Soon she was in his embrace as they cried together. After a moment, she pulled back from him.

"Rulina, who has done this? Who attacked us? Where are the others?"

"The Krahn," she answered, wiping her eyes with the sleeve of her clothing. "The Krahn are responsible for this. I haven't seen anyone else since they took us. Zanth and a few others escaped, but most of us were captured when we left the basement shelter."

"Krahn?" he asked. "But why?"

"No one seems to know," she responded. "The Krahn haven't done anything except lock us up in the old prison."

"We're in the prison?" he asked, confused.

"The courtyard," she said. "They ran out of cells for all of us. It's horrible, Tumaani. They have so many of us packed in here, and there's no food or water. No medicine for the sick and injured. Some have already died from their wounds. It's been two days since the attacks began."

"I must speak with the other Elders," he said, beginning to stand.

"It's not allowed," she said, placing a restraining hand on his chest. "They're keeping all of the Elders separated. They said any Elders who are caught talking to each other will be killed immediately."

Tumaani paused and then stood up. "I have to see." He helped her to stand as well, and, together, they walked out of the tent and into the sunlight. What he saw made his stomach lurch, leaving him sure he would vomit or begin to cry again, though he wasn't sure which. He stopped just outside his tent to look around. There were hundreds, maybe thousands, of Rajani filling the courtyard of the prison.

Some had small tents similar to what he had woken up

in, or shelters improvised from pieces of clothing, but most either stood or sat in large groups. He could also see some were bandaged, and some looked like they had succumbed to their wounds and had been left where they'd died. He couldn't remember ever seeing so many Rajani gathered in one place before. If what Rulina said was true, there were many more locked in cells within the interior of the prison. He could also see some of the males were shaved bald, as he was. They must be fellow Priests, he thought.

The Krahn had attempted to take away all symbols of leadership, like his Ralik, the large braid of hair that symbolized a Priest of the Kha. All Elders were Priests, though not all Priests became Elders. The Elder Council was very selective when it came to membership. Tumaani saw Krahn warriors patrolling the high walls of the prison, their weapons pointed down at the mass numbers of Rajani below. He had heard of the Krahn, but had never seen a picture of them. They were an ugly species, all teeth, claws, and scales. He could see some wore slipshod, ill-fitting armor that looked pieced together. Others wore thick clothing under bandoliers of ammunition. They were dressed for the cooler spring Rajani weather.

He looked over at Rulina, who had a worried look on her face. "It will be fine," he finally said, placing his hands on her shoulders. "We'll get through this, somehow, I promise." He hoped with all of his heart his words were true.

◊

It had been three days since Ries had been arrested aboard the *Interceptor* and confined to his quarters. He'd been given meals four times a day, as was his custom, but had heard no news, and he was out of kolan. He didn't know which one irritated him the most. His lieutenant refused to speak to him, and the officers who brought his food had looked terrified at the prospect of telling him anything. They must have been given a briefing by someone high up in command for them to be so afraid to answer even the most simple of questions.

Finally, his door chime sounded, and he waited expectantly for whomever it was to open the door. When the door opened, he saw that it was an Asnurian. He was wearing the rank of First Admiral, the second highest rank achievable in the Alliance Society for Peace. Ries stood and saluted smartly with his top left arm, dreading what was to come and suspecting it wouldn't be good. He'd spent hours thinking about what would happen to him. He was well aware the Alliance Society for Peace was not a forgiving organization. Although the Alliance didn't have a death penalty for crimes, the ASPs did, and had the authority to carry out punishment without Alliance review.

The Asnurian returned the salute and sat down in a chair across from Ries's desk. "As you were," he said in Talondarian Standard after a moment. Reis was afraid to show any signs of disgust at the Asnurian's odor, which was foul, due to a religious belief held by the Asnurians that forbade bathing. Now was not the time for putting on airs of hygienic superiority.

"I assume you know why I'm here?" the Asnurian asked without preamble, his blackened teeth sitting like diseased tree stumps inside his mouth, forcing Ries to look away as he spoke. The worse off the Asnurians were physically, the more highly regarded they were in their society.

"Sir, we had no warning the Rajani ship was armed," Ries said. "Our complete scan of their ship picked up no signs of weapons. Even when I warned Commander Complin of the danger the ship posed, he failed to take the appropriate security measures when he confronted the ship—"

"I've read the reports," the Asnurian said, interrupting him. "Both his and yours. That is not why I'm here." He let this fact sink in before continuing. "I'm here because of your attempts to gain access to classified Alliance files."

"I swear, I didn't know they were classified until my ship's computer told me," Ries said. "I was only attempting to research the Rajani to discern their capabilities in disabling a ship, as they did mine and the *Waverider*. Especially when the two ships were disabled in entirely different manners. I assure you—"

"I don't want your assurances, Commander," the Asnurian said. "I want to know why one of my subordinates was sticking his antennae where they don't belong."

"I told you," Ries said, almost gagging from the smell emanating from the Asnurian. "I was only attempting to investigate—"

"Enough," the Asnurian said, standing up and beginning to pace in front of the desk. "Now, normally, you would have simply disappeared on your way to your court martial, saving us all time and money. It would have been a simple solution, and one I would have preferred."

Reis felt his hearts sink at the admiral's words. He had hoped there would at least be a trial, where he could plead his case and throw himself on the mercy of the ASP court. Now it didn't look like it would ever happen.

The admiral sighed before continuing on. "But, my nephew Shinto tells me he owes you his life. So, effective immediately, you are transferred to Asnuria Central Command. All holdings on Mandaka are hereby forfeit. You are demoted to Administrative Specialist. You report tomorrow to Commander Jando Kan. Is this understood?"

"Yes, sir," Ries said, stunned by the turn of events. He would live, but his houses, his bank accounts—all would be gone. It had taken him years to amass what the Asnurian had taken away in mere seconds, but Ries had always been a survivor. As long as he still lived, he could always earn or steal more.

"Good," the Asnurian said. "Then you'd better hope I've buried you deep enough that Galactic Intelligence doesn't dig you back up. I don't think I need to tell you what would happen then."

"Thank you, sir," Ries said, standing and saluting. He definitely did not want a visit from GI. He really would disappear then, as he knew very well.

The Asnurian returned the salute. "As far as I'm concerned, my family's life debt is repaid. I wish you luck." He turned and left quickly, leaving Ries standing behind his desk in silence.

◊

Tumaani had been in the Krahn prison camp for five days when the announcement was made over the prison's intercom system. There would be a briefing by the Krahn soon. The Krahn had steadily been adding captured Rajani to the prison's population, and the courtyard was now very crowded. He'd been pleased to find four of his five mates had survived. The missing one, his fourth, had not yet been found amidst the sprawling population of the prison, but he hoped she would be discovered safe soon. He'd also met up with the two sons of the Elder named Delataan, and learned the Keeper of the Promise had been killed on the first night of the attack. Maska and Torile were still only younglings, though they were old enough to Pledge to a House if they chose.

"What do you think it will be about?" Maska asked. "Will they let us go?"

"Of course they won't let us go," Torile said. "Don't be dense."

"We won't have long to wait," Tumaani said, seeing a handful of Krahn warriors enter the courtyard, carrying a square piece of wood about two standard feet tall and six feet on each side. They placed it against the wall of the prison and then surrounded it, pointing their weapons toward the crowd of Rajani. Another Krahn, this one dressed somewhat more elaborately than the other warriors, entered the courtyard and climbed aboard the piece of wood. He held a large translating device in his hands and placed it on the makeshift stage before addressing the crowd.

"For security purposes, we must separate all Rajani males over the age of twenty Talondarian Standard years from the rest of the populace," the Krahn announced to the gathered crowd of captives, his voice translated to Talondarian Standard by the device in front of him. "We've run out of space to safely house all of you, so we must send some of you to another holding facility to ensure overcrowding does not result in a breakout of sickness amongst your members.

"You can understand our concern, yes?" the Krahn continued. "All Rajani males over the age of twenty Talondarian Standard years, please stay in the middle of the courtyard. All other Rajani, please exit the security enclosure in an orderly manner. You are to be processed by our attendants. I can assure you, you will be reunited when our time here is finished."

Some of the Rajani females and young ones were starting to exit out of the enclosure already, herded along by armed Krahn guards. A few of the females were holding their mates, weeping and hysterical. One of the male Rajani turned and struck the Krahn guard who was attempting to separate him from his mate. Another guard stepped in and hit the Rajani in the head with the butt of his gun. The Rajani dropped to the ground, blood streaming down his face from a cut on his forehead. Another Rajani male, this one with a bandage already covering one of his eyes, attempted to wrestle away the Krahn's weapon. He was surrounded by a group of Krahn guards and beaten down to the ground with their weapons and fists. The first Rajani male screamed as his mate and offspring were ushered out, crying and calling his name. This caught Tumaani's ear. He knew who the Rajani was, another Elder named Welemaan.

The Krahn who had been speaking to the crowd clicked off the machine in front of him and spoke to one of the armed Krahn, who was standing near the dais. "Give the males enough food to keep them calm. We don't want them too unhappy."

"The females and young?" the guard asked.

"Take them to the field we prepared," the Krahn replied. "Get it done quickly and quietly."

"Yes, sir," the guard replied with a salute. He turned to carry out his orders.

◊

Dreben had been in charge of the farm for almost thirty years. He'd been hired when he was still a young Rajani; unsure about what he wanted to do with his life. Because the Rajani were mostly self-sufficient, there were numerous endeavors available for someone who had already decided he didn't want to be a Priest of the Kha. Which also meant he would never be chosen for the Elder Council, he knew. However, because life on Rajan was rather simple and plain, there weren't many endeavors Dreben found interesting. There were manufacturing jobs making everything from clothing, to furniture, to the simple ground transport vehicles used by most Rajani. There were medical fields and dentistry. There was maintenance, where he could repair city infrastructure, such as roads, parks, bridges, or buildings.

There were no new buildings being built, though. The architecture was from thousands of years before, when the Rajani had built fantastic spires and tall buildings that touched the sky; but most of those buildings had been modified to fit the modern needs of the Rajani; dwelling areas, prayer centers for the Priests and their Pledges, manufacturing facilities, and medical suites were now the norm, with very little upkeep needed. There were food industries; merdin hunting off the coast of Melaanse, farms used to raise pulko, an animal grown for its meat, and farms and orchards providing the plants used as food for the Rajani, Sekani, and Jirina. There were also the turvien farms producing a small, hard fruit fermented to create the drink known as fernta.

Dreben had found he couldn't stomach working on a merdin vessel, the pulko were disgusting to raise, and the turvien farms hired almost exclusively Sekani and Jirina workers. It seemed Rajani did not possess the needed craftsmanship to brew the drink correctly, or so it was rumored. He finally found something he enjoyed when he was hired as a farmhand at one of the largest farms on Rajan. He'd slowly but steadily risen in the ranks until he'd been placed in charge of the large orchard next to the farm. A few years later, his boss and owner of the farm and orchard, Nebraani, had promoted him to Chief Farmhand, when the old one had died unexpectedly.

Dreben had been in charge of the farm and orchard's operations ever since. He'd been saddened when Nebraani had died, but he'd known the boss's son, Tavien, since he was still a youngling, and when Tavien had taken over for his father after becoming a Priest of the Kha, Dreben had been proud to stay on as Chief Farmhand. Tavien, by that time, had changed his name, as was the custom when becoming a Priest of the Kha. When Tavien, who now went by the name of Rauphangelaa, had journeyed out to visit the farm and give him orders for the coming planting season, Dreben had started preparing, as usual. But then, shortly after Rauphangelaa and his Pledge, Bhakat, left, word came that Melaanse was under attack. All communications had ceased from the city.

Dreben had sent a couple of his farmhands into the city to see what had happened, but they never returned. Dreben was afraid to send anyone else for fear of the same result. Meanwhile, he had farmhands coming to him daily, asking if he'd heard anything, to which he had to truthfully answer 'no.' Dreben knew his duty. He knew how important the food he grew was to the occupants of the city. Until he heard otherwise, he would follow Rauphangelaa's orders and plant what he'd been told to plant. At least it kept everyone too busy to think about what may very well be happening in the city. He only hoped Rauphangelaa would come back soon, or at least send word.

Chapter 2

Administrative Specialist Ries an na Van, Chief Protector of Paperwork, and any other mundane task his superior officers wanted to give him, was in a foul mood, even by his standards. He'd reported for duty, as ordered, and had been shuffling duties such as payment reimbursements and payroll inquiries ever since. He supposed his punishment could have been worse; he could've ended up facedown at the bottom of a garbage chute or ejected into deep space. It was still difficult to adjust to a new life on a new planet, especially when the planet's population was so disgustingly dirty. At least there weren't many Asnurians working in the headquarters building itself.

It was all the fault of that blasted Rajani starship, the *Tukuli*. *They were probably responsible for the riot on the Mandakan Space Port as well,* he thought glumly. *No, too much of a coincidence.* He knew for a fact the riot had been caused by a rogue Xerbian, a large creature with a nasty disposition, who had attacked his officers without provocation in the middle of the port's congested main concourse. It happened sometimes; the ASPs were not the most popular organization in the Alliance.

Besides blaming the Rajani for all of his present woes,

he was also curious about what he had almost discovered about the two Rajani planets. His security clearance aboard the *Interceptor* had been high enough for him to see there were two planets, but not nearly high enough to know why. The average citizen of the Alliance wouldn't have been able to access the fact there were two planets associated with the Rajani.

What did it mean? He felt like the answer was just out of his reach. It was becoming an obsession. He found himself thinking of the Rajani the moment he woke up, as if he'd been dreaming about them just before waking. It was driving him to distraction. He'd received two warnings already at work for critical pay errors he committed. If he received a third, he would be demoted to custodial detail.

He needed to find the truth about the Rajani. But how? He'd spent a few days more thinking about it, his antennae twitching ceaselessly as one of his brains pondered the mystery of discovering how to get past the highest level of ASP security, without getting caught, while the other was tasked with the mundane details of his present occupation.

Just then, Commander Kan walked by his cramped workspace, shooting a cold glare at Ries from both sets of his eyes. Ries finally thought of a solution to solve two of his problems at once.

◊

Tumaani had just settled down for the night in his tent when the flap opened, revealing a shadowy figure blocking out the light of the moon.

"Tumaani?" a gruff male voice whispered.

"Who is it? Who's there?" Tumaani asked, sitting up.

"It's Welemaan," the figure said. "Did I catch you before you fell asleep, old one?"

Tumaani ignored the verbal jab. He wasn't much older

than Welemaan. But he was much more practical, and the younger Elders liked to kid him about being so much older in mind, if not in body. It angered him sometimes. He was the same age as Rauphangelaa, but he'd never heard them giving his friend a hard time about being old. He'd found in his weeks in the prison camp, though, he was one of the oldest Elders in the prison. Although he didn't know for sure, because many of them had been locked up in the prison cells with little or no way to communicate with those in the courtyard.

"Yes," he answered, realizing he had been lost in thought and hadn't actually answered Welemaan's question. "What is it? Is something wrong?"

"Other than just about everything? No," Welemaan answered.

Tumaani knew how he felt. He hadn't recognized him at the time, but it was Welemaan who had assaulted the Krahn guard attempting to take his mate and younglings away. He had found the other Elders looked much different bald. He probably did as well, he supposed.

"Then what is it?" Tumaani asked. "If they catch us speaking together—"

"Oh, there will be more than us speaking together tonight," Welemaan said. "Volaan and I are planning to break out of this place, if we can. We're inviting others to join us."

"Which, I assume, is why you're here," Tumaani said. He'd thought about risking everything to go after his mates as well, but had come to the conclusion it wasn't worth the peril. It wouldn't do any of them any good if he was killed trying to escape from a heavily guarded prison. He knew Volaan had been the Rajani trying to help Welemaan when his family was taken away. From what Tumaani had heard, Volaan had lost his mate in the Krahn attack, as well as one of his eyes. "Welemaan, your actions go against the Kha. An escape attempt will only lead to violence. Please reconsider your actions."

"They took my mate and my younglings," Welemaan said, a bitter note creeping into his voice. "Don't you dare tell me I can't go after them. They took your mates too. I would think you'd care for them enough to try to rescue them. Maybe I was wrong."

"Please," Tumaani said. "Don't do this. There has to be another way."

"There isn't," Welemaan said tersely. "I apologize for disturbing your rest, old one. Good night, Tumaani."

"Wait—" Tumaani said, but Welemaan was already gone. It was a long time before Tumaani could fall asleep. It was not much longer after, he was awoken by the sound of weapons firing. He knelt and prayed for the remainder of the night, though he was unsure what outcome he was praying for.

◊

Ries had taken an immediate dislike to his new boss, Commander Jando Kan. The feeling seemed to be mutual, if Kan's attitude toward him was any indication. So the decision to implement his plan to steal the officer's identification chip wasn't difficult for Ries to make. Each computer used by the Alliance Society for Peace had a scanner that read the identification chip implanted in a user's body. For security purposes, not even the user knew where it was implanted, so Ries knew it would take some time to find Kan's. He needed seclusion if his plan was going to work.

He started slowly, by getting to know some of the officers in the ASP patrol division stationed on the planet over a few days' time, as well as taking long drives outside the city in his free time. He finally settled on a likely candidate. The Tamurian named Koss was like most of his species, friendly, easygoing, and all too eager to please. When Ries asked him if he could borrow his ID chip scanner, he was able to give the simple reason of wanting to know the locations of the chips in all of his family members in case of an emergency. Of course, Ries didn't have a family, but the Tamurian didn't ask any other questions, and Ries didn't divulge any other information.

The chip scanner was a handheld device about the size of Ries's hand. There was a strap on it used by those officers not equipped to hold onto the device tightly due to a lack of fingers or tentacles. Once again, Ries was happy he'd been born with opposable thumbs on his four hands.

"Just don't let anyone know I let you borrow it," Koss said, running a hand through his head feathers. "I'd be in a lot of trouble." Access to the scanners was strictly controlled by the ASPs, and only a few officers were authorized to use them, due to the risk of misuse. It was exactly the kind of misuse that Ries was planning.

"Don't worry," Ries told him, using his best smile. "It'll be our secret." If he got away with his plan, Ries knew, the Tamurian would have to disappear as well. *Not a great loss,* he thought, looking at Koss's large, simple eyes.

The next stage of his plan would need to happen more quickly. Besides the fact the Tamurian expected his scanner back the next day, Ries also knew Kan was going on a planned vacation for two weeks after the day's shift was completed. He wouldn't be missed for at least that amount of time. It was the perfect opportunity.

Kan, an Ontigan, was home alone when Ries rang his door chime. The Ontigan were a species that had no word for 'marriage' or even 'mate.' The males of the species were expected only to donate their sperm to the local fertility clinic. They never saw who received it, nor knew of any subsequent offspring resulting from implantation in a female.

Love in the modern galaxy, Ries thought. He didn't have to worry about any of the Ontigan's family hanging around, at least. But he needed to go somewhere a little less public for what he planned to do. No use taking chances a friend or coworker would stop by to wish Kan well on his trip. When Kan answered the door, Ries immediately shot him with a stun gun, dropping his unconscious body to the hallway floor. Ries looked around and saw no one lurking in the darkness of the night. He hoisted the Ontigan up and walked him to a waiting transport, speaking loudly about Kan having too much to drink before leaving on his trip.

Ries piled the Ontigan into the enclosed back of the transport, not bothering to sort out limbs and other appendages as he did so. He wasn't worried about Kan being sore if he woke up. Ries returned to Kan's apartment and grabbed the two already-packed clothing cases from where they were sitting near the front door. He turned off all of the dwelling unit's lights and closed the front door on the way out. He pulled off his gloves and threw them into the passenger seat as he climbed into his transport, making a mental note to get rid of them later.

He drove out of the city limits to an industrial complex he'd discovered and found the empty storage facility he had scouted out earlier. He walked the Ontigan into the structure and dumped him on the hard stone floor, then returned to the transport for a large box of equipment. He looked around to make sure no one else was about, and then placed the box on the floor next to the unconscious form of his boss.

He returned to the door and set the security code. No one else would be able to open the door without the code. He hadn't seen anyone around the industrial complex for days, so he was pretty sure it was abandoned, but one of the reasons he'd climbed the ranks of the ASPs was his attention to detail and thoroughness, especially when it came to illegal activities.

He began his preparations, laying out his equipment next to the still-unconscious Ontigan. He picked up a pair of neutralizers and placed them on Kan's head. He didn't want a fight if Kan were to wake up unexpectedly. He didn't know enough about Ontigan physiology to guess at how long he'd stay stunned from a single shot from the stun gun.

As he was passing the scanner over the Ontigan's body, starting from the feet, Kan began to stir. Ries made it to his lower thorax before Kan opened his eyes, blearily, and looked at him. Kan tried to jump up, but screamed in pain as the neutralizers kicked in.

"I wouldn't do that if I were you," Ries told him when the screaming had stopped. "I've heard it's quite painful trying to move when you've been neutralized."

Ries continued scanning, reaching the Ontigan's chest and working up and down each tentacle and around the large breathing holes. He was glad he had thought to wear protective gloves, as small pores on the Ontigan's tentacles secreted poisonous mucus at his slightest touch. Ontigans had used the mucus for mating as well as protection from predators somewhere in their past, but at the moment, it was just a gooey distraction in Ries's search. He reached the Ontigan's short neck, concerned he hadn't yet found the identification chip.

"Don't worry, I'm almost finished," he said. He scanned over Kan's head. Nothing. Nonplussed, he began scanning at the Ontigan's feet again, this time going slower and making sure he scanned every part of the Ontigan's body. The chip was small, so he may have missed it the first time. He came to Kan's head once again and scanned it. Again, nothing.

"Blast," he said quietly. There could be only one explanation; the chip was in Kan's head, and the neutralizers were somehow interfering with the scanner. Ries sat back on his haunches and thought for a moment. If he took off the neutralizers, he'd probably have a fight on his hands. He could go back to his transport and get his stun gun, but it would only increase his chances of being seen. There was only one thing he could do.

"Sorry, I lied," he told Kan as he reached for his saw. "There was something to be worried about after all." He smiled, relishing the look on his boss's face as he began to cut.

◊

Tumaani sat and waited for the two brothers, Torile and Maska, to return with the meager food rations given to the Rajani by their captors. By his calculations, it was Araa's day, a day meant for celebrating the life and teachings of Ruvedalin. There were no celebrations, only another day as a prisoner of the Krahn. The brothers soon returned, and Torile handed a small bowl to Tumaani. It was partially filled with a simple broth with a few hard vegetables in it. Yet it was food, and Tumaani ate it quickly, even going so far as to lick the bowl clean. There was no such thing as immodesty when it came to survival.

Tumaani had taken to visiting with the brothers lately. He couldn't speak to the other Elders, especially after the recent escape of Welemaan and the other Rajani. Four Rajani had been killed in the escape attempt, but Welemaan, Volaan, and maybe six more had managed to overpower a few of the Krahn guards and escape, killing two of them in the process. Retribution had been swift. The Krahn had come to the prison with a list of Elders, and had tortured all of them while asking questions about the escape. Tumaani still found it difficult to stand. He had not given up any names, and they still had not been caught.

"It's a pleasant night," Torile said, looking up at the sky. "It doesn't look like it will rain."

"You said that last night," Maska said, irritably. "And we were nearly flooded."

Tumaani was still looking up at the sparse clouds when something caught his attention. A star seemed to be streaking across the darkening sky. After a short time Tumaani could see it wasn't a star, but a ship moving across the atmosphere above them.

"What is it?" Torile asked, standing up.

"It's a ship," Tumaani answered.

"A ship?" Maska said. "Is it Krahn?"

"I don't think so," Tumaani said.

"Why not?" Torile asked.

"Because it's being fired upon," Tumaani answered. As he said this, he could see small Krahn ships following the lone starship and firing at it. Explosions erupted from its frame as it streaked across the sky toward the east. Toward the coast. Tumaani thought about the message he had received from his friend Rauphangelaa, and debated telling the brothers about it. He finally decided against it. No use telling them their last hope may have just crashed into the ocean.

◊

Ries had sneaked into the Commander's office and taken Kan's handheld tablet after disposing of his body and personal belongings. He wanted to be sure if the Ontigan's access was logged by the Alliance central computer, it would be on Kan's own tablet, so as to not arouse too much suspicion. He sat in his dwelling unit after making sure all of the windows were darkened so no one could see in. He'd used the scanner on himself and found his ID chip was located in one of his arms.

Then he'd returned the scanner to the relieved Tamurian, making sure he wiped it down thoroughly first.

He'd marked the spot on his lower left arm where his chip was located, and when he was finally ready, he placed a neutralizer over it and turned it on. That set of arms was now useless, as was the brain controlling them, but, luckily, he had a spare for both. Confident the tablet would only read Kan's ID chip, he turned it on. Kan's identification chip was in his front pocket. It had taken major surgery, but he'd finally dislodged it from the Ontigan's severed head. He'd disposed of the body pieces as well as the box of tools, his gloves, and Kan's clothing cases in a deep quarry on the way back to the city.

Ries began his search for the truth, almost too excited to type on the tablet's screen properly. Normally he would have spoken to it, but he couldn't very well use his own voice while using Kan's chip. He typed the command in to search for information on the Ruvedalin Initiative. Abruptly, a screen came up on the tablet, telling him the following information was classified at Security Level 7K4 and the inquiry had been logged. But unlike his last foray into the Rajani's past, there was a 'continue' command tab on the tablet's screen as well. He pushed it.

A file opened on the screen, and he began to read the text eagerly. It was fascinating. He'd never been aware of the Rajani religious beliefs, and to learn how the religion was created was a shocker. But Ries was not naïve. He knew what the Alliance was capable of, and the ASPs as well. Yet he saw now why it was classified at a level as high as it was. If the Rajani ever learned this information, it was hard telling what they would do.

He closed the file and began a search for Planet A490. Again, a security screen came up stating the inquiry had been logged. He hit the continue tab and began to read the file that opened on his screen. As it went on, he became more and more uncertain about his plan. He shouldn't have done this.

There was going to be more heat associated with this file than he ever would have thought, but there was no changing things now, so he read on, unable to stop. There had been rumors brought up by other ASP officers, saying there was a hole in the yearly budget of the ASPs, but they had been only rumors of overspending or corrupt superior officers embezzling funds. Nothing could ever be proven without catching some admiral with his hand in the bejeweled pot, as his mother used to say.

Now he knew where a great deal of money was going to, and it made his antennae vibrate as the fear spread throughout his body at what he'd discovered. He decided he'd read enough for the night. He signed off of Kan's tablet and sat thinking for a moment. He would have to destroy the tablet as thoroughly as he had Kan's body. The Tamurian named Koss would have to disappear. Then *he'd* have to disappear. He wasn't sure where he would go, but he needed to get out. That night, if possible.

There was a loud crashing noise as the door to his dwelling was smashed in. Ries heard the sound of running feet and the barking of commands and knew he would disappear that night, just not how he had hoped. He slowly put down the tablet he was holding, took off the neutralizer from his arm, and raised both sets of hands over his head.

◊

Tumaani and his fellow Rajani had fallen into a routine within the prison. In the morning, he and a few others would meet and begin to pray. After prayer, they would talk for a while, just to pass the time until the lunch chime sounded and they would receive a small portion of food from the Krahn.

The rest of the day was spent sitting, standing, or walking around the courtyard, alone or in groups, making sure the Elders didn't pass too close to each other. Then dinnertime, when they usually received the same vegetable and broth soup, and maybe a hunk of grainy bread as well. Tumaani didn't think the Krahn ate bread.

Rumors were rampant about what had happened to the group of Rajani who had escaped the prison, what had happened to the females and younglings, and what had happened to the Sekani and most of the Jirina. There had been no word about any of them. There was also speculation about the ship that had been shot down over Melaanse and who it could have been, and there was conjecture of ASPs or a rogue Krahn ship. Tumaani had his own theory, though he hoped he was wrong.

He thought about the message he'd received from Rauphangelaa on the first night of the attack and hoped Rauphangelaa had been able to escape past the Krahn ships and contact the Alliance Society for Peace. The Rajani desperately needed help. There were rumors the Krahn planned on killing all of the Elders to ensure there wouldn't be another escape attempt. Tumaani knew this rumor was untrue. He knew, or at least guessed, why the Krahn had attacked. They wanted the Johar Stones.

He was sure they wouldn't simply kill the Elders. They would torture them first.

◊

Ries woke up in a cell the size of his closet back on the *Interceptor*. There was barely room to stand next to the thin bed he was lying on. He looked around, unsure of his surroundings, and saw the room had bare white walls and a door with a small window in it and a speaker beneath the window.

He sat up slowly, still feeling the effects of the stun gun used on him by the black-clad intruders who had broken into his apartment. They hadn't said a word to him as they forced their way into the room and pointed their weapons at him. A voice had barked out, "Take him alive." It was the last thing he remembered.

He was about to stand up and stretch his legs when he heard a click from the door and a voice spoke to him.

"I see you're finally awake," the voice said in Talondarian Standard. "Good. There are some questions I would like you to answer."

"Where am I?" Ries asked.

"Not important," the voice answered. "What is important is you need to be truthful with me the first time. Any other answers will only lead to suffering on your part. Do you understand?"

Ries stood up and looked out of the small window in the upper middle portion of the door. He couldn't see anyone standing outside the door, only an empty hallway with another closed door at the end, this one with no window at all.

"You haven't answered my question," the voice said quietly.

A bolt of excruciating pain exploded through Ries's entire body. His muscles clenched painfully, and he dropped to the floor of the room, trying to scream, but unable to make a sound.

"Answer the question," the voice said. "That was the pain inducer's lowest level. You don't want me to turn it up."

"I...understand," Ries said, breathlessly.

"Good, you're learning," the voice said.

Ries pulled himself up to a sitting position on the floor of his cell, but couldn't go any farther. His muscles felt like wet paper, and his antennae felt twisted in knots.

"Why were you accessing files several security levels above your rank?" the voice asked.

"I wanted to know about the Rajani," Ries said. "They disabled my ship and led to my demotion to that garbage hole called Asnuria." He winced, too late hoping the voice on the other side of the speaker was not Asnurian.

"You're saying this was a simple case of out-of-control curiosity on your part?" the voice asked, with no discernible reaction to Ries's harsh summation of the planet.

"It's the truth," Ries said, expecting another shock from the pain inducer. It didn't come.

"How many of the files did you read?" the voice asked. "What was your understanding of their content?"

"I...didn't see much," Ries began, before pain seared through his body once more. His antennae curled up almost to the top of his head as his entire body spasmed.

"You're lying. Answer the question, please."

"I only read two documents," Ries said after a few minutes, finally able to speak. "I...didn't understand at first why there were two planet designation numbers for Rajan. Until..."

"Until what?" the voice asked when Ries hesitated.

"Until I saw...there are two planets named Rajan, both with a designation number," Ries said, still trying to speak clearly with a tongue that felt like he had bit it in half. The entire tip was numb, and his mouth seemed devoid of spit.

"Proceed."

"The...original planet named Rajan has been under strict quarantine for two thousand Standard years," Ries said. "There are still ten ASP star battle cruisers patrolling the system, ensuring no one comes near it. And no one escapes."

"The other file?" the voice asked.

"The Alliance created a fiction, a story, in hopes of inspiring a religious awakening among the Rajani transplanted to the second planet," Ries said, trying to remember everything he had read. He didn't think he'd survive another jolt from the inducer, and he didn't want to find out if he could. "The current inhabitants of the planet now known as Rajan," Ries continued, "are living a lie."

"Yes," the voice said. "A necessary lie. You understand the reason for this, yes?"

"Yes, yes, of course," Ries said. "If they ever found out, who knows what could happen?"

"Correct," the voice said. "They must never discover the secrets of their past. Which is why you are here, and not roaming free somewhere, divulging the information you illegally obtained using a stolen identity chip. Did you really expect to be simply demoted to the planet of Asnuria after your initial offense without being monitored? Do you believe Galactic Intelligence is a misnomer of some type?"

"Galactic Intelligence?" Ries asked, a wave of cold passing through his body. Had GI taken him prisoner? If so, he was in more trouble than he originally thought.

"Yet, you still live," the voice said, cryptically.

Ries had been wondering about that. Why keep him prisoner and ask him all of these questions if all they were going to do was kill him?

"You're fortunate," the voice said. "I've taken an interest in your obvious...talents. You've shown remarkable ability in intelligence gathering."

"Commander Kan—"

"Is of no concern," the voice said dismissively. "Oh no, where will we ever find another mid-level officer for such a mediocre assignment?" The speaker's voice had taken on a mocking tone.

"Then, why am I here?" Ries asked, confused.

"If it wasn't already obvious," the voice said. "You are being recruited by Galactic Intelligence. To be more specific, by myself."

Ries pulled himself up onto his bed, his body still aching. *Recruited,* he thought. He felt a smile appear on his face at the same time tears of relief began running from his many eyes.

◊

Rulina had been scared beyond words when the Krahn had separated her from her mate, Tumaani, but she'd been comforted by the fact she had been surrounded by other females and younglings she knew, including Tumaani's other mates. As senior living mate to an important Rajani Elder, she tried to stay as calm as she could, attempting to set a good example for the others to emulate.

The Krahn had steadily marched them from the prison toward the south of Melaanse. She'd been appalled by the devastation she witnessed while walking through the city. Everything she had ever known had been destroyed. Many of the females she was with cried the entire walk; some too exhausted to eat or drink the pitifully small rations they were each given. One female she didn't know had fallen and refused to get up. The Krahn guard nearest to her had shot her in the back of the head as if he were swatting an insect. Through the screams that had followed, the Krahn had started them walking again. To the south; always to the south.

She had been relieved when they had finally called a stop. They had walked all the way through the city, and had come to a large field far enough west, away from the city, that she could no longer see or even smell the ocean. If they continued on their present heading, the grasslands would soon give way to the sands of the Desert of Ambraa. Almost all of the Rajani had fallen to the ground in exhaustion when the Krahn made it clear they were stopping. Their relief was short-lived, however, when the Krahn warriors pulled out their weapons and took aim.

Chapter 3

It was night in the Rajani capital city of Melaanse, the sun having set some time earlier. Little could be seen of the debris from the recent Krahn invasion, except a shadow here from a large piece of building and a darker hole there on the ground that could be a crater, or possibly a body. The moon illuminated very little of the devastation, and there were no lights visible from the broken buildings. The Krahn were thorough in their devastation of the city; not many of the buildings left reached higher than the third floor. Transport vehicles were thrown about haphazardly, some on their tops or sides, some with their inhabitants still inside, the vehicle now serving as their coffin.

The cone-shaped escape pod lay half on its side and half on its bottom, propped up against a large slab of rock, a remnant of one of the beautiful Rajani buildings in the northern part of the city, where it had landed. The hatch to the pod opened, emitting a soft, glowing light. The pod's large parachute lay against the ground like a coiled snake, wrapping itself around the still-hot metal of the pod.

It was spring in Melaanse; the cold winter rains had passed only a few weeks earlier. No sound broke the silence of the mild Rajani night. The fighting had long been finished before the Rajani starship *Tukuli* had returned, ejecting four escape pods before crashing into the planet's largest ocean. The city seemed to be holding its breath, waiting for something to happen, with not even a breeze in the air to stir the various pieces of trash strewn about the ground.

James Dempsey, leader of a team of human beings brought to Rajan to help free it from the Krahn invaders, stood in the open hatchway of his escape pod, having just regained consciousness. He shook his head slowly, trying to clear his thoughts. He powered up, his body covered from head to toe in a protective suit of energy. He fell half in and half out of the pod, and then lost consciousness again. His energy field disappeared once more.

Out of the darkness stepped a Krahn warrior, its eyes glowing, reflecting the light from the escape pod. It tentatively approached the object that had fallen from the sky, from the ship that had screamed overhead just a few moments earlier on its way toward the ocean. Slowly, it crouched over James and hissed softly, looking around for any other potential threats. A short distance away, another Krahn appeared from the darkness, followed by another.

◊

Yvette Manidoo was unconscious as well, lying on the inside wall of her escape pod. There was a large bang from outside the pod, which startled her awake. Another bang sounded as something struck her pod, and her eyes flew open wide. She reached for her head, thinking, *Oh, damn. Where...?*

The door of the pod was open, and she could see it was pointing up toward the dark night sky. Yvette could hear a hissing sound coming from outside, as the pod was slowly pushed right-side up by whoever was on the other side of the pod's walls. She powered up quickly, remembering what

James had told them just before they had all ejected from the ship. Her power field surrounded her in a dark yellow armor. James had told them it was better to be safe and stay powered up, even at the risk of scaring the inhabitants of the planet, and Yvette agreed with his advice. They hadn't been sure what would await them when they reached the planet's surface, but she was about to find out.

As the pod landed on its bottom, she did her best to move with it, landing with her feet on the floor as it came to rest, right-side up. She looked out of the hatch and was immediately met by a face out of a nightmare. The Krahn, for surely that was what it was, hissed at her, bringing up its weapon to fire. She never gave it the chance. Instantly, she formed a spear out of her right hand, pulled back her arm, and thrust it through the Krahn's still-hissing face and out through the back of its skull.

She pulled back her hand, dissolving the spear as she did so and watching the still-jerking body of the Krahn disappear as it dropped to the ground. She was disgusted by the sound it had made as her spear pierced its head. Her strike had been instinct alone, but it had been effective. She re-formed her spear as she began to hear more of the hissing sound coming from outside the pod. She wasn't sure how many there were, but she was ready to fight. She had no qualms about killing every Krahn she saw if she had to. Soon, she had her chance.

◊

Inside another of the *Tukuli's* escape pods, Kieren Gray and Gianni DeMilo were still unconscious from the forceful ejection of the pod from the Rajani starship. They had fallen to the floor of the pod when it landed on the planet's surface. The pod's safety harnesses were built to unclasp when the pod came to a stop after ejection. Whether it was the result of their being tossed about by the crash landing or something more subconscious in nature, they were almost embracing as they lay on the floor of the pod. The door had opened immediately after impact, another safety device, guaranteeing any inhabitant of the pod would not become trapped inside. The pod had come to rest in the middle of a grassy park in the north of Melaanse. The grass below the pod was singed black from the heat of the metal, which had just passed through the atmosphere of the planet.

The sun was just coming over the horizon. A group of six Sekani males had gathered around the pod in the early morning light. The diminutive, cat-like aliens were badly dressed and dirty. Some had filthy bandages covering parts of their body; blood smeared some of their short blue fur. All had makeshift weapons of some sort, though most consisted of homemade clubs or sharp pieces of metal they had found lying amidst the debris. Weapons of any kind were banned on Rajan.

"What are they?" the first Sekani asked, looking in through the hatch at the unconscious Humans, his red eyes turning almost black as the pupils expanded, adapting to the gloom of the escape pod's interior. Its emergency light had turned off with the light of dawn. "I've never seen their like before. They're not Krahn."

A second Sekani, this one with a large bandage over his wounded forehead, answered, "I don't know. What are they doing in a Rajani escape pod? And where did it come from?"

A third Sekani, this one equipped with a large improvised club, waved them on. "We don't have time for this. I say kill them and grab their supplies. They're probably Krahn spies. I'll bash in their heads myself."

The first Sekani pointed at the third. "You're not the leader here, Botran. Take them and their supplies to the temporary compound. Watch them closely. If they turn out to be unfriendly, or in league with the Krahn, kill them both. Otherwise, we'll let Zanth decide their fate."

The Sekani named Botran sniffed in the first Sekani's directions, but he also put down his club along with the others and entered the pod cautiously. It wouldn't do to be surprised in the close confines of the pod if the creatures woke up unexpectedly. They stripped the pod of emergency rations and other supplies before finally bending to the task of bringing the strange-looking creatures out. The pair seemed to be a male and female, though none of them could tell for sure. Until the female opened her eyes.

◊

The last escape pod, which held David Morris and Janan'kela, the Sekani pilot of the *Tukuli,* was lying where it had landed, in the Desert of Ambraa, northwest of the city of Melaanse. The desert stretched for miles from the western outskirts of the city to the middle of the Rajani continent. Sand dunes were all that could be seen around the pod in the morning light. The sand beneath the pod had turned into a thin layer of glass from the heat emanating from the base of the pod. A large furrow led up to where the pod had come to rest, evidence of a hard landing.

The wind blew the sand endlessly across the dunes. It also whipped the pod's parachute away from the pod, like a caged animal trying to escape its tormenting captor. There was already a large drift of sand on one side of the pod. The sun was rising slowly in the east, and the heat from outside the pod was starting to build.

Inside the pod, both of the inhabitants were still unconscious from the sudden G-forces experienced when the pod was ejected from the *Tukuli.* David began to stir gradually. He suddenly sat upright, remembering where he was. He looked over and saw his companion still sleeping.

Standing slowly, he staggered over to the open hatch of the pod and looked outside.

"Oh, crap, you've gotta be kidding me," he said, seeing the seemingly endless blowing sand of the desert. His voice broke, his throat dry from the desert air. It was difficult to swallow at all. He turned and knelt next to the small form of his Sekani companion.

"C'mon, Janan," David said, checking where he thought a pulse might be found on the small alien's wrist. He found one and smiled, and then the smile disappeared as he began to worry. What if he couldn't wake Janan up? What the hell was he supposed to do if Janan was really hurt? Leave him here? Where the hell was here?

"Wake the hell up already," he said, gently shaking his friend. "We're stuck out here. I don't know where we are, or even what direction I should go to find help."

Janan, his eyes still closed, finally spoke. "Shut up, Earth man." He threw one of his arms over his eyes, shielding them from the sunlight streaming in through the open hatch.

"Janan!" David exclaimed, a smile on his face.

Janan moved his arm from his face and squinted up at him, then pointed at a cabinet in the side of the pod. It had fallen open, and David could see a metallic bottle inside. "Softly, please," Janan said. "Can you get me the bottle of water?"

"We have water?" David asked softly. "You mean I've been dying of thirst and there was water here the entire time?"

Janan smiled up at him. "Get a clue, man," he said as David handed him the bottle. He took a long drink of the tepid liquid inside.

"Ha!" David said, watching his friend drink. "Give me some, at least."

Janan grimaced and handed him the container. "Oh," he said in Talondarian Standard. "I think I need some time to heal. Maybe a year or two."

David drank some of the tepid water and made a face. "Ugh. This tastes awful."

"It won't kill you," Janan said. "It's probably been in this pod for quite some time. Plus, it's real Rajani water, not the stuff constantly recycled by the ship. Different minerals, I guess."

"Sure. Great," David replied, taking another drink. "I don't suppose you've created beer on this planet?"

Janan smiled. "No. Not yet."

"Just tell me one thing," David said, serious now.

"What?" Janan replied, already knowing what the Human was going to ask him.

David was looking at Janan now with a painful expression on his face. "Tell me you didn't know about the other human beings on the ship. Tell me you didn't know about the testing they did." It wasn't the loss of human life bothering David, but the thought his new friend had not told him about the first humans taken aboard the *Tukuli*. David had felt a real sense of betrayal when he'd learned about the bodies aboard the ship.

"I cannot lie to you," Janan answered. "Although I didn't know about it, there was nothing I could have done to stop it if I did. I'm only a pilot. A mere servant of Rauphangelaa's House. I have no say in what he can and cannot do."

They looked at one another for a moment, before David spoke. "I hoped that was the case. I'm glad you didn't know. It does make a difference to me." He stood and looked out of the hatch once again. "Let's get out of here."

"No," Janan replied. "It's better to rest now. It'll be cooler at night, you'll see. We'll go then."

"Where?" David asked, turning back to look at him. He still did not know which way was which when looking out of the hatchway.

"East," Janan said, pointing at the pod's internal compass, which was affixed to the wall of the escape pod, just over the hatch. "Toward the capital city, Melaanse." The Sekani stood up slowly and walked to the open hatch. He stood next to David, looking out at the endless sand. "We just have to hope we're close enough to make it to the city in one night. If morning finds us once again in the desert, we won't survive the day."

◊

Under the ocean of Rajan, aquatic creatures swam, ate, and were eaten. Savage and beautiful were the life-forms found in the depths of the ocean on Rajan. It was a harsh planet whether on land or in the sea, and the animals had survived by adapting appropriate defenses. Air bubbles floated gently through the bright blue water near the surface.

The *Tukuli,* or at least what was left of it, was lying on the bottom of the ocean, just off the coast of the Rajani continent. Air bubbles trickled out from holes in the hull; some formed by the crash, others by damage caused by Krahn weapons as the ship passed through the blockade orbiting the planet. More aquatic creatures cavorted amid the wreckage of the once-powerful starship.

Bhakat tuc Rathaan was exhausted. He was giving himself a mental pep talk to keep from passing out on the floor where he stood.

My ancestors were warriors, he thought as he worked at winding a cloth bandage and placing it in a small bag. *Their code was one of conquest. They were feared throughout the galaxy. Entire planets cowered at the mere mention of our name: Rajani. Our ships searched all points of the known universe, exploring and conquering any planet they found. The time for war was long ago. Our ways have turned toward a peaceful existence. A better way of life, where the Rajani are in harmony with ourselves and our world. The Kha says discussion and understanding will work where force of arms may not. I'm losing my faith in the Kha and its teachings. An enemy is out there. They have taken away everything I believed in. They've killed almost everyone I care for in the world. The Krahn Horde cannot be placated. They will not negotiate. I must do all I can to rid our planet of their presence, but I cannot do it if I'm trapped down here.*

Bhakat bent over Rauphangelaa's bandaged and unconscious body. The injured Rajani was on one of the beds of the medical bay, his head pointed toward the medical robot in the middle of the room. The ship's emergency lights were still working, but the inside of the ship was now cast into shadows. The *Tukuli* was dying. Bhakat had turned off any non-essential system he could to conserve the last remaining power in the ship.

I have a choice, he thought. There's enough power left for one operation. I can either heal Rauphangelaa and we'll both die slow deaths under this ocean—or I can do what no Rajani has done for thousands of years, and damn myself forever in the eyes of my species.

He looked down at Rauphangelaa again. There was really no choice at all. There was one Johar Stone left aboard the ship, and one Rajani left to use it. If he implanted himself, he would break the highest law of his planet. His life could be forfeit. He stood there a moment, thinking. *I'm willing to take that risk,* he finally decided.

He walked slowly across the corridor into the medical bay's control room and began to input the parameters into the medi-bot for insertion of the Stone into his skull.

He'd made detailed studies of the Humans' skulls for the operations, but he had to guess about his own operation. He'd gathered as much food—mostly in the form of protein bars and other emergency stores—and water as he could. He placed it in close proximity to his Master, in case he should awaken while Bhakat was still unconscious.

Bhakat had placed Rauphangelaa in a state of hibernation, but he couldn't be sure it would last the entire time he was recovering from his operation. The Humans had been asleep for days after their own operations. Bhakat didn't have the luxury of taking that much time. He estimated the ship had approximately thirty-six Standard hours of breathable air left, as long as there wasn't a major structural failure in the next few hours. It would have to be enough.

Chapter 4

James slowly opened his eyes, adjusting to the bright morning light of Rajan. He opened them wider in shock at what he saw standing over him. The Krahn was bent over, looking James straight in the face. "What manner of creature are you?" it asked in guttural Krahnish. "Not Rajani. Not Jirina. Not Sekani. No matter. Get on your feet." The Krahn pulled out a handgun-like weapon from a holster at its side and pointed it at James's head. "I said, get up!"

James stood up slowly, guessing what the Krahn wanted by its arm motions. His head was telling him he'd been knocked unconscious, and his stomach was telling him it had been a little while since he and the others had abandoned the *Tukuli* to her fate. He didn't know if he could power up fast enough to stop a bullet. Hell, he didn't know if the gun even fired bullets. The Krahn was smaller than James had pictured they would be. It was perhaps five and a half feet tall at the most, and thinner than a human being. But James could see its muscles ripple under its scaly skin every time it moved. Rauph had briefed them about how dangerous the Krahn could be. He wouldn't underestimate it.

While its body looked like he had imagined, dark green outer scales with lighter yellowish scales under its arms and on its throat, the Krahn's head reminded him more of a bird than a reptile. Its eyes were olive-colored and slit like a cats. They were nestled deep in the Krahn's face, with bone-like protrusions around the sockets to protect them. Its snout looked like the beak of a parrot, and its nostrils were slits on either side.

James saw that what he first thought was hair was more like long, thin feathers that came off the top of its head and could be raised and lowered. The first word he thought of was 'hackles,' and this Krahn's hackles were raised in what looked to be dominant posturing. The Krahn's mouth looked like it had more teeth than an alligator and a tongue that could reach the tip of its snout easily. All in all, James thought the Krahn was pretty damn ugly.

The Krahn was pointing off to their right. "You will come with me to Nestbase Two." James could see each of its fingers ended in long, sharp claws. He started walking in the direction the Krahn was pointing. Then he got his first real look at his surroundings and stopped dead.

The escape pod had landed on a small hill within the city limits. The land gradually sloped down to either the north or south, James guessed, by the location of the sun overhead. This was the direction the Krahn had pointed. James could tell the city had once been an awe-inspiring place. He'd spoken with Rauph about Rajan, and Rauph had explained the city had been built long before on the eastern coast of the Rajani continent, next to the only ocean on the planet. Many of the buildings had been converted over the years to dwelling units for the Rajani and Sekani, or places of prayer and solitude for the Rajani Elders and their Pledges.

There wasn't a commercial export industry on Rajan, and the Rajani, Sekani, and Jirina were relatively self-sufficient. There were large farms outside of the city providing their food, as well as what could be caught in the ocean. Anything needed from off-planet was purchased at places like the Mandakan Space Port, which the *Tukuli* had been forced to stop at on the way to Rajan from Earth.

James had seen pictures of Melaanse on the *Tukuli's* central computer. There had been huge buildings with intricate facades and thin, sparkling spires, smaller temples with glistening towers, with roadways winding between them and beautiful parks with colorful, exotic flora and fauna. They had all been destroyed. Some of the structures stood, but none of them were whole. Black smoke still billowed from some of them. The beauty of the city had died.

There were destroyed buildings and vehicles all around him. Some of the vehicles had Krahn warriors in them, looting and pillaging. Some of the vehicles still held the bodies of Rajani and Jirina. Krahn were coming out of the various buildings clutching scavenged items. The Krahn Horde had thrived on scavenging other ships; it's what they'd been raised to do, and they did it with gusto. James was dumbstruck. The magnitude of the destruction hit him like an electric shock. The city was like a dead carcass, and the Krahn were quickly picking the bones clean. Crumbling facades and dead bodies would be the only thing left.

James and the Krahn warrior walked for maybe a hundred yards before they came upon a patrol of Krahn. The group of Krahn had a live Jirina, its arms tied up in restraints behind its back, and a dead Sekani, which one of the Krahn carried over its shoulder. Their hackles were lowered and their heads were bowed in submission as they stopped before their commander.

One Krahn warrior saluted, with the arm carrying a weapon across its chest, and bowed to the Krahn who had captured James, whose hackles were still raised as it looked over its subordinates. "Sir. We've captured these beasts trying to escape the city," the warrior said in Krahnish.

"Good," the Krahn commander said. "I've also caught something interesting. We will take them both to Nestbase Two."

"And the Sekani?" the second Krahn asked, practically drooling in anticipation.

"You may share it between yourselves," the Krahn commander answered magnanimously.

"Thank you, sir," the second Krahn said.

The group of Krahn crouched down in a circle and tore the body of the Sekani apart right there, eating it raw. It reminded James of a pride of hungry lions eating a zebra. He couldn't take his eyes off the spectacle. These Krahn were the most barbaric things he'd ever seen. The body of the Sekani was turned into so many bones and scraps before his eyes. He finally turned away from the gruesome feast and looked at the Krahns' other prisoner. The Jirina was a pitiful sight. It was bruised and bloodied from its capture. It kept its eyes on the ground throughout the entire exchange, unwilling to watch the Krahn eat. James wondered if he'd been friends with the unfortunate Sekani.

James made up his mind and powered up. For a second, everyone stopped what they were doing to stare at him in amazement. Even the Jirina lifted its eyes, an expression of wonder—or perhaps terror—on its face as it saw the alien become encased in the black power field resembling a suit of stone-like armor. Yvette had told him on the ship that his energy field reminded her of lava rock; black yet translucent. He'd had enough of being a Krahn prisoner. It was time to test his powers against the Krahns' weaponry. The Krahn commander lifted its gun and shot James point-blank in the chest. The projectile ricocheted harmlessly off his energy field.

James smiled. "Oh yeah. All I needed to know." He grabbed the Krahn commander and threw it ten feet through the air, where it slammed against the side of a burned-out building and fell to the ground in a heap. The Jirina screamed in terror and ran, heedless of its Krahn captors. They paid him no mind. Their attention was on the black specter suddenly standing in their midst.

He attacked the Krahn warriors in the same way he had their commander, tossing them about the area or just punching them in the head, watching their teeth fly and their skulls fall apart as he did so. He didn't stop. He couldn't stop, even when the Krahn warriors lay broken and bloody at his feet. He picked up their bodies and bashed them against the building remnants until they were almost unrecognizable. He'd seen just about every perversion, every crime possible that one being could inflict on another. Yet the Krahn had done something to him that had not been done in a long time. They'd seriously pissed him off.

◊

Gianni and Kieren were both cut, dirty, and exhausted. The Sekani had awakened them and led them to a burned-out building a few city blocks from where their escape pod had landed. Kieren had attempted to speak to them along the way, but they'd only looked at her and Gianni suspiciously and told her to keep moving. When they arrived, the Sekani had told them to stop and sit down. They had complied, and a short while later, one of the Sekani had brought them each some food and water.

Now, they were sitting, leaning against the inside wall of a building. The building had once had ten floors, but was missing all but the bottom floor now, the top having toppled over onto a smaller building next to it. They were eating the food the Sekani had provided from wood-like bowls with utensils made from the same material. It was a thin stew with small chunks of what Kieren thought might be some type of vegetables. At least she hoped they were. A small band of Sekani had replaced the group who had brought them there. This group had gun-like weapons and stood a few yards away. They looked as ragged as the previous group. They weren't pointing the weapons at Kieren and Gianni, but they were being careful, some casting worried glances toward the humans.

"This stuff tastes like shit," Gianni said, putting the bowl down with a disgusted noise and wiping his hands on his shirt.

"Gianni!" Kieren exclaimed.

"It's not like they understand me," he told her, nodding toward the Sekani. He sighed and pushed his hair out of his eyes. He hadn't cut his hair the entire time he had been on the *Tukuli,* and it was growing long.

"So what?" Kieren said. "*I* can hear you, and it's rude."

"So, what are they doing?" Gianni asked her, deftly changing the subject. "You told them we're here to help them, right?"

"Of course I did. They're discussing us," Kieren told him. "They think this may be a trick. I can't hear everything they're saying, especially if you keep talking to me."

"I haven't seen a Rajani here," Gianni said, looking around.

"Me either," Kieren said, her own food now forgotten. "Gianni, I think these Sekani are runaways or something."

The Rajani considered the Sekani and Jirina to be what Rauph had referred to as 'helper species,' but James and the others had talked about it, and they all suspected the two species were considered little better than slaves. Rauph and Bhakat both had suspected an element within the Sekani had helped the Krahn invade Rajan. James had raised the possibility their status in the Rajani society had led to it, but had never brought it up to Rauph, as far as Kieren knew.

Gianni ran both of his hands through his hair. "The Rajani were invaded by the Krahn and got a full-scale Sekani revolution as an extra bonus." He picked up his bowl once again and began to disinterestedly stir the remaining contents. "Do you think the Krahn and Sekani are working together?"

Kieren scrunched up her nose. "Um...no."

"Why not?" he asked, puzzled by her answer.

"Well, from what I could pick up from their conversation on the way here, the Krahn consider the Sekani...delicacies."

Gianni placed his bowl on the ground. "I think I lost my appetite."

A Sekani female walked up to them and retrieved the bowl from where it rested at his side. She bowed to Gianni. A Sekani male who had just entered the room yelled at her. "No! Don't bow to them. We'll bow to no other species from now on." He'd introduced himself earlier as Zanth, when they were brought before him by the small group of Sekani. He seemed to be their leader.

The Sekani female looked shocked. "Zanth, they're guests—" she started to replied.

"I know they're guests, Tiella, but it's time for new customs," Zanth said, walking over to the female and placing a small, clawed hand on her arm. "We are no longer helpless slaves to the Rajani oppressors. Do you understand?" The female Sekani nodded, though it looked like a reluctant response to Kieren. The female walked away, looking back over her shoulder at them before finally disappearing around a corner.

Kieren stood, not knowing exactly what to say. "We're

sorry if we've offended you in any way, Zanth. Have you found our story to be true?"

Zanth was standing a few feet away from them, studying both her and Gianni. "If Rauphangelaa the Elder did escape Rajan aboard his ship, then he was the only one who did. He left his entire household of Sekani, an entire family group, dead. Except for one member; his pilot, if what you say is true. More than likely the family was killed in the first wave of the Krahn attack. Nevertheless, they're all dead."

Now it was Gianni's turn to stand. He was getting tired of not being able to understand the conversation. This was how he felt every time his family got together and his uncles began to talk in Sicilian to each other: like an outsider.

"No," Kieren said, saddened by the news. "Poor Janan."

"What about Janan?" Gianni asked, recognizing the name, at least. "What the hell are you telling him?"

Zanth kept talking, ignoring the protests. "We buried those we could find, but many others are still beneath the rubble of the buildings on Rauphangelaa's estate. We couldn't be sure who was alive, and who was dead, but none have shown up since then, and we've sent out a great many search parties."

"At least Janan is still alive," Kieren said. "Or at least he was when we arrived here. His entire family?"

"I'm afraid it's true," Zanth said, bowing his head in respect for the dead. He raised his head and once again turned his penetrating gaze on them. "Now, explain to me how you came to know our language. We are *not* speaking Talondarian Standard."

Zanth crossed his arms over his chest, looking at them. "Ours is a language tracing back to our home world," he continued. "It's the language we spoke before the coming of the conquerors. It's one of the few traces of our culture still left to us. How have you learned to speak it so fluently?" He pointed at Gianni. "Why doesn't he know it?"

Kieren looked at Gianni, not knowing what to say.

"What?" Gianni asked her. "I didn't do anything."

"They want to know why I can speak their language and you can't," she replied.

"Might as well tell them about the stones," he said, smiling at Zanth. "It'll be worth seeing the expression on his face."

Kieren turned toward Zanth. "We...we both, well, that is, all of my companions and I were...implanted...with Johar Stones, aboard the *Tukuli*."

There was an immediate uproar from the Sekani in the room. Zanth's face was incredulous. "By the Goddess! No."

Most of the gathered Sekani now held their weapons at the ready, pointed at the two humans standing before them.

"Quiet! Leave us!" Zanth yelled, pointing toward the exit.

One of the armed Sekani, this one with a bandaged head, whom Zanth had called Belani, stepped forward. "But they—"

"I said, leave us!" Zanth yelled. He pointed at the other Sekani. "And tell no one what you have heard here. You all know your objectives for this week. Go fulfill them. This gathering place is no longer safe for us. Go, now!"

◊

James was no longer powered up as he walked down a narrow alley near the area his recent fight had taken place. He was going against his own advice, but he didn't want to scare the Jirina any more than he already had. The Jirina recently held captive by the Krahn was cowering in a corner; his frightened eyes were wide as he looked at James. It had taken James a few minutes to track the alien down after he'd finished his battle with the Krahn. Luckily, he'd seen the direction the Jirina had fled after he'd first powered up, and the battle had been short.

"Hello," James began, trying to remember his Talondarian Standard from the classes Rauph had given them back on the ship. "There's no need to be frightened," he continued in English, knowing the creature couldn't understand what he was saying, but trying to sound soothing, at least, so as not to frighten it away. "I won't hurt you. You must be a Jirina. You've been through enough already, I'm sure. I'm afraid I'm in need of your services. I need a guide."

The Jirina pointed to himself, uncertain. "Jirina."

"Right," James said, able to understand the highly accented word. "Jirina." He pointed to himself now. "Human. Friend," he added in Talondarian Standard.

"Hu-maan?" the alien said, now looking up at James's face.

"Yes," James said, surprised a little the alien could quickly form a word it had never heard before. They'd been told on the ship the Jirina were not very intelligent as a species. This one must be an exception to the rule. Or else the Rajani had underestimated their servants a great deal.

"James. My name is James. What is your name?" he asked, now pointing at the alien.

The Jirina pointed to himself. "Mazal. My name is Mazal, J-jamess the Hu-maan."

"Good," James said quietly, not wanting to spook the alien. "Good. We're getting somewhere now."

Suddenly, the Jirina fell to its knees before him. "I pledge my life to you, in accordance with our law. My life is yours to do with as you wish, James the Human."

"Well, great," James said in English, looking down at the prostrate alien before him, its hands still in the restraints placed there by the Krahn. "Now what do I do?"

◊

Gianni hadn't known what to expect when he'd told Kieren to tell the room full of Sekani that they'd been implanted with the Johar Stones, but their reaction was a little more than he had imagined. The atmosphere of the room seemed to have changed immediately as Zanth shouted out orders and the Sekani abandoned the building they'd been using as a temporary shelter.

Zanth then spoke to Gianni and Kieren. "Come with me, both of you. We don't have much time." He led them deeper into the building, and finally stepped into a small room. "This will have to do for now. Sit, please."

They all sat on what were once finely woven and crafted chairs. Now they were tattered and covered with dust.

"We won't have long to speak," Zanth began. "Word of your presence is already on the way to the Krahn, I'm sure."

"What?" Kieren asked, looking surprised at this statement from the Sekani leader. "How do you know?"

"We have a traitor or traitors in our midst," Zanth explained. "It could be any of those who were just here, or none of them, I don't know."

Gianni was perturbed. He was tired of not knowing what they were saying. "What's going on! God, I hate this shit."

Kieren reached over and grabbed his hand, trying to calm him down before he once again did something stupid. "Be patient..."

Both of their powers fields flared around their clasped hands, which were now powered up. The energy field reached to about their wrists before thinning out and disappearing, making them look like they each had a glove on one hand made of their energy fields.

"What the...?" Gianni began, now speaking fluent Sekani.

All three of them had surprised looks on their faces as they looked at the clasped hands.

"The legends are real," Zanth said in quiet wonder.

"Hey," Gianni said. "I can understand you!"

"And you speak our language now, as well," Zanth told him. "The Stones are real, and they are everything the stories say they are."

Kieren smiled. "You haven't seen anything, yet."

Zanth still had both hands clasped on the armrests of his chair, as if afraid he would fall out of it. "We must evacuate this place before the Krahn attack. They will stop at nothing to obtain the Stones, I'm sure. Unfortunately, this means I must now trust you enough for us all to escape this place."

"Don't do us any favors," Gianni told him. "Just point us in the direction of Melaanse, and we'll be on our way."

"Gianni!" Kieren said, appalled at Gianni's lack of good manners.

Zanth stood and threw his hands up in the air, an angry expression on his face. "You are in Melaanse! Behold! What was once the greatest city on Rajan is now ashes! It's gone!" Zanth lowered his hands to his sides and looked down at the ground. "All of it, it's gone. All of it gone," he said quietly.

They heard the muffled sounds of weapons discharging outside of the building.

"They're here!" Zanth yelled, his eyes growing wider. "We must go now, before it's too late."

Both Kieren and Gianni powered up all the way now. They were no longer holding hands. Zanth jumped back and screamed at the sight of the two of them; startled at their sudden transformation.

"You go with the Sekani," Gianni told her. "I'll cover you both while you escape."

Kieren had an angry look on her face as she turned to look at Gianni. "Like hell you will. We go together. We can't afford to be separated."

"Just can't live without me, huh?" Gianni asked, a mocking smile on his face. He stopped smiling, and they looked at each other for a long moment, each unsure what the other was thinking, without being able to see the other's face clearly through their power field.

Zanth broke their contemplation of each other. He was standing in the doorway, looking down the hall. "Hurry! They'll be coming down the hall at any moment."

Gianni stepped out into the hall. He could see armed Krahn warriors coming toward their position. He fashioned his hands into guns and formed a red force shield in front of him. "Get behind me!" he screamed at the others as he started shooting bolts of energy through his shield. The Krahn bullets and lasers bounced off of it, unable to penetrate. "Go!"

Kieren and Zanth swiftly moved down the hall away from him. Gianni gradually backed up, following them slowly. His force shield followed him, staying about ten feet away from him, though there were spaces between it and the uneven walls and floor. He was afraid that a stray bullet or lucky shot would find its way between the wall and the shield, but there was nothing he could do about it at the moment. His shield wouldn't bend or change shape, no matter how hard he'd tried back on the *Tukuli,* and it was no different on Rajan. At last, he came to the end of the hallway and left his force shield blocking the doorway, while he followed Kieren and Zanth away from the building.

He looked back once to see two or three of the Krahn warriors standing on the other side of the shield, looking at him. He gave them the finger, and then turned quickly and followed after Kieren. He kept his shield up for as long as he could, which was difficult once he could no longer see it with his eyes, and only felt it in his mind. It was difficult to concentrate and run at the same time. He carefully followed

Kieren and Zanth as the Sekani led them along twisting paths between piles of debris and vehicles and through alleys surrounded by the remains of Rajani buildings.

Finally, they came to the end of a long alleyway, and Zanth motioned for them to stop. "You must wait here, out of sight, for a moment," he told them. "I have to go on ahead to let them know I'm bringing guests."

"Tell whom—?" Kieren began, but Zanth had already stepped around the corner of the nearest building.

"Now what?" Gianni asked her.

"I don't know," Kieren replied. "He just asked us to wait here a moment."

"Do you think we can trust him?" Gianni asked, looking around the alleyway. He had been so focused on Zanth's back as they walked that he hadn't had a chance to just look around at his surroundings. He thought that if Melaanse had a shady side, then this was probably it. He could also smell salt water, and figured they must be close to the ocean.

After a few minutes, Zanth returned. Gianni put his hand on Kieren's arm, and their fields flared once again, as their powers connected. "I must ask you to trust me as I trust you," Zanth said, his eyes wide once again at their appearance. "I would ask that you please make your shielding disappear."

"Why?" Kieren asked, sounding unsure. Gianni shared the sentiment. Their encounter with the Krahn had been too close for comfort.

"Because I'm afraid you might frighten them if you came around the corner looking like that," Zanth replied. "Please."

Kieren dropped her energy field and looked at Gianni. "I think we can trust him, Gianni. Can you drop your field before we go any farther?"

Gianni looked from her to Zanth and back. "I don't trust him, but I'll trust your judgment." He dropped his field.

Kieren smiled at him. "Thank you."

"Come," Zanth said, motioning forward. "They're expecting us." He led them around the corner of the building, and they saw that there were a number of armed Sekani guards in front of a large iron gate set in a wall that looked about six feet tall and was made of thick stone. The wall surrounded a collection of buildings that were mostly in good shape, from what they could see. The large buildings were directly on the waterfront. Zanth walked past the guards and motioned for Kieren and Gianni to follow him. The guards acknowledged Zanth with deferential nods of their heads and looked up at the two humans with suspicious expressions.

Once past the outer gate, Zanth led them to the nearest building, a large structure that seemed to have been some sort of warehouse. Zanth passed through the doorway and stopped a moment, letting his eyes adjust to the dim light inside the building. Gianni and Kieren stepped through the doorway and stopped as well, but more from surprise than the bad lighting. The building was full of Sekani. There were hundreds of them. It must have been some sort of emergency shelter. There were beds set up, and personal possessions, such as clothing and other items, were scattered around the beds.

Zanth turned to them. "Do you know now why I needed to be able to trust you with this secret?" he asked.

"Yes," Kieren replied. "I understand now."

"The area outside these storage buildings was once a large marketplace," Zanth said. "Now it serves as home to thousands of Sekani. Any who were found alive have been brought here." He started walking again between the rows of beds, nodding to some of the Sekani and smiling at some of the younger ones, who were looking at the two humans fearfully. "If the Krahn knew of its location, I shudder to think of what would happen to all of these family units."

Gianni could see that many of the Sekani were dirty, and their clothing was torn. Some of them were eating, though not many that he could see. Many just sat and stared straight ahead, still shell-shocked from the Krahn attacks. He heard coughing and babies crying as well, though it sounded more like the mewing of kittens than the cries of human children. It reminded him of news footage he'd seen of natural disasters back on Earth. The Sekani were in desperate need of help.

Chapter 5

It had taken James a while to convince the Jirina named Mazal to stop prostrating himself every time James said something, especially after he'd powered up once again to break off the creature's bonds. He knew that they needed to find shelter before they were rediscovered by the Krahn. He attempted to talk to the Jirina in Talondarian Standard while powered up, but ended up scaring the poor creature even worse, at first. Finally, he was able to get across his need to seek shelter, and the Jirina led him to an abandoned building that was next to the crumbled remains of what used to be a cathedral of some sort. It could have been an outhouse for all James knew of Rajani architecture. One of the walls had either caved in or been blown in, but it had a roof, and the day was still warm. It would have to do.

James let his energy field disappear and sat down heavily on the floor. He ached all over. It had been a rough trip down in the escape pod. On top of that, he was ravenously hungry from using his powers. The Jirina crouched a few feet away. James thought that he looked completely miserable, even though he didn't know enough about the species to truly know what the alien was thinking. Then the Jirina began to cry. Great racking sobs shook his hefty, bovine frame as enormous tears flowed from his large brown eyes. James felt pity for him. He couldn't imagine the horrors the Jirina had been through and witnessed since the Krahn had first attacked.

James waited for the sobs to slow down, and for the Jirina to compose himself a little before he spoke. "Name?" he asked the creature in Talondarian Standard, quietly, not wanting to startle him. The Jirina had been speaking so fast earlier that he wanted to make sure he had his name right before he said it. He couldn't go on thinking of him as 'the Jirina.'

"Mazal," the Jirina answered, not looking up at him.

"I...am happy to...meet you, Mazal," James said hesitantly, or at least, that was what he tried to say. He had never been good at learning foreign languages in school, and absolutely nothing had changed since then. Mazal didn't answer, but whether it was because of James's linguistic deficiencies or because he was still in shock, James couldn't tell.

He decided to just leave the creature alone for the moment and try to figure out what his next move should be. Being separated from the others was a worst-case scenario that he had hoped would never come to pass, but it had happened, so he would just have to deal with his present situation. He had a feeling that Mazal wasn't going to be much help, but he couldn't abandon him to a likely horrible fate at the hands of the Krahn. He was here to help all of the inhabitants of Rajan, so he'd begin one at a time, if he had to.

He stood up, causing Mazal's eyes to open wide in fright. "It's okay," he said, as soothingly as he could. "Just needed to stretch my legs a bit." He continued talking in a low tone of voice as he looked around their adopted shelter, mostly just to keep the Jirina calm. It was obvious that their current position was way too exposed to be defended adequately.

They would have to move on as soon as they could. James guessed that they were somewhere close to the outer city limits. He thought he remembered seeing the ocean after his brief capture, but events had happened so fast, he couldn't be sure. If it had been the ocean, then the Krahn had been bringing him south, farther into the city.

He remembered from his briefings on the Tukuli that the city of Melaanse sat on the eastern shore of the large ocean on Rajan. He must be on the eastern side of the city, but that was about all he could surmise from his brief glimpse of water. He heard the rustling of clothing behind him and turned to see that the Jirina had stopped crying and was now standing up and looking at him. He stopped his low patter and waited expectantly.

"James," the Jirina said, pointing at James with a very large, three-fingered hand. James nodded.

"Mazal," the Jirina said, pointing to himself.

"Mazal," James repeated, trying to copy the alien's accent and inflection.

Mazal pointed to the ceiling and made a slashing motion with his hand. "No good, do you understand?"

James only understood "no," but got the gist of Mazal's meaning. The Jirina knew that they couldn't stay there as well. He pointed to Mazal and then to himself, then out toward the city's remains. "Go," he said.

Mazal smiled, showing large, square white teeth. At least, James guessed it was a smile. He motioned for James to follow him, and then turned and walked to the edge of the knocked-down wall before stopping to look around for any signs of danger. James caught up to him and did his own reconnaissance of the area. He couldn't see anything that suggested a Krahn presence. He had a feeling that the Krahn weren't that subtle.

Mazal sniffed the air a few times, taking in deep breaths through his large nostrils. He turned to look at James and nodded. They both stepped out onto the hard rock of what looked to be a street. Vehicles were strewn about haphazardly, some with holes blown in them, and some with their occupants dead inside, or hanging half out, riddled with holes, struck down before they could even escape the confines of their broken vehicles. It occurred to James that the city seemed awfully deserted. Either the Rajani were in hiding, or they had all been rounded up by the Krahn and were being held captive somewhere. If that was the case, he'd have to find where they were if he was to try to begin a rebellion. Hopefully along the way, he would find the others. He forced himself not to think about what might have happened to them—especially to Yvette. He knew there was nothing he could do for them at the moment.

◊

Kieren looked around at the faces of the Sekani who were sitting, lying down, or standing within the building that Zanth had led them to. She hadn't known Janan well on the *Tukuli,* but she could tell that the Sekani she was looking at now were given over to despair. Their eyes were dull and their expressions listless, for the most part. She also noticed that those who weren't lost in their own misery were looking at her and Gianni with suspicion bordering on aggression. They were unknown, and Kieren had expected that they might not get a warm reception, but what she saw displayed on their faces made her think about powering up right there.

"I apologize if we don't offer you any more food or water than when we first met," Zanth said softly, "but as you can see, we cannot spare any more than we already have." He turned to the gathered Sekani and spoke louder. "Kieren and Gianni are called Humans. They came here to help us and are guests of the Sekani. I expect them to be treated as such."

Kieren was surprised at the change in the expressions on their faces as Zanth spoke. She wasn't sure, but she thought that the naked aggression softened, and in some cases, may have been changed to something bordering on hope. Whether it was because she and Gianni were now considered guests, or because Zanth had told them that they were there to help, she couldn't be sure. At least she didn't feel so threatened, and for that, she was grateful. All she did know was that there was a lot of work to be done in a short amount of time. She looked at Gianni, who probably wore the same expression on his face that she had on her own. But she was also surprised that he was not showing contempt, which seemed to be his usual expression.

What she saw on his face was pity, as well as determination. It also occurred to her that he hadn't said a word since they'd entered the building. He turned to look at her, and she nodded at him, knowing that he was feeling the same things she was. It was time to get to work.

"Zanth," she began, "is there a place that we can talk?"

The Sekani nodded and led her through the building to a doorway. She followed him through the doorway to see a short hallway that led to three other doors. He walked to the end of the hallway and opened the door straight ahead of him. She could see even before they went through the doorway that it was a small room set up with a table and four chairs.

Zanth sat down and motioned for them to do the same. "I apologize for the cramped quarters, but this is the best I can do for now." Kieren sat down on the undersized chair and knew that Gianni must be feeling squeezed by the sides of his, though he didn't say a word about it.

"It's more than adequate," she replied. "I don't want to

seem like I'm questioning your leadership or trying to take over, but it would help us to understand things if we knew the current situation. Before we can do anything to help you, we need to know what has already been done."

"That is understandable," Zanth said.

Gianni leaned forward and grabbed her wrist, their powers flaring together as they had before. "There, that's better," he said.

"Uh, sorry," she said, feeling embarrassed that she hadn't thought to include him in the conversation. "I was just telling Zanth that we needed to know the situation as it stands right now."

"And I agree," Zanth said, his eyes wide at seeing their powers again. "As you can see, I've been collecting together any Sekani that I can find. The Krahn have been picking off small groups, so I've done my best to rescue them before they're discovered. Of course, it doesn't do any good to rescue them if we cannot help them once they've been found. To that end, I've done my best to organize search parties to go out and find what food and water that can possibly be gathered in the immediate vicinity."

Kieren nodded as Zanth spoke. He seemed to be handling events the best he could. She was no expert on coping with disasters. All she knew was from what she had seen and read about natural disasters like Hurricane Katrina and Rita, and various earthquakes, tsunamis, and droughts in other areas of the Earth.

"What about medical supplies?" she asked. "Are there any medical facilities near here?"

"There was one, but it was completely destroyed," Zanth said. "There are a few to the north and south, but up until this time, I've deemed it too dangerous to go and search their locations."

"We can help provide protection to your search teams," Gianni said. "From what I could see just walking through there, if some of them don't get medical treatment, they're going to start dying from infections and sickness."

"And we need to start consolidating water and food supplies and rationing what you have," Kieren said. "The supplies will last longer that way, until we can replenish them."

Zanth looked at them a moment, shrewdly. Kieren wasn't sure if he would appreciate their suggestions until he finally smiled, showing his small, sharp teeth. "I have to admit, when I first saw the two of you, my first thought was there were two more mouths to take care of and that we didn't have the time or resources to do it. I see that my initial assessment was erroneous. At least, I hope it was, Kieren."

"We came here to help," Gianni said. "It was unfortunate that our ship crashed, but there's no time to worry about the others right now. Believe me, James and the others can take care of themselves."

Kieren was once again surprised at Gianni's words. She just hoped that the others were all right. It was too large of a job for her and Gianni to accomplish on their own. She was happy that she'd chosen to argue with James about her and Gianni going together on the escape pod. She didn't know how she would have coped with the almost overwhelming situation she found herself in if she'd been by herself.

◊

Mazal led James through a maze of shattered buildings, debris, and vehicles, to an older part of Melaanse that seemed to have been relatively untouched in the Krahn attack. The light was growing dim as the sun began to set in the west. Mazal stopped in front of one of the buildings. He put his hand out to James and pushed it toward the ground two times. James wasn't sure what the gesture meant, until Mazal said "wait," which James was able to understand. The Jirina wanted him to wait outside while he entered the building.

"Yes," James replied, nodding.

Mazal went inside the building and, only a few moments later, came back out and motioned for James to enter. James was surprised to find that the building still housed Jirina family units. Mazal led him through the building, which James saw was actually more like an apartment complex, with multiple housing units for families of Jirina. They passed doorways full of frightened-looking Jirina males, females, and children.

Finally, Mazal stopped at a doorway and turned to look at James. "Home," he said, pointing at the door. He entered and held the door open for James, motioning for him to follow. James entered and saw that it looked like a typical bachelor pad. He smiled to think that things were different, yet still similar enough between Earth culture and an alien culture located light years away that he could have been in a building in Detroit and not have known it.

The room he entered was furnished simply, with what looked like a couch and small table. There was what looked to be a small stove in one corner. There was a short hallway with a door off to the side and a door straight ahead, where James could see a bed. He assumed the other door was a bathroom. Mazal gave him a short tour of the small dwelling, which confirmed James's assumption that the other door was indeed a bathroom, and then showed him to the bedroom and motioned toward the bed.

"Sleep?" Mazal asked, pointing to the bed.

"No," James said. "I couldn't take your bed," he said in English, though he knew the Jirina couldn't understand him. He pointed toward the couch in the main room.

"No," Mazal said, shaking his head. "Yes," he said, pointing back to the bed.

James finally relented, but only because he was tired, sore, and hungry. The bed looked fluffy, and very inviting. He just hoped that the Jirina didn't have fleas or something similar. "Yes," James said, and sighed.

Mazal nodded, copying James's movement from earlier. He closed the door to the room and left. James waited a moment, wondering if he would be safe there. He looked at the bed and decided he was too tired to care at the moment. He had just entered the first level of sleep when there was a soft knock at his door that brought him swiftly back to consciousness. He slowly rose and made his way to the door. He was surprised to find Mazal waiting apprehensively in the hallway.

The stout alien had a translating device in one hand and a bottle of a dark liquid in the other. Mazal placed the bottle on the ground next to him and pushed a button on the translating device. He motioned at his throat with his free hand, and then pointed to James. From past experience, James knew that the device needed to hear him speak so that it could calibrate his speech patterns. "My name is James Dempsey," he said. "I come from the planet Earth, and I'm very happy to meet you."

The device beeped once, then spoke in Talondarian Standard. "Analyzing language patterns." There was a pause, then it spoke again. "Analysis complete. Language log created." Mazal smiled and picked up the bottle of liquid once again.

"I have brought you a present, James the Human," Mazal said, holding the bottle out to James. "I hope that I am not disturbing you, but I have not had the chance to formally thank you for saving my life." He bowed briefly before motioning toward the translating device. "I was lucky enough to know where one of these devices was kept. It only took me a short while to travel from here to there and back. The fernta was a lucky find."

James had to smile. Mazal looked much better than he had when they had first met, but he still looked as tired as James felt. He grasped the neck of the bottle of fernta and clapped Mazal on the shoulder. "Please, come in and have a drink with me. I'm pleased that I can finally speak to you with more than hand gestures and strange facial expressions." He laughed at the expression of confusion on the Jirina's face. "Okay," he said. "So maybe there are still some things that don't translate well. No matter. Please, sit." He motioned toward the chair next to his bed. "Don't tell me you left the safety of the building again just to get this," James said.

Mazal placed the translating device on the floor. "I needed the way between us to be cleared, James the Human," Mazal said, his speech translated in the stuttering flow of words James remembered from first waking up aboard the *Tukuli*. James knew the device would become smoother as it heard James speak English more. "My getting caught earlier was a bad coincidence. I went needlessly to an area where the Krahn regularly patrol, looking for food. The Krahn do not patrol around here—at least for now."

"I meant to ask you if you knew the Sekani that the Krahn had along with you earlier," James said. "Were you friends?"

"No," Mazal answered, frowning. "He was already dead when the Krahn captured me." He looked around the room, seemingly unsure about being there.

"Is there something wrong?" James asked.

"I apologize," Mazal told him. "It is not our custom to have servants invited in for drinks with the Master."

"Where I come from," James said, "saying something

like that would start a fight."

Mazal's eyes grew wide. "If I have offended—"

"No, no," James said. "Please, why don't you get a couple of glasses and then sit, and I'll explain." James waited while Mazal left the room and came back a moment later with two crude plastic bowls. Mazal sat on the edge of the bed, though James could see he was still uncomfortable.

"You see," James began, "my people were once slaves. It took a long time for them to be freed, and even longer for us to achieve anything close to equality. Even now, the subject is a very sensitive one on my planet. Race relations there are still not what you would call a non-issue. Do you understand?"

Mazal sat for a moment, thinking. "Why did your Masters free your people?" he finally asked.

"It took a war, followed by years of struggle," James said. "But it wasn't like you may think. My ancestors didn't overthrow our oppressors so much as our oppressors fought amongst themselves over whether it was right to own other human beings."

"What?" Mazal asked, looking highly agitated. "Your ancestors were owned by others of your kind?"

"Yes, it's complicated, I know," James said as he poured two bowls of fernta and handed one to Mazal. "On my planet, humans have evolved into different races. Our skin and hair colors and some other cosmetic features differ, but yes, at one time, my race was seen as being second-class, if human at all."

"That is..." Mazal began, not finishing his thought. He took a sip of the liquid and grimaced. Or at least it looked like a grimace to James, who was surprised when Mazal followed this up with, "Mmm, that is quite good."

It occurred to James that the bovine alien's smile from

earlier may have meant something completely different. This was going to be harder than he thought. He took a small sip of the liquid and felt it burn all the way to his empty stomach. He would have to be careful not to drink too much of the heady liquid. He needed to sleep, not to pass out.

"It's very difficult to speak about this," Mazal told him after a moment of silence. "My people have served the Rajani for thousands of years. It is hard to keep our own identity, our own culture."

"I understand," James said, thinking of the cultures back on Earth that had gone through the same situation. He realized that at least three members of his team were from races that had been discriminated against at one time or another in the past. He'd never thought much about making a big deal about being black. He wanted to be thought of as a man first. But it had come up a few times over the years; a Southern drill sergeant, who thought he was still fighting the 'war of Northern aggression,' or a skinhead wannabe he'd busted for killing a young Iraqi-American boy in the name of racial purity. There were even some within his own department who seemed to treat him differently than his white colleagues. But he'd always been able to see past colors to look at the person, a mindset his mother had imparted in him from an early age. He'd learned to deal with the ignorance of humanity out of necessity, but it didn't mean he would ever like it.

"We are not fighters," Mazal said, interrupting James's contemplation. "We never were. This war we find ourselves in goes against our very nature."

"You cannot be afraid of change," James told him. "I was brought up to believe that things happen for a reason. Perhaps it's time for the Jirina to assess their place in this world. After this, if we're capable of defeating the Krahn, maybe it's time for you to demand your freedom. The Sekani most certainly will, from what I've learned from one of them I've met."

"I must think on this more," Mazal said, standing again. "I'm happy that you found me, James the Human."

"I'm happy that we met as well," James replied, holding out his hand. "And it's just James. Please, call me James."

Mazal looked at the proffered hand a moment, puzzled, before extending his thick muscular arm. James clasped the Jirina's thick hand, feeling the strength of it.

"This is a gesture between friends on my world," he explained. "I hope that you'll consider me your friend."

"Yes, of course," Mazal said. "I will speak with you in the morning, my friend, James the...James, but now I think it's time for us both to rest." He left the room with another smile that showed his full complement of teeth, but still bowed once he got outside, where James couldn't see him do it. James took one more sip of the fernta before finally lying down, still fully clothed, and quickly falling into a deep sleep. He didn't dream.

Chapter 6

Yvette was powered up and wielding a sword made out of her dark yellow energy field. She was surrounded by the bodies of dead and dying Krahn. Their blood had formed puddles of crimson around her feet.

"Okay," she said, while stabbing another Krahn through the abdomen and hearing it shriek as its intestines were thrust out through its back. It hissed at her, still trying to reach her face with its clawed hands, even as it died. She reared back and punched it in the throat, sending it flailing to the ground, where it was still. "I'm bored. Let's try something different."

She dissolved her sword back into her energy field and stood waiting for the next Krahn to attack. They held back, wary of her now. A large group circled her. She closed her eyes.

They attacked in unison.

Long blades shot out from her entire field in every direction, impaling and killing all of the Krahn around her. She opened her eyes and smiled before dissolving the blades and letting the Krahn fall to the ground. It felt good to finally be able to use her powers without fear that she would hurt someone. She hadn't been able to on the ship, with the others also training in close proximity.

She took in her surroundings. She hadn't had a chance to actually just look at the devastation caused by the Krahn, but now that there didn't seem to be any of them in her immediate vicinity, she stopped and rested next to the escape pod. She stayed powered up, aware that there could still be Krahn snipers around. She saw that she was in what was left of a city district, in what she assumed was Melaanse, but all of the buildings were now piles of rubble. The small park had a fountain filled with the bodies of Rajani and another species that she assumed were Jirina.

Now that she had a moment to think, she knew that she needed to try to find James and the others. Suddenly, her reverie was broken by the sound of a weapon firing. She saw something ricochet off her energy field, and was glad she'd decided to keep it up. She looked around, unsure where the shot had come from. She saw a muzzle flash as another shot was fired at her. She bent down and picked up one of the Krahn rifles lying on the ground near her feet. It was a crude-looking weapon, with a barrel about three feet long and a short trigger at the top of the handle.

She had gone hunting with her father on many occasions while growing up in Michigan, so she was familiar with guns, and especially rifles. Her father had taken her deer hunting every fall. It took her a minute to get comfortable with the grip, but the next time a Krahn fired at her, she turned and fired back, seeing dust explode from the stone a few inches from the Krahn's head.

The firing back and forth went on for a while. She would run out of ammunition in a weapon and throw it away, picking up another lying near her. She had killed at least two of the Krahn snipers that were firing at her, but there were still at least three more. The Krahn were now too afraid to fight her hand-to-hand. Yvette found a Krahn energy weapon that must have belonged to a higher-ranking warrior, and fired back at them, while their weapons just bounced off of her energy field. She was starting to get frustrated at the pesky Krahn, who still insisted on firing at her.

A small Krahn ship came in over her position. It was about the size of a large SUV. She could see the pilot through the windows of the cockpit. The pilot started firing. The bullets peppered the area all around her, some hitting her and bouncing off. She dropped the weapon and held her arms out in front of her, palms together and pointing at the ship. A large lance of energy extended from her arms, shooting straight through the ship and the pilot. She spread her hands, and the ship and pilot were torn apart, falling from the sky. She brought the lance back into her field as she slowly bent over and picked up her weapon, leaving debris burning in her wake.

◊

Janan and David had been walking for nearly an hour, carrying improvised backpacks made from the escape pod's parachute. It was dusk; the sun was a bleary red orb at their backs. The wind had died down now that it had cooled off, and they had both pulled down the strips of cloth they had tied around their lower faces to help with the choking, blowing sand.

"Maybe a song will help us on our journey" Janan said after a few minutes of walking in silence.

"Uh, sure," David replied, wondering what type of song Janan would sing. He half expected it to be some strange alien ballad with words and emotions that he couldn't understand.

Janan started bellowing in a loud though not unpleasant voice. "She'll be coming 'round the mountain when she comes!"

David laughed before joining in. "She'll be comin' 'round

the mountain when she comes!"

Later on that night, it was dark, and they were still singing, though their voices now sounded a bit hoarse. They were both playing air guitars as they belted out a late eighties hair band song. David had spent at least half an hour explaining to Janan why classic eighties rock was the best music.

Suddenly, a long, thick tentacle snaked out of the sand and wrapped around Janan's neck. David didn't notice—he continued singing and walking at the same pace, putting more and more distance between him and his friend. "C'mon, Janan, sing along." He stopped, suddenly aware that something wasn't right. He was the only one still singing. "Janan?" he asked, his smile disappearing.

He looked around and saw that Janan had been pulled off of his feet and was slowly being dragged toward a large swelling in the sand. He was fighting, but clearly losing the battle. He wasn't making any noise, unable to take in any air through his constricted throat.

"Janan!" David screamed. He powered up and, in a blur, raced to Janan's side. He tried to pry the tentacle away from Janan's neck. The thing felt like a large muscle covered in sandpaper. Janan's eyes were beginning to bulge. David couldn't budge the tentacle, even with the augmented strength that the Johar Stone afforded him. He could feel the muscle tighten as it slowly began to pull his friend beneath the sand.

If only I had some type of weapon, he thought, desperately. Then he thought of his time in the Boy Scouts. It had never really appealed to him, but his father had always insisted that it would build character. He didn't earn many badges, but one that he did earn was for starting a fire without matches. It was all about friction.

"God, please let this work," he said quietly. He began to rub his hands quickly on the tentacle. The tentacle started to smoke as the thick outer layer of the creature's skin was scoured away. He rubbed faster and faster, until the smoke really started to billow, and he could see some type of ichor frothing under his hands. The tentacle unexpectedly let go of Janan and recoiled back under the sand.

David bent over his now-gasping friend. "Are you okay?" he asked.

Suddenly, the sand erupted behind them, and a large creature started pulling itself up out of the ground. It was tentacles and teeth and not much else, below a crown that matched the surrounding sand. It looked like a sand dune come to life, and it seemed very hungry, and very angry. It made a roaring sound as it rose from its pit.

"Oh shit!" David screamed. He grabbed Janan and ran, in a panic. His force field extended around Janan, protecting him and allowing him to breathe at the high rate of speed that David was traveling within seconds. David kept running, a blue blur, into the distance.

◊

Yvette was exhausted. She'd been fighting Krahn warriors for hours, maybe even as long as a full day; ever since she'd woken up in her escape pod. She'd found in her training on the ship that her powers had their limits. Or at least, her energy field would only extend so far. They had measured it at about a hundred feet before it would stop. She had tried hard aboard the *Tukuli* to extend it farther during training, but so far, she had been unsuccessful. At least she could form just about any shape with her field that she could think of, which had already helped her a great deal. She wasn't surprised when it finally occurred to the Krahn to stay outside of her kill radius. Now there was a stalemate; they stayed away, but wouldn't leave her alone, and she couldn't be hurt as long as she stayed awake and powered up. She had moved from her pod to a half-demolished building that was located to what she figured was the east of where she had landed; opposite the sunset.

The night was growing dark as she sat leaning on an inside wall of the building. It was definitely not the way she thought events would transpire when they reached Rajan. All she knew was that the ship was moving west to east when she ejected in her escape pod. If the Rajani were able to land the ship, it would be somewhere to the east, so that was the direction she needed to keep heading. But she was so tired, and starving as well. Another side effect of using their powers, they had found, was how much energy it drained from them. After every training session, they all had devoured a few protein bars each.

It occurred to her she could still see well in the darkness of the Rajani night. There was no moon up to aid her, yet she could still see the details in the rubble of the building. *Another power?* she wondered. The team had talked about the fact that some of them had inherited two distinct powers from the Johar Stones, while she and David had only one. Of course, they had never tried training in the dark before, either. If this was her second power, then she wondered if David had one that had so far gone undiscovered as well. She hoped she'd see him again to find out.

She caught a movement out of the corner of her eye and instinctively struck with a lance of energy from her hand. But it was not a Krahn. It was a rat. Or at least, it was something similar to a rat. The creature was about ten inches long, sleek and dark-furred. It didn't have a tail that she could see. It had a long snout, and its ears were nearly three inches long and laid back against its skull. She had skewered it through the middle of its body, and it still twitched feebly. Yvette had never been the squeamish type, even as a child. Her father had taken her hunting with him from an early age, and had taught her the proper way to dress a kill, whether it was deer, bear, rabbit, or squirrel. She guessed this thing was close enough to a squirrel.

Yvette didn't dare start a fire, and she'd never tried eating a kill raw (except for her first, when she was forced to eat the rabbit's heart—a tradition, according to her father). Her stomach turned as she watched the creature end its twitching for good. Then her stomach growled from the ceaseless hunger brought on by the Johar Stone, and she knew what had to be done for her to survive. She always had.

◊

David was wearing down quickly. The heat of the desert and the lack of drinking water and food were taking a toll on his body. There had been plenty of supplies in the escape pod, but they both had come to the conclusion that carrying too much would only weigh them down unnecessarily. They had brought along the remaining drinking water, but that had only lasted for a few hours, even in the cooler temperatures of the night.

It was now day, and David found that his ability to run, especially while carrying Janan, was depleting, the task becoming more and more difficult. He was taking ever more frequent breaks, and not feeling as rested afterward. He knew that if they didn't find water and food in the next day or so, that it might be the end. Not to mention the dangers posed by the local wildlife. Besides the thing that almost had Janan for a snack, there were large insects that lived in the sand and would suck blood from any exposed flesh that came in contact with the ground. There were things that looked like snakes that would shoot straight out of the sand to capture anything small enough that passed by. All in all, he thought the desert might be the worst place he'd ever heard of, let alone visited personally.

They had stopped singing after the thing had attacked Janan. The Sekani's throat was sore, and all he could seem to coax from his injured vocal chords was a pained whisper, but David thought he'd be all right, as long as they got out of the desert soon. David's own throat was raw from lack of water and the blowing sand that seemed to find every crevice of his body. In the end, he just wasn't in a singing mood, and didn't have the energy, even if he had been.

It also bothered him that his power to catch a glimpse of future events didn't always seem to work. If it had, they could have avoided the incident with the keg beast, or whatever Janan had called it. It seemed to work well for short-term events, such as when he was running quickly and needed to avoid obstacles (much better than on the ship when Gianni had tripped him). But he only had the infrequent visions, and most of the time, they were confusing and non-linear.

He couldn't worry about it now. They needed to find shelter. Night was quickly descending, and most of the really scary creatures would come out then. He'd thought, the first night, that he'd be able to rest a little without the heat of the sun baking his thoughts away with his energy, but had found that he needed to be even more alert. He'd ended up running for far too long. His arms and back ached from carrying Janan while he ran. The little alien was solid muscle, and must have weighed at least ninety pounds. Finally, he asked Janan to just start talking, anything to keep his mind occupied while his body was in such agony. Janan told him about his family, about becoming Rauph's pilot, and about life on Rajan.

The only thing that seemed to stick in David's mind was a whispered conversation they'd shared earlier that day.

"I can't believe how much your planet sucks, Janan," David had said, only half joking.

"Oh, it's not my planet," Janan had said in his new, whispery voice. "I may have been born here, but my species didn't originate here, remember? We were brought here by the Rajani, long ago." He had chuckled painfully then. "From what I've been told, there could be Sekani still out there somewhere on our home world, wherever that may be."

"You don't know?" he'd asked.

"No," Janan had answered. "All records of it were destroyed by the Rajani after we were brought here. You want to know the worst thing?"

"What?" David had asked, wondering what could be worse than their present situation.

"Most Sekani believe this isn't even the Rajani's planet of origin, either," Janan had answered. "This planet is just where they stopped running when they were done conquering other planets, and basically being the scourge of the galaxy. There's a reason the only major Rajani city is along the coast. Everywhere else is basically uninhabitable. This desert takes up a good portion of the continent." He had pointed listlessly out at the seemingly never-ending sand.

"The Kha may have taught the Rajani to limit their numbers because of a need for peace with other inhabitants of the galaxy," he'd finally continued, "but it was also a safeguard against overpopulating this sorry excuse for a planet. The only ones that seem at home here are the Jirina, and for all I know, they might be the original inhabitants of this place, except the Rajani destroyed all records of their past as well, so there is no way to know."

"That does suck," David had said. "It would be like growing up in Topeka and later finding out your parents had moved there from LA after they were done partying with rock stars and then got pregnant with you, and they were forced to move and settle down because of it."

"Whatever," Janan had said. "I have no idea what you just said, but I'm tired of talking now. Maybe later you can tell me what a Topeka is, but right now, I just need to sleep."

David had carried his wounded Sekani friend for what seemed like hours across the blowing sand, but now he couldn't go on any farther. He dropped to his knees and set Janan down. "I'm sorry, Janan," he said, lying down next to him.

"It's fine, David," Janan whispered, propping the Human's head with his backpack to keep it out of the sand. "You rest. I'll watch over you."

◊

On board the *Tukuli*, Rauphangelaa was still lying unconscious on one of the examination tables in the medical bay. The lights of the room were very low as the ship slowly lost the last of its power. In the shadows was the form of Bhakat, now powered up and even more imposing than before, his power field making him look taller and broader than he had been.

I'm ready, he thought, as he picked Rauphangelaa up as gently as possible. The operation had been a success, and while he was experiencing a major headache, there were no other symptoms he could attribute to not taking long enough to recuperate. He could deal with the pain for now. He left the medical bay just as the lights of the ship failed for good.

The *Tukuli* was dead.

He walked toward the section of the wing where he had collected all of the supplies in an escape pod. He figured ejecting a pod manually would be the easiest way to leave the ship. He put Rauphangelaa down gently inside the pod and closed its hatch securely. He disengaged the holding clamps and pushed as hard as he could. There was a wrench, and then a flood of water, and then he was swimming free of the ship in a flurry of bubbles.

Chapter 7

Ronak, High Vasin of the Krahn Horde, was sitting on his throne aboard the Krahn colony ship, listening to reports from his counselors; mainly from his chief counselor, Kalik. He had set up his throne room to mirror the same room on Krahn itself, which he had vowed would one day be his. He was tall for a Krahn, a trait of his family, though he was not as tall as his hated brother, Maliq, who was currently in control of his home world.

The counselors were all standing before the throne, which was slightly raised on a dais in the middle of a large chamber. The throne was made of a light but strong metal, and covered with cushions, unlike the original throne back on Krahn. That throne was made from a solid block of native rock, and had no cushions. That seat had been worn smooth over the years by those who had sat, and ruled, from it.

Ronak had left Krahn in somewhat of a hurry, and he'd had no time to collect enough rock for a proper throne. He liked his little comforts as well. It helped appease him when he thought of his exile at the hands of his brother. He yawned as he leaned on one elbow, as Kalik droned on before him. Yet his followers had learned he was at his most dangerous when he seemed inattentive or close to sleep, and they knew better than to wake him up with bad news.

"...Sekani rebellion was quashed in the southern region, with a negligible loss of one hundred and sixty-four warriors," Kalik was saying in his deep, steady voice, giving his daily report on the state of the Krahn warriors who had been sent down to the planet's surface. "This brings the total list of Krahn casualties to eight hundred and ninety-nine."

"Bah!" Ronak yelled, standing up and pacing before his throne, a common occurrence. Usually his bloodmate was present to keep his quirkier behaviors in check, but she had gone down to the planet herself to assess the situation. "I asked about the ship that was shot down attempting to return across our blockade of Rajan. Were there any survivors? It's been long enough for your investigation to have told you something."

The counselors conferred together in a circle, knowing that they needed an answer, and the wrong one could be fatal.

Ronak returned to his throne. After a moment, becoming impatient, he yelled again. "Well? Speak!"

"There may have—" Kalik began.

"May have?" Ronak yelled. "I *may have* to kill you all now. Find out."

"There were survivors, bloodmate," said a voice from the doorway.

They all turned to see Mariqa, Ronak's bloodmate, standing in the doorway of the throne room. She was tall, statuesque, and quite imposing in full battle gear. Next to her was a Krahn warrior. The Krahn was badly beaten, and had blood dripping from cuts all over its body, as well as its face. One side of its face was swollen and discolored.

"This one captured one of the aliens who were aboard the ship," Mariqa continued. "It was not a Rajani, though the alien was found next to a Rajani escape pod within the city below."

"Excellent!" Ronak said, sitting back in his throne. "Bring it before me."

"Unfortunately," Mariqa said, disdain dripping in her voice as she pushed the Krahn before her closer to the throne dais. The Krahn warrior stumbled and almost fell to his knees. "This one also let the alien escape."

Ronak stood up and screamed. "Am I surrounded by fools? You! What do you have to say? Come forward and kneel."

Ronak sat back down on his throne. The warrior approached and knelt before him, its hackles almost touching the floor as it bent low before its leader. Mariqa stood behind him, a look of derision still on her face for the pitiful-looking warrior.

"Mighty Qadira," the Krahn began through puffy and torn lips, using the honorific for the leader of the mightiest clan on Krahn. "This creature had powers the likes of which I have never seen."

"Powers?" Ronak asked, glancing up at Mariqa. She nodded slightly, knowing the question that he was asking. He felt adrenaline rush into his system at the implication. They were close to their goal.

"Yes, mighty Qadira," the Krahn continued. "It overcame and killed all of my warriors. I was knocked unconscious."

Ronak rubbed his throat casually and looked down at the warrior before him. "It killed all of the others, and yet you, you survived."

"Yes, mighty Qadira," the Krahn replied. "Please allow me to return to the planet's surface and find the creature once again."

"Is that what you were preparing to do when I found you

hiding in the medical facility like a coward?" Mariqa asked disdainfully.

"I was only seeking medical treatment before I took another patrol out to look for the creature," the Krahn said weakly, looking from Mariqa to Ronak fearfully.

"Enough! Rise and approach my throne," Ronak told him. The Krahn warrior slowly rose and walked to stand before his leader, keeping his head bowed.

Ronak leaned forward and placed his hand on each side of the Krahn's head. "You are the offspring of my nephew Karel, are you not?" he asked, looking the warrior in the eye.

"Y-yes, mighty—" the warrior began.

Ronak snapped his neck with a swift, violent turn of his hands. "I will send my condolences." Ronak turned to his counselors, pointing toward the dead Krahn lying before his throne. "Clean that up."

Two of the Krahn stepped forward and dragged the body away.

Mariqa still stood before the throne. "Ronak, do you think he was talking about...?"

"Victory," Ronak said. "He was talking about victory."

Kalik walked up and stood before them on the top step of the dais. "Mighty Qadira, about—"

"That made nine hundred dead," Ronak told his chief counselor. "Do you wish to be number nine hundred and one?"

"No, mighty Qadira," Kalik answered with a sigh, unfazed by the threat. He received so many throughout the day that they hardly meant anything to him anymore. He could tell when Ronak was serious about the threats, and he wasn't at the moment, having just sated his bloodthirst on the unfortunate warrior.

Ronak clenched his hand into a fist. "Then bring me the

creature that so easily defeated my warriors, fool! And any others that are not from Rajan. I want them now!"

Kalik bowed and left the throne room, followed by the other remaining counselors in the chamber. Ronak waited for a moment before turning to his bloodmate. "The Johar Stones are here," he said to her, a smile on his face. His voice was changed from the angry, contemptuous tone he used before others. This was a voice he only used while alone with Mariqa.

"The contact was true to his word," she said. "It will only be a matter of time before we find the Stones and return to Krahn in glory."

"My brother will die slowly before me for what he has done," Ronak said, his smile now gone. "I promise you."

◊

David and Janan walked down a crudely paved road lined with tall, scraggly plants with long, hanging branches. The area was a flat plain with rolling hills in the distance. They had finally escaped the Desert of Ambraa. No other living things made a sound around them, which gave David hope that they might be able to rest that night without worrying so much about becoming something's late-night meal.

"I should be able to run again in a few minutes," David told his friend.

"There's no hurry," Janan replied with a whisper. "I'm enjoying the peace and quiet."

"Yeah, I am too. How's your throat?"

Janan rubbed his neck. It still had welts on it from where the tentacle had been wrapped around it. "Better. I should have remembered the danger of the Kleng beast. I was just so happy to be home." Janan had told David about the creature that had almost killed him. They were nasty customers, from what Janan had said, and plentiful in the deep desert that bordered Melaanse.

David was looking around him. "I know. I'll be happy to get back to Earth, I guess. This area reminds me of Montana. At least the pictures I've seen of it; I've never actually been there. Except there are no buildings here, of course. I don't think there are any areas back on Earth that don't have some type of man-made structure. I've always wanted to hike through Montana."

"Why?" Janan asked, taking a sip from their canteen. They had found a small creek a few miles back, and had filled up the canteen again before moving on. David had wanted to stop there and rest for a while, but Janan had convinced him they were very close now, and they should keep moving. David had finally relented after drinking his fill directly from the creek.

David was looking down at the ground. "I don't know, really. It doesn't matter anyway. My father never would have stood for it. All of my time was spent training for football or working. Then I blew my knee out playing football in college. After that happened, it didn't matter anymore. I had a hard enough time walking to the fridge and back."

"That which we love the most shall in turn hurt the deepest," Janan said.

"Something like that, I guess," David said. He smiled. "It's strange, though; my knee hasn't hurt since...you know."

"Kartan said that, by the way," Janan explained. "He was a famous phil...phila...uh, thinker? A ghoshal."

"Philosopher?" David offered.

"Yes," Janan replied. "That is the Human word. Although all of the Elders are Priests of the Kha, there are other leaders in thought on Rajan. The Sekani have their own religion, though it's banned by the Rajani, but we have also had those who were able to think without the trappings of religion."

"So he was a Sekani philosopher?" David asked.

"Yes," Janan answered, stretching his arms over his head.

"Are you ready to go?" David asked, sensing that was all he was going to get on the subject from his friend.

"Yes," Janan replied. "Let us burn some rubber, as you Humans say."

Janan jumped up on David's back piggy-back style. David powered up, his force field once again surrounding both of them. He started running and was soon a blur moving down the road, heading east toward the city.

◊

Bhakat knew he didn't have much time left. Rauphangelaa needed medical attention, or he would die. It was that simple. Bhakat suspected that his Master had a broken leg and at least a few broken ribs. There were probably some internal injuries as well as some internal bleeding, and, more than likely, a slight concussion.

The *Tukuli* had run out of power shortly after Bhakat's operation, so he had been forced to place Rauphangelaa and whatever food supplies he could find inside an escape pod and swim, pushing the pod toward the surface of the ocean as he did so. He wasn't used to his new powers yet, but he did know how to swim well, so it only took a moment for him to break the surface of the ocean. He took a moment to catch his bearings before finally setting off westward toward where the coast should be. The water was full of floating pieces of the ship, as well as lubricating liquids and other chemical substances, which had formed a large slick.

Bhakat swam on, pushing the escape pod ahead of him, and saw land in the distance after swimming for what seemed like an hour or so. He was amazed that he'd been swimming for so long and still felt like he'd only just started. He had a slight headache from the effects of the operation, but he wasn't too worried about it. He needed to get Rauphangelaa to safety. He could see why his ancestors had placed a high value in the Johar Stones. An army implanted with the Stones would be almost unbeatable. But he could also see why they were so feared. There was no way to negotiate with an enemy who saw you as no threat to them. There was no leverage against invincibility.

A short time later, he was standing in the shallows of a secluded cove as the sun slowly set, casting everything in shadow. The cove was dominated by a tall cliff that overlooked the small sandy beach he had pulled the escape pod onto. He knew from the territory that he must be a ways north of the city. The coastal area along the city's borders consisted of sandy beaches. He also knew that the only direction he could go was south, to Melaanse. He strapped a bag with food onto his back and then gently picked up his Master and began his search for a medical facility. He hoped he wasn't already too late to save Rauphangelaa.

◊

Yvette was sitting in an alley between two partially destroyed buildings. There was rubble and trash strewn all around her, but she didn't pay it any attention. She was used to the destruction by then. She was hugging her knees to her chest, crying. She had powered down and found a spot that was as secluded as she could manage. There hadn't been a Krahn attack for at least an hour. She didn't know how much longer she could hold up. She was exhausted, and her last meal had left her still hungry. The meat had been gamy and stringy and not very palatable, but she had eaten as much as she could find on the creature, even gagging down its brain. Despite the unexpected protein boost, she knew she'd have to eat again soon, or else she might pass out from lack of nourishment.

From around the corner peeked two children, a Sekani girl and a Jirina boy. Both had the look of combat survivors, their faces dirty, and a vacant look in their eyes. They walked away a little from the mouth of the alleyway. They were holding flowers that they had picked in a nearby park.

"What's wrong with it?" the Sekani asked in Talondarian.

"I don't know," the Jirina answered, absent-mindedly chewing on a flower. "Maybe it's hurt, or lost."

They slowly came out into the open. Yvette was startled by them at first, but then saw that they were only children. "Oh! It's...it's okay. I won't hurt you," she told them in English.

They slowly walked toward her. She smiled, wiping the tears from her face. "Oh, James," she said quietly. "Where are you?"

The children came closer to her. The Sekani began to hand her the flowers from her hand. Yvette reached out for them. Then she saw a Krahn warrior walk around the corner. She screamed, "No!"

The hand that was reaching out to grasp the flowers now extended into a spear from her force shield, racing between the children and killing the Krahn instantly. The flowers fell to the ground, forgotten. The two children ran away, disappearing around another corner.

"No, wait!" Yvette yelled after them. "Wait...please."

She stood there, next to the fallen flowers and the body of the Krahn, its blood slowly seeping under a pile of trash.

◊

David and Janan were finally entering the outskirts of Melaanse. The road they were walking on was in much better condition than it had been when they'd left the desert. The sun was shining brightly, though it was much cooler nearer the coast than it was inland. Janan was aghast at the destruction surrounding him. David was no longer powered-up; his attention was on his surroundings as well. They moved past the wreckage of buildings and various-sized transport vehicles, the smell of dead bodies almost overpowering.

"By the goddess, no," Janan said. "It...was once so...it was beautiful."

"I'm sorry," David said quietly, unable to look away from the expressions of terror on the faces of the Rajani and Jirina that were scattered among the rubble and trash left over from the Krahn attack.

"There's truly nothing left for me here now," Janan said, a tear tracing down his furry cheek.

They passed by a dark alleyway, unaware that there were Krahn warriors crouched down, watching them from the darkness of the alley.

Janan stopped to look at a broken-down vehicle, hoping that it would be operable. If not, they would have to continue to rely on David's legs. There were still a few miles until they would reach Rauphangelaa's estate. Janan figured that was as good a place as any to begin their search for survivors. And Janan needed to see it with his own eyes. David kept walking a little, and then stopped to look at the broken statue of a Rajani. Janan wasn't aware that a Krahn warrior had crept up and was standing behind him. His mind was still overwhelmed by the destruction of his home world, as well as thoughts of his family, and the guilt of being the lone survivor.

"Janan, is this Ruvedalin?" David asked, still looking down at the destroyed statue. He knelt next to the statue pieces. There was little left of the body but rubble and dust. He picked up the almost complete head of Ruvedalin, and began acting out a scene from Shakespeare. "Alas, poor Yorick, I knew him..." He smiled, remembering the cute girl from his college acting class; a memory from another time.

That's when he heard the reptilian hiss coming from behind him. It was already too late for David to react as the Krahn hit him in the back of the head with the butt of its rifle. The Krahn stood over David's unconscious form, looking down at him as if making sure that the human was not going to get up again.

Two other Krahn came from ahead of them. One of them was holding the unconscious body of Janan. The Krahn held him up by one of his ankles. "What about the Sekani, Sendok?"

The first Krahn was still standing over David. Its tongue hung out of its mouth in satisfaction. "Bring it. We may get hungry on our way to Nestbase One." He smiled, knowing that this was one of the aliens that Ronak had ordered the capture of, and that it could only mean a promotion for him. He pulled out his communication radio and called into the base. "Sendok to Nestbase One," he said.

"This is Nestbase One," a voice replied softly. The communication radio's reception was notoriously bad on Rajan, for some unknown reason.

"I'm returning with an important prisoner and his Sekani companion," Sendok said. "Let Toruq know it was I who caught it."

"Reminder," the voice said, "your orders are that you return all prisoners *alive* to Nestbase One. Orders are from Ronak himself."

"Both prisoners will be brought in alive," Sendok said. He couldn't keep the note of disappointment out of his voice. He'd been looking forward to a good meal as a reward for his efforts.

Chapter 8

Yvette was sleeping inside the ruins of an abandoned building. She was dirty, and her clothes showed wear and tear from her adventures amongst the Krahn. She was curled up as small as she could make herself. The night air had developed a chill, and she didn't have any other way to stay warm.

Two Krahn warriors outside of the building were debating whether or not to go in to capture her. They'd been following her from a distance, staying out of her kill radius. They knew she would have to get tired after a while.

"Why do we have to do this?" the first Krahn said. "Ronak already has one of them."

"We do what we're told," the second Krahn responded. "If he says he wants more, we get more. You should know that by now."

The first Krahn pointed toward the building, referring to the sleeping form of Yvette. "But this one is dangerous! It killed many from my unit. It brought down one of our ships, Jpak curse it!"

"All the more reason you should take your revenge," the second Krahn said. "As unit leader, it's your responsibility to make sure the alien is captured. Fail, and Ronak is liable to skin you alive."

"Don't remind me," the first Krahn said.

A shadowy form, huge and dark, appeared behind the Krahn. Bhakat, now powered up, was determined to keep Yvette safe.

"I didn't like them that well—" the first Krahn started to say, crossing its arms before it.

A powered-up hand grabbed both Krahn around their faces from behind, and neither one made another sound. Yvette heard none of this. She was exhausted, both physically and mentally, and remained asleep, oblivious to how close she'd come to being captured or killed.

◊

Janan was scared. He didn't know what had happened to David after they were separated. The Krahn had split up, taking the still-unconscious Human to the east and Janan south, toward their main base. He wasn't even sure why he was still alive. He'd been told by his captors, with longingly hungry looks, that Sekani were considered food by the Krahn, and that he looked delicious. There were times he wished he could turn off his translation implant. After listening to more of their conversation between each other, he had come to the conclusion that Krahn would eat just about anything, but his kind were considered especially tasty. His stomach roiled at the thought of being eaten by the creatures.

Janan was puzzled, then, by the fact that he had not yet ended up as the evening meal for his captors. They had spent time talking on a communication device, but he hadn't heard what was said, only that his Krahn guards were seemingly disappointed they had once again been ordered not to eat him, and to deliver him quickly to their base.

The group trekked through the heart of Melaanse, Janan in tow, and wasted little time in bringing him to the main

Krahn headquarters, which they referred to as Nestbase One. He was led to what could only have been the house and grounds of a Rajani Elder. He saw that the Krahn had housed many of their troops in the surrounding quarters, which had previously housed the Elder's Sekani and Jirina workers and servants. Janan was led straight to the main house. By this time, he was both exhausted and starving. He hadn't eaten nor slept for two days. He was dragged before a Krahn, who seemed to be in charge of the house, judging by the respect shown to him by the others. The Krahn was sitting on a large chair that had been set in the middle of the largest room of the house, almost like a throne.

"You have a translation implant?" the Krahn asked him, while leaning back nonchalantly in the large chair. Janan didn't reply. The Krahn nodded to the guard closest to Janan. The guard hit Janan in the small of his back with his weapon. The pain exploded as his legs buckled. He fell to his knees, gasping from the agony in his kidneys.

"I will ask you once again," the head Krahn said. "Do you have a translation implant?"

Janan nodded slowly. "Yes," he whispered.

"Good," the Krahn said. "My name is Toruq. I'm fortunate enough to have risen in the ranks of my cousin's army to the point that I am important enough to have had one installed as well. Luckily, I haven't given Ronak cause to question my usefulness. I mean to keep it that way."

Toruq stood and walked to where Janan still knelt. "What is your name, Sekani?"

"Janan'kela," Janan replied. His back hurt too much for him to attempt any subterfuge.

"Were you aboard the ship that attempted to get past our blockade? The one that eventually crashed into the ocean?" Toruq asked, walking slowly around Janan.

"Yes," Janan said, looking down at the stone floor. A tear escaped his left eye and fell to the floor, creating a dark spot. He hadn't known what happened to the *Tukuli* after he'd escaped, but if it really had crashed into the ocean, then Bhakat and Rauphangelaa were more than likely dead.

"Were there other survivors besides you and the alien creature that you were discovered with?" Toruq asked.

"He and I were in an escape pod together," Janan told him. "I don't know if any others survived. I don't know anything else."

"I don't believe that," Toruq said. "Let's delve a little deeper, shall we?" He stopped in front of Janan. "Be thankful. If I thought you had nothing to offer me, your remains would already be sitting in the bellies of my warriors. Now, the creature you were with was taken to the only medical facility in Melaanse not destroyed in our initial attack." Toruq walked back and sat languidly in the chair once again. "I'm afraid that some of our pilots became a little carried away with their strafing runs. They do so like causing wanton destruction. Ah, to be young once again. There's nothing to be done about it now, though. Anyways, the creature you were with; was it by any chance implanted with what is known as a Johar Stone?"

Panic flooded Janan's mind for a moment. *So this is why I'm still alive,* he thought. *But how could they know the Humans were implanted?*

"I'll take your silence as a yes," Toruq said. "Don't worry, we will find out soon enough. We have a medical team prepared for your friend's arrival at the facility. If there is a Stone, it will be found when it's examined. And then it will be cut out. Messy, yes, but again, there's nothing for it, I'm afraid."

Janan looked up at the Krahn finally. Toruq was smiling

at him, one leg propped up on the arm of the chair. "You will not win this war," Janan said. "Whether you kill me or not; whether you kill a thousand of us, it doesn't matter. You've woken the sleeping beast, and you'll pay for it with your lives."

Toruq placed both feet on the floor before him and sat forward. "Your threats mean little to me, snackmeat. When we find the Stones, we will leave this ball of dirt, and all of you can rot, for all I care. For now, you will be our...guest until we know more about your friend and the role it plays in all of this." He sat back once more before continuing. "Guards, take him below and make sure he's as uncomfortable as possible."

◊

Yvette was now sleeping on a pallet inside a different building, although it looked much the same; partially destroyed and full of rubble. She was covered with a blanket, and her head was propped on one of the Rajani robes. Bhakat had tried to make her as comfortable as possible. She awoke suddenly with a gasp. She sat up and was powered up instantly before she realized Rauphangelaa was sitting next to her. Bhakat was standing next to the wall; he'd been acting as a lookout while the other two rested.

"Hello, child," Rauphangelaa said, softly in Rajani. "We did not wish to disturb your sleep. You looked as though you needed it."

"It was damn sloppy—" Bhakat began, not turning to look at them.

Rauphangelaa smiled at Bhakat, even while admonishing him. "Silence, Bhakat. She was exhausted. I doubt she has had any nourishment at all since she landed."

"I hate to tell you this," Yvette said, "but I can't understand a word you're saying to me."

"That's all right," Rauphangelaa told her. "Please, Bhakat,

give her some water, and some food, also. We must find James and the others."

Rauphangelaa turned toward Yvette. "James?"

Yvette shrugged, holding out her hands. "Sorry. I don't know where anyone else is. I've done nothing but fight Krahn since I got here."

Rauphangelaa suddenly grabbed his side. "Ung!"

Bhakat reached out to hold him steady. "We need to find a medical facility. You have broken ribs and—"

A yellow hand, about two feet across, reached out around his Master's midsection. It flattened out, forming a kind of bandage, though it was still attached to the end of her arm.

"What?" Bhakat exclaimed, his eyes wide. "What are you doing?"

Yvette was now standing, and powered up. One of her arms had created the bandage. "I'm trying to help him. Do you comprende help, you big jerk? It's why we're here. Why you brought us here in the first place."

A cot formed out of her other arm and went underneath Rauphangelaa. It linked together with the bandage, forming a sort of stretcher.

"So, please don't give me any shit," Yvette continued. "Because I finally get to use these powers to help!" She lifted Rauphangelaa off of the ground. "Are you ready to go?"

His Master laughed softly at suddenly finding himself carried like a youngling in the cot Yvette had created.

"Hmmph," was all Bhakat replied as he walked away. He was fine with her carrying Rauphangelaa, as long as she could keep up and not injure his Master any more than he already was.

Rauphangelaa soon fell to sleep as Yvette carried him, rocked by the swaying motion of her impromptu stretcher. Bhakat was relieved to have found one of the Humans, and surprised he found himself happy it was the female named Yvette. He wished that he knew more of her language so he could tell her this, but he didn't. All he could do was communicate using hand signals and his limited vocabulary. He could sense her frustration, which matched his own. He wondered, also, how she would react when she found out that he had implanted himself with a Johar Stone. He didn't have long to wait.

As they turned a corner, they came face-to-face with a band of four Krahn on a security patrol. Bhakat saw the Human pull Rauphangelaa into a protective embrace as the Krahn began to fire at them. He instinctively powered up as he ran toward the four Krahn. He was still unsure of what he was going to do once he reached their position. Although he had trained with the Humans aboard the *Tukuli,* he was still a novice fighter—he'd never been in a real fight in his life. He had only knocked out the two Krahn who were outside of Yvette's earlier sanctuary, unwilling to kill them.

He made his way toward the closest Krahn and did as James had instructed him, aiming a blow to the creature's throat. He was surprised when his hand passed through it, punching out the back of its neck in a spray of blood. He pulled his hand back and ran toward the next closest Krahn, dispatching it just as quickly. In the back of his mind, he could hear a voice crying out for him to stop, but he did his best to ignore it, even though he felt the nausea rising within him. He quickly killed the other two Krahn before just as quickly dropping his energy field and throwing up what little was in his stomach. When the clenching and unclenching of his midsection had finally ceased, he turned to see Yvette standing close by, a look of concern on her face.

"Bhakat, are you okay?" she asked.

He nodded, another dry heave racking his body. He

didn't know if he truly was, but he didn't want to tell her that. He was embarrassed enough as it was at his reaction to killing the four Krahn. From what she'd said, she had killed countless Krahn already.

"You've implanted yourself with a Stone," she said. He looked up quickly to see if there was any recrimination in her eyes, but he saw only understanding. "You're very brave," she continued. "I know how much you've given up by doing this. You must have had no other choice."

He nodded again and stood up shakily, struggling in his mind for the correct Human words for thank you, but he couldn't remember them. He wished Janan was there to translate, but in the end, the best he could do was place his hand on her shoulder and gently squeeze it, hoping she would understand the meaning of the gesture. By her smile, he knew it was close enough.

◊

David was still unconscious, lying on a table much like the ones used on the Tukuli. His shirt was gone now, and his pale white skin was relatively unbruised. The Krahn wanted him alive for this examination. Krahn guards stood watch outside the door of the room he was located in within the Rajani medical facility. There were two Krahn standing over him. They were looking at a small monitor screen that was centered over David's head. The Krahn were not dressed like most of the others of their kind. These Krahn were not warriors, they were Krahn healers, though their talents were not always used for the good of their patients. The screen showed the inside of David's skull. It showed almost nothing where the stone should have been. There was an intricate filament winding throughout the entire brain and down toward the spine, but the stone itself was gone.

"This cannot be," the first Krahn said.

"Where is it?" the second Krahn replied, looking at his companion. "Ronak will kill us if—"

Suddenly, there was an explosion of debris from the doorway that cut off any other musings by the two. The Krahn guards turned toward the large hole that had appeared where the doors once were. Each of the guards were impaled by one of Yvette's yellow arms, which were now formed into spears.

Bhakat walked toward the two Krahn healers. He was powered up once again, and he towered over the two Krahn. One of the Krahn ran for the doorway, and Yvette killed it, nonchalantly, while leaning against the edge of the hole in the wall. Her arm lashed out, slicing the creature's head from its body in a spray of blood. The other Krahn stood its ground, facing Bhakat and hissing. It jumped, screaming, its claws extended at Bhakat's head. Bhakat easily caught the Krahn by the neck, picking it up over his head and bending its body in half, backwards, feeling its spine and vertebrae break with a loud crunch. He threw the body into the corner.

Yvette walked over to the operating table and stood over David's unconscious body, which was still lying on the examining table. "Oh my God, it's David!"

Bhakat looked at the screen, which showed David's skull contents. "He has a slight concussion. He will live." He chose to ignore the fact the Stone had transformed, as Rauphanagelaa had explained to him it would. His own Stone was probably not quite as advanced in its change, he knew. Bhakat gently picked up David. He pointed toward the hole in the wall that he had made. "Rauphangelaa, please." He walked over and placed the still-unconscious Human on the floor, making sure he was comfortable. He looked up to see Yvette had walked out to get his Master.

As he waited for Yvette to return, he inspected the

medical equipment, noting the Krahn had hooked it up to a small, portable generator. They'd been lucky; the power was knocked out in the rest of the city. The Krahn had saved him the time it would have taken to find another generator; time they didn't have, if Rauphangelaa would survive.

Later that night, Rauphangelaa was on the table. The arms of the medical robot moved over his midsection as Bhakat directed their movements from the operating panel on the table's side. David was sitting up against the wall and drinking water from a bottle. Yvette stood next to him, leaning back against the wall and watching as Bhakat attempted to repair Rauphangelaa's broken ribs.

"So, you weren't even looking for me?" David asked, smiling and holding the bottle up to her.

"No. Sorry," Yvette answered, taking a swig from the proffered bottle. "We needed to use the medical equipment. This is the only hospital we could find that wasn't totally trashed."

David looked around him at the blood and destruction. "Well, it is now." His eyes went wide as it finally occurred to him that Janan wasn't there. "Where's Janan? He was with me."

"I don't know," Yvette answered. "You were alone when we found you."

"We have to find him," David said, trying to stand and wincing at the pain in his head. "Ugh. Damn it!"

"You're in no condition to go anywhere yet," she said, looking away from him at the approaching form of Bhakat.

Bhakat walked over to them. "Rauphangelaa. Okay. Soon."

"Hey!" David said. "I didn't know he was learning to speak English."

Bhakat placed his hand on Yvette's shoulder. "I know you

cannot understand me, Human," he said, reverting to Rajani. "But I thank you. It's...difficult for me to rely on others. But I thank the Kha you are all here to help us."

Yvette placed her hand on his and smiled. "I don't think I need the translation, Bhakat. Thank you."

◊

The darkness was complete around him as Janan sat against the wall of his small cell. The Krahn had converted the basement of the Elder's house into a prison. The cells had bars on the doors, though the walls were solid. From what Janan had seen when they'd first thrown him in the cell, its walls dripped moisture and had web-like white plants growing in various spots along the walls and in the corners. It looked to him as though the Krahn had hastily built the cells using materials from an old fernta cellar.

Janan was the only prisoner at the moment. He sat with his legs pulled up protectively against his body, his arms around his knees. He'd already been bitten twice by the small creatures known as masagas. He couldn't see them, but he could hear them as they rustled through the trash in the basement. One of the masagas darted toward him and bit him on the foot, and Janan was forced to kick the creature away, yelling as best he could to scare the others he knew were waiting for their chance to strike from the darkness. Suddenly, a blade of light crossed his face as the door to the basement opened. Janan saw a row of masagas, their eyes glinting in the new light, before they ran off, screeching, to the dark corners of the room.

A shadow blocked the light on his face as a Krahn guard walked over to the cell. "It's dinner time, slave," the Krahn said as it tossed a hunk of bread into the cell. It fell into the muck next to Janan with a soft splat. Janan didn't stir. The guard laughed. "Toruq tells me that you can understand me, even though I don't speak your language. Be grateful that you're important to Ronak, or it could have been the other way around. Instead of us feeding you, you could be feeding us. Personally, I think your eyes look delicious."

Janan sat still, with his head hanging down to the tops of his knees, unwilling to give the guard's taunting any encouragement.

"What?" the guard asked him. "None of that Rajani spiritual drivel about how your faith will get you through this? I thought you were all a bunch of holy creatures here on Rajan. Or maybe you're praying right now. Is that it?" His guttural laugh made Janan's head hurt.

Janan looked up at the guard. His face was bruised and swollen on the left side, a final gift before he'd been tossed bodily into the cell. "Where's my Human companion, filth?" he asked with all the anger and contempt he could summon. "If you've hurt him, I will kill you."

"Ah," the guard said, smiling down at him with a mouth full of teeth, "that's what I'm looking for, a little spirit. Don't worry, you'll soon meet the same fate as all the others of your kind." The guard began to walk away, calling back over his shoulder. "And I'm sure you'll taste just as good."

Janan sat in the dark, hearing the Krahn's cruel laughter echo off the walls of the basement. Then there was only darkness and the chittering of the masagas as they once again approached his cell. His head lowered slowly to rest on his chest once more as tears rolled down through the dirt on his cheeks.

◊

Yvette, David, and Bhakat sat in the medical clinic eating protein bars that Bhakat had brought from the *Tukuli*. Bhakat had successfully set and mended Rauph's leg and ribs, using the medical device to join the ends of the bones together with a temporary adhesive until they mended on their own. The device had luckily detected minimal internal bleeding from a small tear in Rauph's spleen, and Bhakat had stitched that up as well. While Bhakat worked on Rauph, Yvette and David had cleaned up the clinic, removing the dead Krahn and sweeping up as much rubble and trash as they could.

"We need to leave as soon as we can," Yvette said.

"Why?" David asked around a mouthful of food. "We're sheltered here, and Rauph is going to need some time to recuperate."

"The Krahn know the location of this place," Yvette replied. "When they don't hear back from the ones who were here, they're going to send someone to find out why."

"Does it matter?" David asked. "We've all been implanted with the Stones. As long as one of us is awake, it's not like they can get the jump on us. I say we stay here, where at least we can see them coming. We can't move Rauph for a while anyway."

"Are you going to stay up all night on guard duty?" Yvette asked. "I mean, you have a concussion, for God's sake."

"If I have to, I will," David said defensively. "Look, this is pointless right now. The fact is that, at least for the next few days, we're going to have to stay here, so we might as well come up with a plan for defending this place."

"You're awfully quiet in all of this," Yvette said, looking at Bhakat. "Who do you agree with?"

Bhakat looked from one Human to the other before finally pointing at David.

"Well, that's just great," Yvette said disgustedly, before standing up and leaving.

Bhakat and David looked at each other for a moment. Then David shrugged, and they both went back to eating.

A short time later, Yvette returned to find David asleep

in the corner, while Bhakat was checking in on his patient. Yvette walked over to Bhakat. "Sorry I got upset earlier," she said. Bhakat smiled in reply, looking like he was either going to be sick or bite her. He didn't smile often.

"You know," Yvette said, "if we're going to be stuck here for a little while, we've got to work on your communication skills. It's very annoying trying to have a conversation with someone who can understand me, but I can't understand in return."

Bhakat shrugged, mimicking David's actions from before. He then nodded.

"Okay." Yvette sighed. "Where should we start?"

Chapter 9

James spent his days speaking with Mazal and trying not to make too many appearances outside of Mazal's dwelling unit, in an attempt to not upset or disturb the other occupants. He'd told Mazal all about how he'd come to be on Rajan, about the other humans who were somewhere close to Melaanse, if not somewhere within its limits, and about the Johar Stones. Mazal had taken it all in stride, eager to please the human who had saved him from the Krahn.

James was amazed at how resourceful the Jirina was when it came to finding the things that James needed. He had asked Mazal for some large pieces of paper and something to write with, and Mazal had brought him a large role of parchment and a box of thin, black writing utensils that seemed to be made of some type of wax and wrote like crayons. He guessed that the Jirina was searching through the surrounding abandoned buildings that had once belonged to Rajani or Sekani. The Jirina themselves seemed to live in sparsely-furnished dwellings, with little as far as luxury items and no electrical appliances, as far as James could see.

James had Mazal do his best to draw a map of the city and point out their location, which was toward the center of the northern part of Melaanse. Mazal had crudely drawn a map, though he told James that he wasn't good with distances, so the map wasn't to scale. At least it gave James an idea of where he was at the moment. He spent a great deal of time poring over the map with Mazal and drawing out the approximate location of landmarks, such as where he was found, where the individual Rajani Elders lived, and where the Krahn usually patrolled. He also did his best to help Mazal and the other Jirinas look for food and fresh water. He ventured out more often as the days went along, and soon, the Jirina were unafraid if he made an appearance, and some actually began to smile or nod to him when he passed by in the hallway.

The Jirina, he found, were vegetarians, so many of them already had a small plot of land outside their buildings to grow their own food, which helped. Unfortunately, not many of the plants had produced fruit or vegetables as of yet, because it was still early in the season. Most of what they were able to find were dry stores and preserves. He'd also had them go out and retrieve the weapons from the Krahn that he had defeated earlier. The Jirina brought back three rifles and a handgun, as well as two small, wickedly barbed knives.

Not much to start a rebellion, James thought. *But they're better than nothing.* He looked over the weapons and saw that they were crude, though effective. They fired egg-shaped projectiles made of a dark metal. He showed Mazal how to fire one of the empty rifles, though the Jirina looked like he might not be able to hit the broad side of a barn with it; he would cringe every time he pulled the trigger, even though he knew the weapon wasn't loaded.

James was surprised that the time was going by so swiftly, and he vowed that he would soon have to leave the hospitality of Mazal and the other Jirina and strike out in search of his companions. He had plotted on the map what he thought the *Tukuli's* course was when they had crashed and hoped to follow the line on his map and find them.

One day, after James had counted back and figured out that he had been in the Jirina's company for approximately three weeks, he made up his mind to set out. He bade goodbye to the Jirina neighbors that he had met while there and packed a small bag with some of the preserved fruits and vegetables that had been found. He waited until Mazal returned from a scavenging mission so that he could say goodbye.

When Mazal came back, James was waiting for him. "I need to leave," he said, standing up and picking up his supplies. "My friends are out there somewhere." The translating device echoed in the small apartment. "I want to thank you for allowing me to stay with you. You can't imagine what it meant to me."

Mazal nodded. "Yes," he said in Talondarian. "I knew you would finally need to go. I am ready."

"Ready?" James asked. "Mazal, I can't ask you to go with me. The Krahn are still out there. It's too dangerous."

"You do not ask," Mazal said. "You saved my life. My place is at your side. It's simple. Plus, you need a guide."

"Yes," James said, sighing. "I do need a guide, but I also don't want you to get hurt out there. I have powers. You don't."

"If it is my fate to die in your service," Mazal said, "then that's my fate. I cannot change it." He smiled and picked up the translating device. "Shall we go?"

James laughed. "I suppose we should. I'd ask you if that's too heavy, but I know you wouldn't tell me, even if it was."

"We Jirina are strong," Mazal said, still smiling. James had no doubt that he was telling the truth.

They made their way down the hallway of the apartment

complex, with the other Jirina standing in their doorways and smiling and nodding now at the human as he walked past. James smiled back; amazed at how much their dispositions had changed since the first night he'd arrived.

They headed north, winding their way through the maze of destruction once again. After about an hour, James realized that they had left the confiscated Krahn weapons back at Mazal's place. He hoped they wouldn't need them. It seemed a pleasant time of the year as they walked through the remains of the dead city. The air was warm, and there was a slight breeze. It helped reduce the smell of death emanating from the bodies that been left where they had fallen by the Krahn.

"What season is it here?" James asked his companion.

"The rainy season had just ended when the Krahn attacked," Mazal said. "We're now in the planting season. Soon will come the sunny, hot season."

"So there are basically three seasons on Rajan?" James asked. He figured if this was the case, they were probably toward the end of spring or beginning of summer. He knew by the briefings Rauph had given them aboard the *Tukuli* that Melaanse was located close to the equator of the planet, so they didn't get any snow, the worst weather being the occasional hurricane-like storm that would blow in from the ocean.

Suddenly, Mazal stopped and hurriedly motioned for James to take cover. James instinctively powered up and disappeared just as a small group of Krahn walked past their location. James had a chance to study them and saw that each had slight differences that he hadn't noticed in his initial dealings with them. Whether it was the shade of their skin or length of their hackles, or even the shape of the bony protrusions around their eyes, there seemed to be as many variances in the Krahn as there were in human beings. From the description that Rauph had given them, he had expected them to look like alligators walking on their back legs, but that wasn't the case at all. When the Krahn were a sufficient distance away, James reappeared and crouched down next to Mazal. He noticed that Mazal's eyes were wide as the Jirina watched him, and realized that he hadn't disappeared before in his presence.

"It's okay," James said, smiling. "Just another power from the Stone." When James had first told Mazal about his trip from Earth and his implantation with the Johar Stone, the Jirina had been amazed, but seemed to take it well enough. The legendary status of the Stones was enough that all of the inhabitants of Rajan knew about them, even though they hadn't been used in a very long time.

Mazal turned toward where the Krahn had disappeared. "They're headed toward the old prison," he whispered, with the translating device's sensors lowering its volume automatically to match.

"Prison?" James asked.

"They've taken over the Rajani prison in the north of the city," Mazal continued. "No one is sure why—they don't house their troops there, and no ships land there, either. We stay away from it as much as we can."

James thought for a moment. "I need to see this prison," he finally said.

Mazal nodded. "I'll show you."

They walked about four city blocks, being careful not to be spotted by any Krahn warriors. Finally, they made their way to a high-walled building. They saw Krahn guards walking the tops of the walls, and a few outside of the structure as well. James motioned for Mazal to follow him and then backtracked to their original position; before they saw the Krahn troops.

"What is it?" Mazal asked. "What's wrong?"

"I think the Krahn are using the prison to hold at least some of the Rajani captive," James replied.

"How do you know?" Mazal asked, looking confused.

"I don't know for sure," James said. "But the guards on top of the wall were pointing their weapons toward the inside of the prison. They weren't guarding against someone getting in, they were guarding against someone getting out." He thought for a moment before sighing. "This changes things. I'm going to go for a look inside the prison. I need you to go back and get the Krahn weapons, and if you can, maybe some of your Jirina friends. If things go badly inside, I might need a rescue."

"I understand," Mazal said, though he looked uncertain.

"I'm sorry to place you and your fellow Jirina in this situation, but I can't do this by myself," James said.

Mazal looked him in the eye. "You saved my life. Anything I can do to help you, it's expected. I will bring the weapons and as many Jirina as will come." They shook hands and went their separate ways.

◊

Gianni and Kieren had been living with the Sekani for weeks and had fallen into a familiar schedule while they assisted the Sekani in everything, from cleaning up their compound to taking turns at guard duty when needed. Many of their days were spent speaking with Zanth and going over tactical plans with him that dealt with everything from raids on Krahn patrols to cleaning up the dead bodies still littering the area around the Sekani compound and ensuring that they had proper burials.

It was difficult work, and Kieren went to bed each night exhausted. But she always felt exhilarated at the thought of how much she was able to do to help, and likewise overwhelmed by how much still needed to happen for the Sekani to return to any modicum of normality they could hope to achieve. She worried also about the fact that they hadn't heard anything from James, Yvette, or David since they had arrived. She hoped that they were okay, but as the days passed with no word, she began to fear that she and Gianni were the only ones who had survivedve.

Kieren had tried to bring up her fears to Gianni, but he had just shrugged her off, most of the time saying, "we'll see what happens," or something just as noncommittal. It drove her nuts. The worst thing for her was the thought that she might never be able to return home again. It still hurt to think about her brother, Dennis, and what he must be going through. She'd never had a chance to say goodbye before leaving with the Rajani. At least she was usually too tired at night to care.

◊

Imposing stone walls surrounded the large courtyard of the former Rajani prison. Krahn troops patrolled the tops of the walls, and there was a guard tower on each of the four corners. The prison camp was located in the north of Melaanse. The city's desolation surrounded the camp on all sides. Inside the camp, Rajani and a few Jirina males milled about and sat within shelters made from a canvas-like material. In one of the larger shelters, there was a gathering of three Rajani discussing recent events in low tones.

"Torile, I tell you, he escaped," one of the younger Rajani said. "He sent a message as he left our atmosphere. Tumaani said so."

"And I say you are a fool, Maska," Torile, another young Rajani, replied.

Maska and Torile faced each other, looking like they

wanted nothing better than to fight. It was natural to them; after all, they were half brothers.

"The cursed Krahn have an impenetrable blockade up there," Torile continued. "Even if Rauphangelaa did escape, there is no way he could get back through."

"By the Kha," Maska said, raising his fist toward the other. "If you weren't my brother, I would pound some sense into your head."

Tumaani was sitting down not far away from them. He had been a Rajani Elder for longer than the two sibling combatants had been alive and was growing tired of their constant arguing.

"That is enough of that kind of talk, Maska," Tumaani said. "Would you be like the Krahn? You say 'by the Kha,' yet in the same breath, you threaten violence against your brother."

"I'm sorry, Tumaani," Maska said, his eyes downcast.

"I'm not the one who requires an apology," Tumaani answered. "You were both wrong in your behavior. Be grateful that you have a brother. There are very few second sons left on Rajan."

Both younger Rajani stood before Tumaani, looking down at the ground. "I'm sorry, Maska," Torile finally said.

"Now," continued Tumaani, "as to whether Rauphangelaa escaped, I have meditated a long time upon this subject. I believe that he did. But, I'm afraid that the ship that was destroyed last Araa's Day was not attempting to escape."

"What do you mean, Elder?" Maska asked, confused. They had all seen the explosion in the sky. They had assumed that it was a ship trying to get past the blockade and find shelter among the stars.

"I believe the ship was attempting to come back," Tumaani said. "We can only pray that it wasn't Rauphangelaa's. He was our last hope."

Suddenly, there were shouts outside from the Krahn guards. "Line up! Line up!" came the mechanical voice of the translating device.

"Come," Tumaani said. "It's time for headcount. We'll speak more on this later." Speculation was one of the few pastimes they had left in the camp.

Outside, there were rows and rows of Rajani and Jirina prisoners. There were no Sekani. It was the only time of day that all of the prisoners were let out of their cells to join those who were already in the prison's courtyard. On a large wooden stage in front of these rows stood the Krahn prison warden, who had become as fat as he was sadistic, a rarity among the usually slim Krahn. The Rajani had come to hate him in the time that they'd been in the prison. In front of the warden was a table with a translating device, similar to the one on the *Tukuli*.

"Good evening, slaves of the great Krahn Empire," the warden said. "I hope that you continue to find your accommodations comfortable. I was quite distressed by the attempt to escape our lovely camp by some of your Elders. Do we not provide food and shelter to you? Did we not release all of your women and children as a show of good faith and promises of their safety if you all behaved in a civilized manner?"

Tumaani looked at the others when he heard the warden's words. He'd said that Welemaan and the others had attempted to escape. Did that mean that their attempt had failed? After so long, he and the others had assumed that the attempt had succeeded.

They all watched as a line of Rajani was led in to stand before the stage. Their hands were clasped behind their heads. One of them had a swath of clothing over his left eye, covering what looked like a horrible wound. Tumaani felt his stomach tighten at the sight. It was Volaan. He looked down the line of Rajani and finally saw Welemaan among their numbers. They had been recaptured, somehow.

◊

James had turned invisible shortly after leaving Mazal to go back toward the prison. He walked around the entire building, which turned out to be about the size of a city block back on Earth, looking for a way in. There was only one, the main gate, and it looked like a thick piece of wood. He stood a moment before the gate, wondering if he would have to tear it from its hinges to gain entrance to the prison. He had been hoping for a more subtle entrance, so he was happy when he saw a line of what looked like Rajani prisoners led by Krahn guards heading toward the gate. The gate opened, and the prisoners were led through the doorway.

James followed close behind, just barely making it through before the door began to close. He could see that many of the Rajani in the line had been beaten recently. Some had bruises and cuts on their faces, and some held a hand or an elbow in a protective manner, as if it pained them to move it. He stood inside the door for a moment, amazed at the mass of Rajani and Jirina prisoners inside the courtyard. He looked around and counted the number of Krahn guards. Surprisingly, there were only about a dozen guards in the courtyard, and another six lining the tops of the walls. If he could get the Rajani to fight, then they could easily overtake them out of sheer numbers.

"These slaves were found to be a part of this conspiracy to escape, though, as you can see, they ultimately failed in their attempt," he heard a Krahn saying to the crowd in the courtyard. "Because of their actions, I'm afraid that an example must be made."

The prisoners in the line were stopped and left to face the rest of the camp's occupants. The Krahn guards lowered their weapons into firing position.

"But I do not want this example wasted on the dead," the Warden said. "So, each of these slaves will pick another from the crowd to take its place." The Rajani in the line were amazed. Stunned and frightened faces looked around at each other in the large crowd. They had not expected this. One older Rajani in the crowd fell to his knees.

A guard near him yelled at him in Krahnish. "Get up! I said, get up!"

The warden stood there with a grin on his face. "Kill it."

The guard walked up to the Rajani, who was still on one knee, but starting to rise. The guard placed a gun to the Rajani's head and pulled the trigger before he had a chance to rise fully to his feet. Blood sprayed thickly on the ground as the Rajani fell on his face. There were now more looks of anger among the occupants of the prison, especially on the faces of the Rajani in the line up front. James cursed under his breath; he hadn't been quick enough to save the old Rajani. He quickly made his way toward the Krahn speaking near the front of the assembly.

The warden kept the smile on his face. He did so enjoy his job. "Such are the...mercies...of the Krahn for those who are too weak to survive. Now, slaves, pick, or we will pick two for every one of you."

Suddenly, the voice of James came from right next to the warden. "You bastard." James materialized next to the warden, his arm already cocked back. He punched the Krahn so hard that its head almost disintegrated. He looked at the crowd and stepped over to the translating device to make sure they understood what he said. "Fight, damn you! Don't just stand there looking stupid."

Some of the Rajani and some of the Krahn were too stunned to react. Then the Rajani with the eye patch grabbed the Krahn next to him. He wrapped an arm around the Krahn's neck and lifted it, picking the Krahn up off the ground, and gave a sharp twist to its head, breaking the Krahn's neck. All hell broke loose, as almost all of the rest of the Rajani began to fight. Some of them refused to fight, James saw. It was to be expected, he knew. The Rajani had been preaching peace for thousands of years; he couldn't expect all of them to start fighting right away. The Jirina milled around in a frightened crowd, unsure what to do.

Krahn guards began firing into the crowd, not bothering to aim. They hit Rajani and fellow Krahn alike. Many of the Krahn in the crowd were overpowered by the mass of Rajani. James didn't know how long they had been held in the prison, but the Rajani seemed to have a lot of pent-up aggression toward their Krahn captors. The guards on top of the walls were also firing into the crowd. Suddenly, the guards were fired upon from outside the prison camp.

Mazal and some other Jirina were outside the wall of the camp. "James!" Mazal screamed. "We are here! I have brought them as you said!" He looked around him at the others. "It is time to fight. To fight for our savior. For James the Human!"

They all screamed, holding up their weapons, which they had taken from the patrol of Krahn that James had defeated after he'd first arrived on Rajan. "For James the Human!" they screamed, aiming their weapons at the Krahn guards above them.

◊

Tumaani had been surprised to see the creature appear next to the Krahn warden, but as soon as it did, he knew what it was. Somehow, it had been implanted with a Johar

Stone. It was the only explanation. That meant that either Rauphangelaa had done it, or he had been captured by this creature and compelled to hand over the Stones. Either way, Tumaani's heart sank at the sight, even though the creature seemed to be trying to free them all. When the Krahn began firing into the crowd indiscriminately, he ducked down the best he could to avoid their fire. He heard a grunt to his left as Torile fell to the ground.

"Torile!" Maska yelled, running over to where his brother had collapsed. He wrapped his arms around his brother's shoulders in an attempt to protect him. Suddenly, a red burst of blood appeared on the side of his head, and he slumped to the ground as well.

"No!" Tumaani screamed, running to where the two brothers had fallen. He knelt down next to them as the fighting raged around him. He bent over them and saw that it was too late. They were both dead. He bent his head, tears streaming from his eyes. He decided that he wouldn't leave them. He closed his eyes and began to pray, laying both hands on the two brothers as he did so.

◊

Later, inside the camp, the fighting was over as the last Krahn guards were killed, despite James's protests that the Rajani should keep at least one alive to question. The Rajani only looked at him with suspicion in their eyes. James wasn't surprised; they didn't know him. There were bodies and wounded Rajani and Jirina lying everywhere. Tents were burning, and most were filled with holes.

James looked around at the devastation, sickened by the wanton violence, but knowing it was the only way to free the Rajani from their captors. He walked around the camp, his energy shield now down, carrying the translating device that had most recently belonged to the Krahn and asking to speak to an Elder. Finally, the Rajani with the eye patch walked up to him. James had noticed that this Rajani had been the first to start fighting the Krahn when he'd appeared. Like most of the Rajani James had seen there, his hair was closely cropped to his skull, as if it had been shaved recently.

"I heard that you were looking for an Elder," the Rajani said. He towered over James by a good six inches. James thought that he was even bigger than Bhakat, though he would have imagined that to be impossible.

"Yes, are you one, or can you lead me to one?" James asked. "I came here with Rauphangelaa, though we became separated when his ship was shot down."

"So, that was the *Tukuli* we saw," the one with the eye patch said. His face was bruised and bloodied, either from the recent fighting or earlier treatment at the hands of the Krahn; James wasn't sure.

"You saw it crash?" James asked.

"We saw it fly overhead, yes," the Rajani said. "We didn't see it crash, though. I was hoping that there were survivors. By the way, my name is Kedar."

"James," James answered, pointing to himself. "I understand by your name that you're not an Elder. Can you lead me to one here?"

Kedar smiled. "No, I am no longer an Elder, nor a Priest of the Kha. That time in my life is over now. If you'll follow me, I can lead you to the Elder Tumaani."

As James walked behind the tall Rajani, he pondered his words. 'No longer an Elder,' he'd said. James didn't understand what that meant, but he didn't feel like he should ask. The Rajani had spoken with a bitterness that was palpable. Kedar led him over to a Rajani who was knelt down beside the bodies of two other Rajani, cradling one in each arm. "The Kha save us," he was sobbing.

"Oh no," Kedar said when he saw them. He reached out and squeezed Tumaani's shoulder. "Cry not for the fallen," he said softly. The Rajani named Tumaani looked up at Kedar, and then gently laid the two bodies down on the ground. He wiped his eyes and stood shakily.

"I'm glad to see that you're alive, Volaan," he said.

James caught the fact that Tumaani had addressed the other by a different name than he had given. He must have changed it recently, or at least hadn't told anyone that he was going to do it. James wasn't sure how to proceed. He didn't really want to barge in on their private conversation. He needn't have worried.

"This is..." Kedar began, looking at him.

"James," he replied.

"James," Kedar said. "He came here with Rauphangelaa."

"I could have guessed that by his entrance," Tumaani said, turning an appraising eye on James.

"Yes," James said. "But now is not the time to speak of this. We need to get all of you to shelter somewhere before the Krahn return. We're too open here in this courtyard; this isn't a defensible position."

Just then, Mazal and the other Jirina that had come with him entered the courtyard. He rushed up to James. "James, I'm happy to see that you're unhurt."

"Thank you, Mazal," James said. "I feel the same about you. Thank you for returning to the prison." He turned back to Tumaani. "We have to leave now, I'm afraid. It isn't safe here."

"I agree," Tumaani said, looking down at the two dead bodies lying next to his feet. "Volaan, can you find someone to carry the dead? I'm afraid I'm not quite up to it at the moment. But we need to bring them with us for proper burials."

Kedar nodded. He looked at James and nodded again. James nodded back to him. Kedar walked away, beginning to bark orders at Jirina and Rajani alike, to start preparing to leave. James wondered when he was going to inform Tumaani that he had changed his name.

Doesn't matter right now, he thought.

The real work was about to begin.

Chapter 10

Gianni and Kieren were leading a group of Sekani on a quest to find food and water, walking down a narrow alleyway that was choked with debris. They were both powered up, aware that they were in the heart of Krahn territory. They came to a dead end; the passage was blocked with all manner of building pieces, abandoned vehicles, and trash. It was the detritus of war that they had become all too accustomed to since arriving on Rajan.

The food situation was becoming desperate for the Sekani. They had begun to ration what food stores they had, but they knew that it wouldn't last long, even at the current rate of consumption. Zanth had suggested that they expand their search area, but asked the two humans to come along for protection with the search party, which was larger than any they had sent out before.

"Tell them to wait a second," Gianni whispered to Kieren as they neared the end of the alleyway.

Kieren started whispering to Zanth, who was the first Sekani in line behind them. "Hold on for a second."

"Hold on to what?" Zanth whispered back. "What is a second?"

"No," Kieren said, feeling her cheeks turn red. "I mean stop. Please." It wasn't the first time she had used a common phrase from Earth that didn't translate well. She turned to Gianni. "Okay, now what?" she whispered. "And why are we all whispering?"

"I was attempting to keep things quiet," Gianni answered her, now talking in a normal volume. "We need to know what's behind all this junk," he said, looking at the piles of debris that blocked their way. He turned to look at Kieren. "Why don't you fly up above it and check it out?"

"Oh, sure," Kieren answered. "I get to stick my neck out while you all stay here safe."

"That's right," Gianni told her. "If I could fly, I'd be the one doing it. Would you rather have one of the Sekani try and climb over this mess? Quit whining and go."

Kieren started to rise. "Whatever," she said, exasperated.

"Kieren?" Gianni said quietly.

Kieren was about three feet off the ground next to Gianni when she stopped rising. "What?"

"Be careful," he answered.

"Thanks," she said, rolling her eyes. "I guess."

She rose up over the top of the debris to look around, hovering about twenty feet off the ground. Suddenly, a shot from an energy weapon came from the other side of the wall and hit her square in the chest. She screamed, her power field disappearing at the same time she let her concentration waver. She started falling toward the rocky debris below.

"Kieren!" Gianni screamed.

She fell until she was only about ten feet from the ground, then regained her composure and powered up again, pulling out of the dive.

They all heard a loud voice from the other side of the wall yell, "Stop!" in Talondarian Standard.

Kieren landed next to Gianni and almost lost her balance. Gianni caught her in what was almost an embrace, stopping her momentum before she ran into the side of a burned-out vehicle.

"Are you all right?" he asked her, real concern sounding in his voice.

"I...think so," she answered. She wasn't very sure about it, though. She'd had problems keeping her energy field up back on the *Tukuli* as well. She thought she'd overcome the problem during her training on the spaceship, and was disappointed that she hadn't.

A large piece of stone from a building was tossed aside in front of them. Gianni's hands, which were still on either side of Kieren, were pointed toward the wall and ready to fire. "Son of a bitch," he said, angry now. "I'm going to kill whoever it is."

James walked through the small crack in the debris that he'd made. He was powered up. "Hold your fire! Kieren, tell them all to hold their fire."

Kieren was still in Gianni's embrace. "James!" she yelled. She turned to the Sekani. "Hold your fire! He's our leader."

James came fully into sight; he had dropped his energy field. Kieren ran to him and hugged him. She was crying.

"It's all right, girl," he told her softly. "Shhh...are you okay? Where's the rest?"

Gianni walked over to them, still powered up. "Of course *we're* okay," he said. "We would have been even better if you hadn't fired on her."

"It wasn't me," James told him.

"Then who was it?" Gianni asked.

"Them," James answered, pointing in the direction he had just come from. They all turned to look and saw a much larger force of Jirina and Rajani, with Mazal and Tumaani in the lead.

◊

James was relieved to see that Kieren and Gianni had survived the crash on Rajan, even if Gianni was still being a pain in the ass. But he knew that the hard work had just started. The situation on Rajan was worse than they thought it would be. The three races, the Rajani, Sekani, and Jirina, were scattered and disorganized. The recent liberation of the Krahn slave camp had released a few thousand Rajani and a few hundred Jirina from their bondage, but there had to be other camps that hadn't been found yet. For one thing, the camp had only held Rajani and Jirina, and only Rajani males. The young and female Rajani must have been held somewhere else.

Tumaani had told him that the Krahn had herded them out of the prison, and had reportedly released them as a sign of good faith. *If so, then they should be easy enough to find,* James thought, but he wasn't about to trust that the Krahn were true to their word. For all he knew, they were being held at another site. They would need to be found quickly. Aboard the *Tukuli,* James had thought that they would have to train the Rajani in the methods of warfare, but the Rajani and Sekani had picked up the fighting pretty well without having to be taught. Their methods were still crude, but effective. The Jirina, on the other hand, were still rather timid, but James thought they would come around once the fighting grew more intense. At least, he hoped they would.

Luckily, most of the Krahn seemed to be concentrated closer to the center of Melaanse. Unluckily, if they wanted to defeat the Krahn, there were going to have to take the city back. They outnumbered the Krahn, but were heavily outgunned by the invaders, and they had no ships. They had a few weapons that they had confiscated from the slave camp, plus some that came from Krahn outposts that they had overrun in the days following the escape. But those skirmishes had resulted in heavy Rajani casualties, and the scouts still had brought no word on their search for the other humans and the crew of the *Tukuli,* which weighed heavily on James's mind as the days passed.

James now had to worry about bringing the three races together to fight as one team. So far, the Jirina had only done what he'd told them. They would not take the initiative by themselves. The Sekani refused to fight alongside the Rajani, and the Rajani didn't really seem to care that the Sekani wouldn't fight alongside them. He would have to get across the fact that they needed each other if they hoped to win this war. He determined that he would have to call a meeting between the leaders of each race. The Rajani seemed to defer to the Elder Tumaani, so James thought he would be a good candidate for the Rajani. The Sekani seemed to have elected a leader, Zanth.

The Jirina weren't used to having any type of leadership hierarchy within their own race. They had not been able to hold any type of leadership position in the Rajani society, and were mostly uneducated laborers. Their status seemed to have come from whatever Rajani House they worked for at the time. Mazal seemed to have gained the esteem of his fellow Jirina by becoming James's personal assistant. Not that James had asked him to perform any of the tasks James required. Mazal had taken it upon himself to become James's servant, no matter how many times James protested. *But,* James thought, *maybe I can use that to my advantage.*

James had been led by Tumaani and Kedar to an abandoned building that was once used to make textiles and carpeting. It was large and had thick stone walls. James was sure that it hadn't always been a textile factory, but no one there seemed to know its history. He thought it would serve the purpose of becoming a secure base for the Rajani who had been liberated from the prison. The Rajani had dispersed to various buildings around the factory and had begun the process of cleaning them up and making them suitable for living in. Kieren and Gianni had briefed him on what they had been up to since landing in Rajan, and about the Sekani and the condition their own base was in. James made it his first order of business to secure the locations of the Rajanai, Sekani, and Jirina. They would then need to find the others, as well as clean drinking water and food.

He had deployed search teams to try and discover word of any other slave camps or pockets of free Rajani. He also sent out reconnaissance teams to spy out Krahn troops and where they were located. He needed to know where the enemy was if he was going to fight them. Up until that point, they had just been fighting what seemed to be small patrols of three or four Krahn at various roadblocks and small outposts. There had to be a base of operations that they were using.

Finally, he'd created teams that would be able to begin cleanup efforts to at least bury the remaining bodies from the initial Krahn attack, so that there wouldn't be an outbreak of disease. The last thing he needed was for the resistance, as he had begun to think of them, to be brought down by some type of plague. There was also the fact that having dead bodies around would hurt the morale of the living.

James had been given a dwelling space within the factory building. He wanted to be close to the Rajani to help advise them. He had felt bad that he would no longer be staying with the Jirina; his time among them had been enjoyable. But he knew that even though the three species had split up into individual groups, the Rajani were still the leaders on the planet, and he would need to have their backing if he was going to succeed.

It was early in the afternoon when he left his room to find

Mazal sitting outside in the hallway, next to his translating device. The Jirina hurriedly stood up, smiling. "Where are we going, James?"

"Mazal, you haven't been sitting out here all this time waiting for me, have you?" James asked.

"No, I've only been here about half a standard hour," Mazal said, with no sign of irony on his earnest face.

"We need to talk to the Rajani and Sekani," James replied. "We need to get everyone together and work out a strategy for moving forward." James began walking down the hallway, with Mazal following behind and carrying the translating device. "I'm going to need you there as well," he said, looking back at Mazal. "The Jirina must be represented too."

He found Tumaani in the basement of the textile factory, which had been cleared out and set up as a meeting room, with a large table and chairs, per James's orders. He knew that they would need somewhere to meet in the coming days, weeks, and months, depending on how long the fighting lasted. He prayed the war for liberation wouldn't last longer than that.

"Tumaani," James said, nodding to the Elder. "I'm happy I found you."

"James," Tumaani said, nodding back. He didn't acknowledge Mazal's presence.

"I want to set up a meeting tonight between the Rajani, Sekani, and Jirina," James said. "We need to speak about why the other humans and I are here, and what needs to happen in the future, if we're to help free you all from the Krahn."

"If that is your wish," Tumaani said. "I'm in no position to say no." He sighed and rubbed his eyes. "I apologize; I'm quite tired, and still not recovered from my treatment at the hands of the Krahn. Of course we need to meet. I suggest after the evening meal, at Tamaa's time. I'm sure your Jirina servant can tell you when that is."

"Thank you, Tumaani," James said, deciding not to address the fact that Mazal was not his servant. "I'll see you here, then." He turned and quickly left the basement by the same stairwell he'd used to descend, his mind already working on his plan to have the Sekani come to the Rajani building for a meeting. "Mazal," he said, turning to the Jirina. "Can you lead me to where the Sekani are staying?"

"Of course," the Jirina responded.

They made their way through streets still choked with debris, and finally arrived at the outside of the Sekani compound. Sekani guards with rifles stood outside the gates of the area.

James walked up to one of the guards. "I must speak to the other humans," he said, the translating device conveying his words.

"You cannot enter without permission," one of the guards said.

"I understand that," James replied. "Can one of you please send for either Gianni or Kieren?"

"No need for that," a voice said, coming up behind them.

James turned to see that Gianni and a small group of Sekani males were walking toward the compound. He noticed that the Sekani were ringed around him, either in a protective posture or in reverence, he wasn't sure which. Either way, it was strange to see Gianni shown such respect.

"What do you need?" Gianni said, stopping in front of James.

James clicked off the translating device before speaking. "I'm organizing a meeting tonight between the leaders of the three species," he said. "Do you think you and Kieren can convince the Sekani to send someone? Hopefully Zanth."

"I'm sure we can," Gianni said. "You know relations between the Sekani and Rajani aren't that great, right?"

"Yes," James said. "Just tell them that this is for the best. Actually, maybe you should let Kieren do the talking." He smiled at the other man, letting him know that he was joking. Mostly.

"Ha-ha," Gianni said, scowling.

"You know I'm just kidding," James said. "I need all of us to be on the same page here, Gianni. We need to get them all together to talk, or relations are only going to become worse between them."

"Yeah, I know," Gianni said. "Don't worry, we'll be there."

"Great," James said. "I'll see you tonight. Tell them that the meeting will begin at something called Tamaa's time. I'm sure they'll understand when that is."

"Okay, see you then," Gianni said. He turned to his group of Sekani and spoke some words in a language that James couldn't understand.

As Gianni walked away, surrounded by his group of Sekani warriors, James was surprised at the changes in the man since they'd been reunited. He seemed more mature than he had on the ship. He wasn't sure if it was Kieren's influence, or the Sekani he'd been living with since coming to Rajan, but he was happy to see it. He turned toward Mazal, who was looking at him expectantly. He clicked on the translating device. "Well, I guess that's all we can do for now. How long until this Tamaa's time that Tumaani spoke of?"

Mazal looked up at the sun, seeing its position in the sky. "I would say at least two or three standard hours."

"Good," James said, smiling at Mazal and placing an arm around the Jirina's broad shoulders. "I'm starving. Let's go find some food."

◊

Tumaani, James, Kieren, Gianni, and Zanth were sitting around a table in the basement bunker of the damaged building that the Rajani had set up as their headquarters. Mazal was standing directly behind James with his arms crossed. Kieren was sitting between Gianni and James, holding their hands so that they could both speak and understand Talondarian Standard without using the clunky translating device.

"Thank you for coming to this first meeting," James began. "I know how much things are...strained...between your species."

Zanth leaned forward. "I am here only because I trust Kieren."

Kieren blushed and smiled, looking down at the table. "Thank you, Zanth."

Gianni broke contact with Kieren. "What am I, chopped liver?"

"Shut up, Gianni," James told him without looking at the other man. "You're not helping the situation."

Gianni raised his hands in a fending off gesture, smiling. "Sorry, Boss." He once again took hold of Kieren's hand.

"This course of action cannot continue, James," Tumaani said. "My people have lived by the teachings of Ruvedalin for two thousand years. Yes, we have made mistakes in the past. Yet, to continue with this brutal killing is a larger threat than anything the Krahn Horde could do to us."

"Then why are we here?" Gianni asked.

"Gianni—" Kieren began.

Gianni broke contact with her once again to speak English. "No, Kieren, I want to know." He grabbed her hand again. "Why were we brought all the way out here to fight for a species that won't fight for itself? If you wanted to give up so badly, then why drag us into it?"

"Believe it or not, he does have a point," James said, looking at Tumaani. "We cannot win this fight alone, even with the powers afforded us by the Johar Stones. We need you to help us."

Tumaani looked down at his hands for a moment. He then quietly spoke, still not raising his eyes. "You don't understand."

"Then tell us," Gianni said. "We want to help you."

"Tell them, Tumaani," Zanth said to his former master. "Or I will." Tumaani looked at James. "You don't know what we Rajani are capable of. You have not seen what we could... what we *have* done. The worlds that we have—" He stopped a moment and leaned forward. "Don't you see? We've devoted our entire lives to peace for two thousand years, and yet, the flame of our fury has only been hidden, it has not been extinguished." He looked at his intertwined fingers, held before him on the table. "If we continue along this course of action, it may blaze once again, stronger than ever."

"Once that happens," Zanth said. "No one will be safe. Not even your home planet, Kieren."

"You would condemn your species to extinction," James continued. "Rather than take the chance of returning to what you once were over two thousand years ago?"

"Yes," Tumaani answered, sitting up straighter. "I would."

Gianni threw up his hands. "Well, that's just great. He's crazy."

"I understand your concern," James said, ignoring Gianni. "But I guarantee you, if something is not done soon, your species, as well as Zanth's and Mazal's, will face extinction or slavery. That's a fact."

"I see," Tumaani began, sighing, "that I no longer have a choice. You, James, have reawakened my people's thirst for battle. I cannot stop them now. I can only hope to keep them under control."

"Like you have kept us for so long?" Zanth asked. "I tell you now, we will no longer stand for it, Tumaani. We'll fight, with or without our former masters. Even against them, if need be."

"Zanth, I know what your species has gone through," James said. "On Earth, my people were once in a very similar position. Nobody wants to be treated as a second-class citizen. All I'm asking is that both of you agree to help fight for your planet. And when we kick their ugly asses off it, then you must fight to keep the alliance we forge between your two species. Do you accept these terms?"

"Long have we relied on the Sekani...and on the Jirina, for that matter," Tumaani said. "We have grown lazy, and we have grown even more arrogant. I give my word that I will work to set about changing our ways. The Rajani must become more self-sufficient."

"Tumaani," Zanth replied, "I know you to be a good and wise leader. But until I see proof that my species will be free, I can guarantee nothing."

"But will you fight alongside us all?" James asked. "Will you fight for your planet?"

Zanth smiled. "Oh yes. We will fight. To the death of us all, if it comes to it."

"Let's all hope that it doesn't come to that," James said. He turned to look at Mazal, who was still standing behind him. "And you, Mazal. Will you please sit down? You are *not* my servant."

"But James," Mazal said, "I owe you my life."

James was smiling now. "Fine. If that's true, then I order you to devote yourself to the benefit of your species. Please, sit down. You are among equals here."

Mazal reluctantly sat between James and Tumaani.

"I would ask that you all go to your respective groups," James continued. "If we're to form a plan of action, then we must know who will fight, and who will not."

"That is reasonable," Zanth said.

"I...agree," Tumaani replied, still looking unsure.

James turned to Mazal. "Mazal?"

"The Jirina will go where you lead," Mazal said.

"No, my friend," James said, placing a hand on his shoulder. "From now on, they go where you lead." They smiled at one another.

◊

Kieren was in her small room at the Sekani compound, crying. The room had a makeshift door for privacy; it had not yet been fixed up for her to live in by the Sekani. The door was set in place in the doorway, but wasn't attached by a hinge. She and Gianni had been sleeping in the large building on cots among the Sekani, but since Zanth had invited her and Gianni to live there as his guests after the first meeting between the Rajani, Jirina, and Sekani, they were each given their own rooms to stay in. There was a knock on the door, and she quickly wiped her eyes with her hands, not wanting anyone to know she'd been crying. If word spread among the Sekani that the human woman was crying, it could look bad, or maybe even cause them to lose confidence in her. "Yes?"

Gianni stood in the open doorway. He closed the door as much as possible and turned to her. "Hey. Are you all right? I, I heard you crying."

"You know," she began, "when we got into this, I thought we would be doing this great, heroic deed. We were going to free a whole planet from oppression and slavery to an evil race. But...the Rajani were once the bad guys. They could be again, for all we know."

Gianni sat next to her on the small wooden pallet that

was the only furniture other than the even less comfortable-looking cot in the corner of the room. "I know. It's hard to know who we're fighting for, or why we're even here. But I want you to know something."

"What?" she asked, wiping away another tear as it streamed down her face. She was aware of how close he was sitting next to her; could feel the warmth from him in the chill night air.

"No matter what happens," Gianni said, "we're all here for you. I'm...here for you."

"Gianni—" Kieren began.

Gianni stood up abruptly. "Yeah, I know. Sorry if I got a little corny."

"Don't do that," Kieren said.

"Do what?" Gianni asked, unable to look at her.

"Don't close yourself off from me," Kieren said. She stood and placed her hand on the side of his face. "Just tell me that everything will be all right."

"It will," Gianni told her, now looking her in the eyes.

They embraced, almost cautiously, before settling into it. Kieren rested her head on his shoulder and closed her eyes.

"I promise," Gianni whispered.

They stood there a moment before he pulled back. She looked up at him, noticing how long his hair and beard were getting. She thought it made him look older, but it also softened his features. He had always had a hard look to him, from the first time she had seen him on the starship. "Thank you," she said. "I needed that."

"Uh, anytime," he said. "I...I should be going now. I need to get some sleep."

"Yeah, me too," she said. "I'll see you tomorrow."

"Goodnight," he said softly, looking into her eyes once again before turning away. He moved the door out of the way and replaced it again once outside the room.

"Goodnight," she said softly, not knowing what to think about him. It was a long time before she fell asleep.

◊

Later that night, Gianni was sitting alone in his room in the Sekani compound, having walked slowly away from Kieren's place, kicking himself the entire way for blowing it once again with her. He was tired. Tired of fighting Krahn; fighting with the other people who were crazy enough to have come along on this trip, and tired of fighting himself. He had always been something of a loner, which was difficult, coming from a large family of Italian Catholics. He had four younger siblings and too many cousins, nieces, and nephews to keep track of without a spreadsheet. But he'd always been the outsider; the one who, as a kid, played on his own when the family got together, or later, when he'd grown old enough to have his own car, arrived late to those same family gatherings, and left early.

He'd always had trouble with relationships, and things were no different now, light years away from family and friends. Maybe he was too proud, or just rubbed people the wrong way. He had never been one to cater to other people's wishes or demands. Tact was also a foreign word. Most of the time it suited him fine, not having to care about what other people thought of him. He lived his life the way he wanted. But there were times—not too often, but they came up—when he found it difficult to interact with others, even when he wanted to. The worst part was the fact that he felt strong emotions about Kieren and didn't know how to express them.

Kieren was usually who he was thinking about at any given moment of the day, and it was driving him crazy. She was definitely not like the girls he was used to spending time with back in New York, or even after he'd moved to Detroit. He couldn't let her know that he felt like some teenager with a crush, though. He had too much self-respect for that. So instead, he made an ass of himself most of the time they were together. He threw his hairbrush down in disgust and looked at himself in the mirror. *You'll never change,* he thought. But he could see that he *had* changed, at least physically. He'd lost weight and gained muscle since coming to Rajan.

Physical exertion and a lack of food supplies had helped toward that. He'd been a little overweight back on Earth—too many rich Italian meals and cannolis—but now he was probably in the best shape of his life. *The interstellar war diet, try it and see the results!* he thought sardonically. He hadn't cut his hair since leaving Earth either, and it was starting to get long. He'd worn it a little long before, but now it hung past his neck and would fly into his eyes if he didn't keep it bound. He'd also grown a mustache and goatee. It was difficult to keep up on the personal grooming in a war zone.

At least he was usually so tired at night that he didn't think much about those he'd left back on Earth, and he didn't dream much, or if he did, he didn't remember anything. It was cold comfort, at best.

◊

James lay down on his cot, ready for bed. He was feeling the exhaustion seeping in from all that had happened to him in the last few days. Since crash-landing on Rajan, it seemed like he had hardly been able to sleep more than an hour or two at a time.

When Rauph had asked him to be the leader of the small band of humans, he had no idea that he would become the military leader of the entire resistance. But there was really no one else who would or could do it; he could see that from the meeting earlier that night. It had been over two thousand years since the Rajani had gone to war. No living Rajani had studied battle tactics or trained for fighting. The same went for the Sekani and Jirina. Hell, the Jirina were not even warriors by nature, and never had been in their known short history on Rajan, from what Mazal had told him.

So far, the resistance had been fighting and winning skirmishes with pure numbers, not out of any type of sound tactics or plans. James sighed as he turned over on his side on the cot. It wasn't very comfortable. He decided he'd have to try and come up with a better plan of battle going forward. They had been able to defeat random bands of Krahn and small outposts, but the main body of the Krahn forces were still entrenched in the inner sections of the city, and the resistance had not dared come out in the open as a large fighting force, for fear of the colony ship that was still somewhere overhead, waiting. If that thing opened up on them, they wouldn't last long.

He finally began to fall asleep, his last waking thought, as usual, about Yvette and wondering if she was still alive out there somewhere. He was heartened by the fact that Gianni and Kieren had survived their crash on Rajan. There was still hope that he and Yvette would be reunited soon.

◊

Dreben was just lying down for the night when he heard the ship flying over the farm, becoming louder by the second. He rose quickly from the bed and looked out of the room's single window, but could see only lights in the darkness above the farm. He walked out of his room to the main bunkroom, where the other Rajani slept at night. The Sekani and Jirina farmhands slept in a separate building closer to the orchard. Dreben saw that a few of the hands were sleeping, but most were still awake.

Terin, who was the senior hand under Dreben, walked

over, a worried look on his face. "What is it, Dreben?"

"I don't know," Dreben answered. "A ship of some sort. Everyone stay calm." He walked to the front door and slowly opened it. He could see a small ship landing in the middle of the jubka field. "Blast it," he yelled as he saw it crushing at least four rows of seedlings.

He was about to run out and yell at the pilot when the rear hatch of the ship opened, and three figures emerged. He could tell right away that they weren't from Rajan; and that they were armed, as well. He watched as they ran toward the other bunkhouse, which was about a hundred standard feet away from where he was standing.

"What are they doing?" Terin whispered from next to him, causing him to jump.

"I don't know," Dreben answered, giving his friend a scornful look. "Why don't you go ask them?"

"When pulkos dance," Terin said. "Did you fail to notice their weapons?"

"No, I saw them," Dreben said. "We need to figure out how to get them to leave without anyone getting hurt."

Just then, a shot rang out from the other bunkhouse. "Blast it," Dreben said.

"Too late," Terin said.

Dreben saw two of the figures come out of the bunkhouse, followed by the third, who was carrying the body of a Sekani over its shoulder. They walked quickly back to the ship, and it swiftly lifted off the ground and flew away.

"Well, let's go see who it was at least," Dreben said to Terin. They walked over to the bunkhouse. Dreben walked through the doorway to see that there were overturned bunks and a spatter of gore on one wall, with a streak of blood leading down to the floor. The Sekani and Jirina were huddled together in the far corner, a look of shock on all of their faces.

"They killed Joran," a Jirina named Gamel said, a look of shock on his face.

"Blast," Dreben said softly. "All right, I want all of you to grab your clothes and gear and bring it over to our quarters. We'll all sleep there tonight."

"I don't think I could sleep after this," Terin said, looking at the red smear on the wall and floor.

"Needless to say," Dreben said, "we'll all be safer if we're in one place together. We'll post a couple of guards."

"And arm them with what?" a Sekani named Maden'ta asked. "They had weapons. They killed Joran!"

Dreben could hear the panic in the Sekani's voice, bubbling below the surface and threatening to overwhelm him. He knew that if it happened to one of the Sekani, there was no telling how the others would react. "Everyone just calm down and listen to me. We'll have to come up with something," he said. "Right now, it's important that you just get your stuff and bring it on over to the other bunkhouse."

He turned to look at Terin. "Terin, I need you to go back to the bunkhouse and start making room for them. It doesn't matter where everyone sleeps, just make sure there's a place for all of us."

"What are you going to do?" Terin asked.

"I'm going to find some weapons," Dreben answered, though he was unsure what he could come up with on the farm. Despite the lack of real weaponry, though, he knew that anything was better than what they had now. Whoever it was that had attacked them would get a surprise if they came back. But he hoped with all of his heart that they didn't.

Chapter 11

James had grown a beard in his time away from Earth. It was difficult to find a shaving implement in a society where no one shaved. His was salt-and-pepper in color, and it made him look ten years older, he knew. Not to mention Yvette had hated it back on the ship. She'd actually offered to shave it by using her powers, but the thought of it had not appealed to him in the least. *Best not to think about her now,* he told himself, looking in the mirror that Mazal had found for him, weeks before. It still surprised him when he woke up in the morning and looked in the mirror to see the beard.

There had still been no word from Yvette since the *Tukuli* crashed. He'd almost be inclined to let her try to shave him if he could just see her again. And if something had happened to her, what then? It had been a long time since he was in any sort of meaningful relationship with a woman. Jenny would always be there in his mind and his heart, there was no way it could be different, but he had truly started to care about Yvette. He wasn't sure he was ready to think about the "L" word, though. It was different, certainly, but there was nothing wrong with that. He wasn't the lovesick pup trying to be a man at too young an age anymore. He knew, though, that losing Yvette would hurt, and so he did everything he could not to think about her, which, of course, meant that he spent most of his downtime doing exactly that.

Not that he'd had a lot of extra time to think about anything else lately. He was still attempting to grasp the Krahns' strategies. He had no intelligence on how they fought and how to counteract them. Everything right now was guerrilla warfare; hit them and withdraw. But he also knew that this type of insurgency could last for years without coming to any type of closure. He needed to come up with a better plan with a definite end in sight, and preferably with that end coming soon, for the sake of all of them.

One problem he faced was that he didn't know how many Krahn were still on the colony ship. He knew there was a finite number of Krahn overall, but didn't know how many were on Rajan and how many were off-planet. He didn't even know how fast they could deploy from space if they called in reinforcements. He'd seen Krahn ships flying over Melaanse, and could tell that it wasn't just the same one over and over again. He had asked the three species to write down details of each ship they saw so that they could start to get an idea of how many there were, but he knew it would be slow going. Luckily, from the ships that he had seen so far, he had learned that the Krahn ships could be told apart by size and type, customized as they were from ships they had captured.

The Krahn had been attacking and confiscating ships for years, so none of them looked alike. They seemed to range in size from something a little bigger than a large SUV back on Earth to about twice the size of a semi. None of them that he'd seen were close to the size of the colony ship, but then, the Krahn could be keeping the larger ships in orbit around the planet. He didn't want to attack the Krahn in Melaanse, only to be sandwiched between them and others coming from the colony ship. There was no doubt in his mind he needed spies, and he needed to capture a few Krahn for questioning. He sighed and grabbed a nutrition bar, knowing that he was going to have to go talk to the Rajani about it.

◊

James and Zanth had met formally, but had not had the chance to speak together extensively. So it was no surprise when the small blue alien showed up at his room to speak with him.

James had just returned from a meeting with some of the minor Rajani leaders—those who had taken up fighting the Krahn instead of bowing to their Elder's wishes to let the humans and other inhabitants of Rajan fight on their own. Kedar and Welemaan were both intelligent and willing to do what they could to free their home world. He'd been somewhat astounded that the Rajani had been a peaceful society for two thousand years, and yet, had taken to warfare as naturally as they had. All they had needed was a catalyst, and James had arrived at the first prison camp to be that catalyst. He just hoped he didn't end up getting burned.

Zanth had been waiting for him to return, and from the frown on the little alien's face as he stood to look at James, he had been waiting for a while. James smiled and nodded to the Sekani, and motioned for him to enter his room. Zanth returned the smile, reluctantly, then nodded at James and entered the room. Unfortunately, the resistance had not yet been able to restore any type of short-range communication that would have allowed Zanth to simply call over to say he was popping by. They hoped to in the future, but, for now, they were mostly using messengers, most of them Sekani, who would carry messages from location to location and were able to go mostly undetected by the Krahn, though there had been casualties. It had also forced them to come up with a code language that was hard for the Krahn to interpret.

James guessed that what Zanth had to say was too important to entrust to a mere messenger, even with a coded message. Either that, or he simply wanted to speak face-to-face, which was fine with James.

He studied the diminutive alien as he motioned for him to sit in the somewhat uncomfortable chair in his room. It was hard to tell his age, though James suspected that he was much older than Janan. He wasn't familiar enough with Sekani physiology to know what their aging process looked like. Did they go bald? Get wrinkles? Lose teeth? He didn't know. The one thing he did notice, and had noticed upon meeting Zanth the first time, was that the Sekani held himself in a more dignified, almost stately, manner than Janan. Whether that was due to age or maturity, he wasn't sure, but as the leader of the Sekani people, he was probably the best choice, in James's estimation. James had requested a translating device installed in his room, and he reached over and turned it on.

"I truly loathe those things," Zanth told James, though he smiled as he said this. "Always make me feel like I'm speaking at the same time as someone else."

"It took me a while to get used to them as well," James replied, returning the smile. "And the device on the *Tukuli* sounded like it had a mouthful of rocks sometimes."

"Yes," Zanth said. "Kieren has told me some of the exploits of your trip from your home world to Rajan after you were kidnapped. Cannot be helped, I'm afraid. The Rajani are not very progressive when it comes to new technology. Even the ships themselves are based on designs that were created hundreds of years ago by a species that is not even around anymore."

James winced at the word 'kidnapped,' but he supposed that word was as good as any to describe what had happened to them. He also knew that Zanth would not be pulling any punches when it came to his thoughts on the Rajani. He'd also learned more about the Talondarians on their trip than they wanted to. James was thinking back to his run-in with the being named Zazzil on the Mandakan Space Port. It had all been a case of mistaken identity, but he'd been afraid that they would never make it to Rajan. Luckily, the situation had been resolved peacefully.

"But your arrival here did serve a purpose," Zanth was saying. "Whether your voyage here was voluntary or not, the fact is, I don't think the Sekani would have survived much longer without intervention, so for that, I am most grateful." He leaned forward and looked intently into James's eyes. "I suppose you've been told of what the Krahn do to Sekani."

"I've seen it first-hand," James told him, remembering back to the day he arrived on Rajan. He almost shuddered at the memory, which was still vivid in his mind.

"Ah," Zanth said, leaning back. "Then you know that our numbers were dwindling faster than those of the Rajani or Jirina. But enough about that. This wasn't what I came here to talk to you about."

James waited, not really knowing what to say. Zanth was different than he had acted when they were in the presence of the Rajani, or even a few minutes before, outside his room. The Sekani seemed more relaxed and comfortable. James had the feeling that all of the bluster Zanth had shown before was an act. He considered that Zanth must have been placed in an enormously stressful position as leader of his species. Not only was there the fight against the Krahn to consider, but also the fight for freedom from the Rajani. It was a lot of responsibility to place on anyone's shoulders, let alone someone who had been a servant only a few months before.

"You are aware, I'm sure," Zanth began, "that some of the

Sekani worked as pilots or crewmembers aboard the Rajani vessels before the Krahn attacked our planet. Many more of us worked for the households of Rajani Elders. Having Sekani and Jirina servants was seen as a sort of status symbol in Rajani society." Zanth sighed before proceeding. "I myself was the head steward for Tumaani's House, which, I suppose, is why I became the de facto leader of the Sekani after the invasion. I had gone from ordering around the servants in my house to ordering around all of the Sekani."

"Which is why," James said, "it must be difficult for Tumaani to accept you as the leader of the Sekani."

"Precisely," Zanth said, smiling. "All he remembers is the servant who updated him every morning with his schedule for the day and made sure his breakfast was hot and waiting. Other than that, I was invisible. But this leads to the point of our conversation. I have a suggestion for a mission that I believe will greatly benefit our cause. Yet I know that if I were to present it before the others, it might not get the consideration it deserves."

"So you want me to suggest it for you," James said, following the train of the alien's thoughts.

"Yes!" Zanth said, smiling again and leaning forward. "I must say, when I first met Kieren and Gianni, I had my doubts about the intelligence of your species." He thought a second before adding, "At least, about the males of your species." Zanth and James both laughed at this before he continued. "But I see that Rauphangelaa at least was smart enough to pick the right one to lead your group of Humans."

"Thank you," James said, nodding his appreciation.

"As for my suggestion," Zanth said, "I think that any final battle will be quite lopsided if we have to contend with Krahn troops on the ground as well as in the air. So far, we have been able to slip in and out of any battles because of the element of surprise and by using small bands of troops to attack and retreat. If we're to prevail in any large-scale battles in the future, we must use a larger force against the Krahn."

"Which, in turn," James said, "leaves our troops open to attacks from the air. If we amass too large a force, they'll be easy pickings for any Krahn ships flying over."

"Right you are," Zanth said. "So what I propose is that we attack the main landing and refueling area in Melaanse and either capture or destroy the Krahn ships. If we do manage to capture any, it shouldn't be too difficult for our Sekani pilots to fly them, either into battle on the planet's surface, or into space against the Krahn colony ship. The sticking point here is that the Sekani alone are not enough to succeed in this mission. We must have the aid of the Rajani and Jirina."

James thought for a moment about the scenario that was being presented. On one hand, Zanth had a point about the Krahn's air superiority; it was something that had been weighing on his mind as well. On the other, who could say that the Sekani wouldn't just leave Rajan if they ever got a hold of a ship that was large enough for them all to fit in? He didn't know the answer to the question. How would the Rajani react to the Sekani being able to fly ships without their approval? Somehow, he didn't think they would be happy with this plan. But it made enough sense. And as Zanth pointed out, if they couldn't capture the ships for some reason, they could at least attempt to destroy them.

◊

Zanth had enjoyed speaking with the Human named Dempsey earlier that night. As he'd told James, he hadn't been sure about the Humans when he had first met Kieren and Gianni. The one named Gianni had come off as both rude and ignorant. But that first impression, it seemed, had turned out to be incorrect. He could understand what Rauphangelaa had seen in these Humans, though he was still shocked that they had been implanted with Johar Stones so quickly by the Keeper of the Stones. The Stones themselves had always been a mystery to the Sekani. Yes, they had known some of the stories surrounding them, but they had never really known what the truth was, and what was merely embellishment from years of rumors. When he had met the Humans and saw their powers, he'd been amazed to see that many of the stories may actually be true.

Zanth got into bed, though he wasn't feeling very tired. His mind was too active to sleep. He knew, though, that the next day would be long and difficult, as they had been since the Krahn attacked. After generations of toiling under Rajani control, this was the first time that the Sekani had even a glimmer of freedom. It was a bittersweet feeling, though, considering what they'd had to experience so far at the hands of the Krahn Horde. Like most Sekani, not only did Zanth thirst for freedom, but also for knowledge. So much of their past had been taken away when they had been conquered by the Rajani. There were hardly any records as to what Sekani society had been like before then. Once they broke away from the Rajani and defeated the Krahn, or at least drove them off, then would come the real work: discovering who they had been, and if they could ever go back to being what they once were.

Most of the traditions, like the Sekani language, were what could be passed down from father to son, mother to daughter. They had their own religion, their own language, and their own customs. Although these had been banned by the Rajani, they were still practiced in private by Sekani families, a secret that had been kept for generations. It would be a secret no more. No longer would they live half of their lives in the shadows. If the Rajani would formally recognize that, then it would be a great day when they finally defeated the Krahn. If not, then a new battle would begin after the Krahn were driven off. Zanth was prepared for both scenarios.

◊

Gianni woke up and couldn't tell what time it was, only that it was still early in the morning. There was someone banging on his door. He wearily got out of bed and walked to the door. Before opening it, he powered up, just to make sure that he wasn't caught by surprise in case the Krahn had overtaken the Sekani base sometime during the night. He opened the door and saw a small group of Sekani waiting outside. They were all smiling. *Typical,* he thought, powering down. They all thought they were so funny, liking to kid him about relying on his powers too much. He wasn't surprised that they would try to get him to power up for no reason, just to prove their point.

"Ha-ha, guys," he said. "Give me a minute to get dressed. You know, clothes?" He motioned like he was putting on pants. They all nodded and still stood there, watching him and smiling. He turned away from them. "Whatever." He walked over and really did pull on his pants, feeling how thin they were becoming from constantly wearing them. He would have to search for new ones soon.

He considered the fact that things might go smoother with his Sekani companions if he learned Talondarian Standard. He sighed, knowing that he would have to, eventually. He'd been relying on Kieren too much to interpret what was being said. *Not that holding hands with her was a bad thing, he thought,* smiling. If he was going to keep spending his days with the small group of Sekani going out on patrols, though, he would have to bend somewhat on what he was willing to do. Although he had learned a smattering of Sekani words, their conversations were still extremely limited. Hell, he didn't even know many of their names.

He stopped at the door to his room and pointed to himself. "Gianni," he said. He then pointed at the first Sekani next to his door.

The Sekani looked at his finger a moment before it dawned on him that Gianni was asking for his name, something that he had not done before. "Joreni," he finally said, bowing slightly to Gianni.

Gianni pointed at the next Sekani. "Golena," he said. Gianni kept pointing to all four of them, learning their names. The other two were named Mandan and Botran. It was a start, at least. He still would rather have had at least a collar translator, like the one they'd had on the Tukuli, but it had been lost even before the ship had crashed.

They made their way out of the Sekani compound, weapons at the ready. Gianni had powered back up, aware that Krahn snipers were sometimes posted around the city in case they were able to catch sight of random bands of Rajani or Sekani. Gianni and the other Sekani had been trying to clean out the Krahn checkpoints near the compound first. He walked along with them, listening to them talk to each other, and could tell that they weren't speaking Talondarian Standard. They were speaking Sekani. He would have a hard enough time learning Talondarian without having to weed it out from another language. He stopped and waved at them all.

"Talondarian," he said, pointing to his mouth.

Mandan looked at the others, and shook his fingers at Gianni. "No, Sekani." The others looked at Gianni, as if wondering how he would respond.

He finally sighed. "Fine, Sekani," he said. The Sekani all

smiled, and Botran even hooted at him, a noise that Gianni had learned meant 'thumbs-up' or the equivalent of clapping. He smiled at them all, shaking his head.

They continued their patrol, with Gianni pointing at things along the way and one of the Sekani saying the word for it. He would then repeat it. In this way, he learned that Mandan and Botran were brothers, and from the looks of it, twins. He also learned that Botran had been one of the Sekani that had first found him and Kieren when their escape pod had crashed on Rajan.

They were walking along, the Sekani hooting from time to time as he attempted to speak more and more of their language, when, suddenly, they heard a weapon fire, and something bounced off of his power field. Gianni saw that there was a group of Krahn standing approximately a hundred yards away from their group. The Sekani had already taken cover behind various large pieces of stone ruins and vehicles. The Krahn continued firing at them, and the Sekani grasped their weapons, unable to move from behind cover. None of them had a projectile weapon, since they were in short supply.

Gianni set up a shield between them and the Krahn, about ten feet away. He called their names and pointed toward the shield, letting them know it was safe to come out. He then began walking toward the Krahn, firing bolts of energy at them through his shield, his fingers pointed like he was firing a gun. As they got closer to the Krahn position, he brought his shield closer to him and the Sekani. When they finally reached the Krahn, he dropped the shield, and they attacked their enemy at close range. Gianni waded into the fighting, firing at the Krahn and helping the Sekani as much as he could.

Suddenly, he noticed there was a Krahn poised to shoot

Golena from a few feet behind. He quickly dispatched the Krahn with a shot to the head and looked around, aware that all of their enemy now littered the ground. The Sekani looked up at him, all hooting now. Gianni smiled back, even though he knew they probably couldn't see his expression through the power field that surrounded him.

"Sedan'ka!" Botran yelled. The other Sekani followed suit, yelling out the word. Gianni wasn't sure what the word meant, but he followed suit. All of the Sekani were laughing, collecting the Krahn's weapons and making sure they were all dead. Gianni was surprised to find that he was happy. He was part of the team.

Suddenly, Mandan called out. He was bent over the form of one of the Krahn warriors. The Krahn was moving its arms, slowly. Mandan stood up straight and raised his club over his head, ready to deliver the killing blow.

Gianni sighed, knowing what he had to do. "Wait!" he called out. "Stop," he said in Sekani, for good measure. Mandan stopped and looked at him quizzically. He walked over and looked at the Krahn, noticing a large cut on its forehead that was bleeding profusely, but that was the only noticeable wound.

"James said he wanted prisoners," he said, knowing that the Sekani probably didn't understand what he was saying. "You know, James," he said, pointing at the Krahn. "For James." Mandan growled, but lowered his club. "Good. Now, who wants to carry him back?" Gianni asked, trying to make motions like he was picking up the Krahn.

The Sekani just stood and looked at him. They either didn't understand, or refused to touch the scaly creature. Either way, it looked like he would be carrying the unconscious Krahn. "Fine," he said, bending to grasp the Krahn's arm. He hoisted him over his shoulder and got it settled before turning to the Sekani. "Let's get out of here."

◊

James was in his room when the Rajani guard came to inform him that Gianni was waiting outside the building with a Krahn prisoner. He thanked the guard and quickly made his way to where he'd been told Gianni was waiting. He went through the doorway to find Gianni and a few Sekani males standing outside, guarding an unconscious Krahn warrior, who had been unceremoniously dumped on the ground.

"He's all yours," Gianni said, pointing at the Krahn. He began to walk away.

"Wait," James said. "Where did it come from?"

Gianni turned back to look at him. "Over by the Sekani compound. We killed the others. Thought we'd killed this one too. I think it's just unconscious, though. You said you wanted prisoners to interrogate, so here's one."

"Thanks," James said, surprised that Gianni had actually thought about what he'd told him. "I'll make sure there's a bonus in your paycheck this month."

"Ha-ha," Gianni said, but he smiled. "I'll tell Kieren you said hello."

As Gianni walked away, James powered up and easily picked up the body of the Krahn and slung it over his shoulder. He had to figure out a secure location where he could ask it questions. Just then, Kedar and a few other Rajani walked by. Kedar stopped and looked at the unlikely sight of James carrying a Krahn over his shoulder.

"I have an explanation," James said in his best Talondarian Standard.

"I'm sure that you do," Kedar said. "Do you need assistance?"

"Yes," James answered truthfully. "I need to find some place that is private."

Kedar turned to his companions. "I'll meet up with you later," he said. He turned back to James. "Follow me."

James did as he was bid and followed the Rajani through a circuit of alleyways, to a building that still had three stories above ground. Kedar didn't speak the entire route, so James kept silent as well. He didn't know the former Rajani Elder that well, so he wasn't sure what to expect when he walked through the front door of the building. He was surprised to find that the interior of the building had been cleaned up and was free of debris. There were a few chairs in what looked to be a reception area. He couldn't see more, though there was a hallway that led deeper into the structure.

Kedar turned to look at him. "As you know, there is a difference in opinions among the Rajani as to the best way to proceed in this fight."

James nodded, doing his best to follow the other's words. He had been around the Rajani long enough that he could have a conversation, but he still didn't feel confident speaking Talondarian Standard.

"There are Rajani who believe in peaceful resistance," Kedar continued, "and make no mistake, the Elders have a right to their beliefs. There is another group, which I've come to call Vaderren. This group believes that if we are to defeat the Krahn, then force must be used, however regrettable that may be."

"I understand," James said. He had met briefly with Kedar and Welemaan before, though they hadn't seemed very organized then. It seemed that things had changed.

"This place is to be the headquarters of the Vaderren," Kedar said. "I'm entrusting you to keep this a secret for now. We have enough problems without having Rajani fighting each other over our ideological differences. That can come later."

"I'm honored that you would trust me with this," James said. "As I've told you and Welemaan in the past, the other humans and I are not here to change your society, just to save it. What happens afterward is not up to us."

Kedar bowed his head briefly. "Thank you. Now, if you'll follow me again, I know of a place in the building that should be secure enough for anything you would need."

James nodded, and Kedar turned and led him down the hallway and past a number of doors. One of the doors was open, and James looked in to see a table and chairs set up for meetings. He followed Kedar down to the end of the hallway. Kedar opened the door at the very end and held it open for James to walk through. As soon as he did, James saw that there were stairs leading down to what he assumed was the basement. He walked down the stairs, careful not to trip. A fall wouldn't harm him in his powered-up form, but it could kill the Krahn before he ever had a chance to talk to it. He reached the end of the staircase and saw that there was a hallway down there as well that led to various rooms. James wondered what they were. Kedar walked past him and then down the hallway to the first door. He pulled a key chain out of his pocket and inserted a key into the lock.

James was surprised to see the Rajani using old-fashioned locks and keys. Every door he'd seen since leaving Earth were meant to be opened by a simple electronic button outside the door. But since they still hadn't restored power, it was probably a good thing these doors were manually locked. Kedar opened the door and motioned for James to enter the room. James walked through the doorway to see a bare, empty room, about ten feet square. The stone floor was even bare of carpet. There were no decorations on the walls, and a single light in each corner gave off a dull glow, just enough to bathe the entire room.

"These rooms were used for storage, from what we could tell," Kedar said. "This building housed a few different industries. They made clothing on one floor, and furniture on another. The top floors were dwelling units for the Sekani and Jirina workers."

James laid the still-unconscious Krahn as gently as he could on the floor, and then powered down. He felt the now-familiar hunger from using his powers for so long. "You wouldn't happen to have any food or drink around here, would you?"

"For...?" Kedar asked, looking down at the Krahn.

"Me," James said, smiling. "I haven't had anything to eat since breakfast, and using my powers really makes me hungry."

Kedar looked at him with an expression that James couldn't read very well. It was a cool appraisal, but he wasn't sure if the Rajani was sizing him up or thinking about the Johar Stone he had been implanted with on the *Tukuli*. The fact that the Rajani only had one eye made it that much more difficult to read him.

"I'll go look," the Rajani finally said.

"And a translating device, if you can find one," James said. "I don't know if this thing understands Talondarian Standard."

Kedar bowed slightly and left James alone with his prisoner, closing the door behind him.

James looked down at the Krahn and saw that it had stopped bleeding from the cut on its head. There was some discoloration around the wound, but it didn't look like a life-threatening injury. He bent over to look closer at the creature. He saw that one of the Krahn's eyes had an old wound over it. One of the bone spurs looked like it had been sheared off sometime earlier. The Krahn was breathing shallowly, but still hard enough for James to recoil slightly at the smell. He didn't want to think about what the creature had been eating recently. He looked at the Krahn's hands. Each finger had an inch-long, thick nail at the end that appeared to be razor-sharp. James had seen the damage they could inflict. Once the Krahn woke up, he'd have to stay powered up, just to be safe.

He stood back up, wondering what was taking Kedar so long, when the Krahn began to stir. He quickly powered up again. The Krahn moaned and slowly opened its eyes. Then it did something that James wasn't expecting: its eyes grew wide when it saw him standing over it. It quickly sat up, and while keeping both eyes on James, scooted itself as far away from James as it could, into the corner of the room.

James was surprised at the fear he saw in the Krahn's eyes. It was unmistakable as it clung to the far wall, as if attempting to become part of it. He wished that Kedar would return with the translating device. From what he'd seen, the Krahn were unable to speak Talondarian Standard due to the mechanics of their mouths. Their tongues were ill-equipped to pronounce the language. He stood and waited for Kedar to return, wary that the Krahn would try to escape, or lash out at him in fear. Finally, Kedar returned with a steaming bowl of what looked like oatmeal but smelled different; more like cooked rice. He also carried a translating device, which James was thankful for.

"I'm sorry I took so long," Kedar said. "It took me a while to find the device, and all we had for food was zephan, so I had to wait for it to cook."

"I'm sorry I put you through such trouble," James said, taking the bowl from Kedar. "Thank you for sharing your food with me." He looked down at the still-steaming bowl of what he assumed was some type of cooked grain, wondering how it would taste. Even more worrisome was how he was going to eat it with his power field still up. His stomach gurgled, telling him that he had better make a choice soon. He sighed and dropped his field, keeping his eyes on the Krahn as he did so. Wary of any sudden moves, he picked up the spoon-like utensil in the bowl and took a small bite of zephan. He was pleasantly surprised to find that it tasted like puffed rice cereal. He had grown up eating the sugary cereal, and it tasted very close to what he remembered, though it was warm and somewhat softer.

"It's good," James said, still keeping his eyes on the Krahn. "Do you want to stay here and help me question it? I don't want to keep you away from any important business you may have."

"I'll stay," Kedar said, looking at the Krahn. "There are some questions I would like the answers to as well."

James could see the hatred on the Rajani's face. There was no mistaking that emotion.

Chapter 12

Fajel was still a young Jirina when the Krahn attacked. His horns had only just begun to come in, a development that had caused much excitement when he'd first discovered the lumps forming under the skin of his forehead. His older brother, Tenel, had given him a hard time about them, of course, telling him that his horns were going to grow crooked. He and his brother had always been close, but Tenel sometimes had a cruel sense of humor. That had all changed the day his brother had been killed in the first wave of attacks by the Krahn. His parents were devastated, and his mother still cried at least once a day. Unfortunately, he didn't get to see his parents as much as he would have liked to since joining the fight against the Krahn, although most of what he'd done to that point was menial work, carrying supplies and cleaning up debris.

He could have stayed in hiding, like many of the other Jirina in his social group, but he just had to fight. He fought for his brother, and more importantly, to help his species to not be afraid of the monsters who had invaded their planet anymore. It didn't feel right to hide in the shadows. So when his Uncle Mazal had come around searching for volunteers for a special mission, of course he had stepped up and said yes. Maybe he would actually get a chance to meet their savior, James the Human.

He was told to meet in an abandoned Rajani residence on the north side of Melaanse. He was nervous and excited, and maybe a little scared, but he was determined to help out the resistance if he could. He arrived alone, the night dark around him, and no stars visible in the sky above. It would be another hour or so before Rajan's sole, small moon made its way into the night sky. He knocked tentatively at the back door, as he had been instructed to do by Mazal. The door opened, and a very large Rajani with a patch over his left eye stood blocking a set of stairs that disappeared into the darkness below the house.

"What's your name, young one?" the Rajani asked, not unkindly.

"Fajel," he answered, a lump forming in his throat.

"Proceed down the stairs and to the right, Fajel. Go to the door and knock three times," the Rajani doorkeeper told him.

Fajel did what he was told and soon found himself knocking on the door to a large underground room that looked like it had once been an office and library. The house must have belonged to a Rajani Elder. No one else would have been able to afford it.

The door was opened by a Sekani, who introduced himself as Belani and told him to take a seat with the others. The room was mostly cleared of furniture, except for a desk and bookcases, so Fajel found a spot among the small group of Sekani, Rajani, and Jirina sitting on the floor. He didn't know anyone. He waited quietly for a short while, until another Sekani entered, followed by the large Rajani who had been guarding the door above. The room grew quiet as the Sekani began to speak.

"For those of you who don't know me, I am Zanth," the Sekani said, and then pointed to his Rajani companion. "This is Kedar. We're here because we need your help. As you know, the resistance continues to fight the Krahn invaders on a daily basis, and, every day, there are more casualties, due to the Krahns' ability to attack from the air." Zanth paused, as there was a murmur of agreement from some in attendance, before continuing. "What we propose now is the formation of a task force. What this force would be expected to do is search out and find where the Krahn are landing and refueling their ships, and then, either take over the ships or destroy them so that they cannot be used against us."

Zanth paused again, looking at everyone in the room, before continuing. "We believe that if we're able to attack the Krahn in force, we will be very close to victory. But we will never achieve this victory without the ability to amass in large numbers to attack the Krahns' stronghold in the north of the city. Are there any questions so far?"

Fajel looked around him at the others, noticing that they had mostly sat with others of their own kind, so that there were really three small groups, not one. No one spoke up. Fajel was just replaying the Sekani's words over in his mind. Attack the Krahn and steal or destroy their ships. It was a scary proposition.

The Rajani named Kedar spoke up. "I see that you have split up along species lines. This will not do. You all need to be on the same team if this plan is to succeed. So what I'm going to do is assign you to a strike team made up of one Sekani, one Rajani, and one Jirina. Your strike team will be responsible for securing or destroying one Krahn ship. The Sekani will act as the pilot, if you're able to take the ship. All of the Sekani in this room have been cleared as having experience as pilots. Because of this, they will be the strike team leader." There was some muttering from the group of Rajani at this proclamation. "If you have a problem with that," Kedar continued, "you're free to leave now. We cannot afford your petty species biases on this operation; it's too vital to the future of the resistance."

Fajel was surprised by the Rajani's words, and even more surprised that none of the other Rajani left. He supposed that they probably would have if it had been Zanth speaking, but Kedar was a well-known and respected Rajani, who had been fighting the Krahn even before his liberation from the Krahn prison by James the Human. That was more than likely the reason he was present at this meeting.

Zanth pulled out a small tablet computer and read aloud the names of each strike team. Fajel learned that he would be teamed with Belani, the Sekani who had introduced himself at the door earlier, and Rachal, a rather small Rajani with white fur on his ears—a sign of aging among his species. Fajel soon learned that Rachal was as ornery as he was old. After the names had been read, Zanth told them all that the entire group would meet again the next day, but for now, the strike teams needed to meet and get to know one another. Zanth and Kedar said their goodbyes, and then Fajel, Belani, and Rachal walked upstairs in the large house, to separate themselves from the others.

Fajel found himself following his teammates into one of the numerous rooms in the second floor of the house. Belani carried a light, but didn't turn it on until they had closed the window coverings in what looked like a spare bed chamber. Fajel was in awe that a house could have a room just in case it was needed. In the Jirina dwellings, every room had a purpose, and overcrowding was a problem even for families like his that only had two offspring.

"Can't see why we had to leave the basement," Rachal

muttered. "Doesn't feel as safe up here. Can't say I like being in another Rajani's bedroom, either."

"We're up here," Belani explained, "because I'm not sure I can trust some of the others."

"What?" Fajel asked, stunned by this admission.

"Zanth doesn't like to publicize it," Belani continued, "but the Sekani movement is as leaky as an old sailing ship. That's why they didn't just come out and tell us tonight the plan for this grand idea of theirs."

"Well, that's just great, isn't it?" Rachal said. "Why did I volunteer for this again?" He snorted in disgust.

"You volunteered," Fajel said, "because you want the same thing as I and everyone else; to kill the Krahn and free our planet."

"Very idealistic, this one," Rachal said, talking to Belani and pointing a thumb at Fajel.

"Well," Belani said, "he's young. He'll learn."

"Look," Fajel said, standing up, "if you don't want me here, I can leave right now."

"Sit down, sit down," Rachal said, smiling. "No need to get angry. We were just having a bit of fun with you. Besides, have you got anything better to do?"

Fajel sat down again, slightly mollified, but still wary. He had not come to the meeting to be insulted.

"Good," Belani said. "The only way we're going to succeed in this is if we work together. Now, I've been a pilot for over three seasons. I have no doubt that I can pilot whatever kind of ship we end up stealing. What useful skills do you two bring to this operation?"

"I'm not afraid to fight, unlike some of those others," Rachal said. "It was Kedar and me who came up with the plan to escape from the Krahn prison camp, though Welemaan likes to take credit for it all." He snorted at this before continuing.

"Probably why I was never granted the title of Elder—I don't back down from a confrontation, and the teachings of the Kha never really appealed to me. All that praying and such seemed like an awful way to spend your days. Never seemed natural to me. So I made my way the best I could, taking any odd job they were offering. You learn a lot of different skills that way. Just tell me what you need me to do, and I can do it."

"Good," Belani said, and turned to Fajel. "And you?" he asked.

Fajel's mind raced as he tried to think of something that would impress them, but he came up blank. Finally, he muttered "I'm a hard worker," and sat there dejectedly. *Maybe I* should *go home,* he thought.

"That's good enough for me," Rachal said. "Can't all be in charge. Need someone to do the heavy lifting." He smiled at Fajel and patted him on his muscular arm.

Fajel returned the smile, grateful for not being made to feel totally incompetent.

"I think that's good enough for tonight," Belani said. "We'll meet here again tomorrow. Hopefully we'll get the full story then."

They made their goodbyes and went on their separate ways. Fajel still felt a little discouraged, but was adamant that he would return again the next evening. He wouldn't give up so easily.

◊

James had called together a meeting with Tumaani, Zanth, and Mazal, to talk about attacking the Northern Krahn base of operations; what his Krahn prisoner had referred to as Nestbase Two. As he sat in the meeting room waiting for everyone to arrive, he ate a lunch consisting of some type of dried fruit and a protein bar. He would have preferred a cheeseburger, fries, and a cold beer. He found that the longer he was away, the more he missed the food of Earth. He was surprised when the first one to arrive was Kedar. James stood from his feast and nodded to the Rajani as he entered. He reached over and turned on the translating device that had been placed in the middle of the table. "I wasn't expecting you, Kedar."

"Tumaani sends his regrets," Kedar said, sitting at the table. "He says that he won't take part in planning for war. I respect his opinion, but I feel there should be a Rajani presence at this meeting."

"Yes," James said, sitting back down. "I should have thought about that when I first invited Tumaani. And I should have invited the Vaderren as well. I apologize for the oversight." He had learned since last talking to Kedar that the word Vaderren was translated literally as 'the Fighters.'

"Don't worry," Kedar said. "These are not normal times for anyone. I can sympathize with your situation. I can't imagine being so far from my home world and trying to plan a war."

James smiled. He was beginning to like the big Rajani. He picked up the last bite of protein bar and ate it, washing it down with a sip of water. His water ration for the day was almost half gone. "Did the Krahn prisoner divulge any other interesting details after I left him in your care?" he asked.

"Unfortunately, no," Kedar said. "I don't think they are told much, except to kill anything that's not them and steal anything that could be valuable."

Just then, Zanth, Gianni, and Kieren entered the room. James stood and gave Kieren a hug before sitting back in his chair. "Hey, Kieren."

"No hug for me, boss?" Gianni said. "I'm crushed."

"Behave, or you will be," James said, but he smiled as he said it. He'd heard that Gianni had been a great help to the Sekani since arriving. Soon, Mazal arrived and bowed to everyone present before taking a seat at the table. James waited while everyone said their greetings, and then called the meeting to order. "Thank you all for coming. As you know, we are planning to attack the Northern Krahn base as a way to divert their attention away from the strike teams that are being sent out soon."

"Do you really think it's a good idea?" Kieren asked. "There still aren't a lot of weapons available to use. We're going to be outgunned, and we could be outnumbered."

"Yeah," Gianni added. "Especially if they call in reinforcements and ships."

"I'm aware of our weapon situation," James said, "but I'm afraid that there's not much we can do about it at the moment. The time must be now, if we're going to keep the element of surprise. If we wait too long, the situation is likely to change."

"And what is the situation?" Zanth asked.

"We know from a Krahn prisoner that Gianni was nice enough to catch for us," James began, nodding toward Gianni, "that the Northern Base, or Nestbase Two as they refer to it, is actually a group of highly guarded buildings that they've been using as a staging area since the night of the attack. Their primary base, Nestbase One, is located somewhere farther south, in Melaanse." He paused a second and took a sip of water, hating the aftertaste from the protein bar. "Our recent raids and ambushes of their patrols have left the Northern base weakened. They have not, as of yet, been resupplied from the colony ship."

"But those reinforcements could be coming within a Standard week," Kedar added. "The prisoner said that a fresh group of Krahn warriors was being trained aboard the ship and would be sent down to the planet soon."

"And you believe what the Krahn told you?" Kieren asked.

"I was being very persuasive," Kedar replied, without a hint of humor in his voice.

James saw her wince at the Rajani's words, but plowed ahead with his assessment. "All of which means that we have to hit them now in conjunction with our strike teams heading south. We don't want them waylaid by Krahn patrols along the way. We want all of their attention on us."

Mazal, who up until that point had sat silently, finally spoke. "Just tell me where you want the Jirina placed, and we'll be there, James."

"Thank you, Mazal," James said.

"Unfortunately, many of the Rajani who are willing to fight are going with the strike teams," Kedar said. "We're getting new recruits every day, but as of now, there won't be many Rajani available to fight."

"I understand the limitations we'll be under," Zanth said. "The Sekani, however, are ready to fight. What's the strategy of the attack?"

James pulled out a sheet of parchment. There was a dark red swath along one edge. "The Krahn prisoner was able to draw a layout of the buildings." *Before he could no longer use his fingers,* James added in his mind. But he would keep that little detail away from Kieren. "As you can see," he continued, "there's a large building surrounded by smaller buildings with a courtyard on one side of the larger building. If we split them up here, and here, we should be able to cut off their forces from making a prolonged defense of the largest building."

The meeting went on for another hour, while they talked

about their strategy and the best way to attack and who should be placed where, and by the end, they had a final plan that everyone could agree on. And the taste of the protein bar was finally gone as well, for which James was thankful.

◇

Fajel showed up early for his appointment the next day, ready to learn more about the mission. He had returned to his dwelling the night before and had hardly been able to sleep, thinking about the impending operation. This time, he was met at the door of the Rajani Elder house by his Uncle Mazal.

"Fajel," Mazal said, smiling. "You're the first one here. Come in. You can keep James company while Zanth and I set up the room for the meeting."

"James?" Fajel asked, walking through the door, his eyes wide. His heart was racing as he walked down the stairs and into the room at the bottom. He was disappointed to find it was empty. He gave a small yelp of fear when James the Human appeared before him, still powered up.

"Sorry to startle you," James the Human said through the translating device that sat in the corner of the room. The Human's energy field disappeared, revealing a large, dark-skinned alien with long, braided hair and a short beard that was speckled black and white.

Fajel had heard about the Humans—everyone had, by now—but to see one up close was still interesting. Especially when it was James the Human himself. For a moment, all he could do was stand and stare. Then he prostrated himself before the hero of Rajan.

"Oh no," James said, smiling. "Not another one."

"Stand up, Fajel," Mazal said, coming into the room. "He really doesn't like that." Mazal hurried off to do some other errand, and Fajel was left alone with the Human once again.

Fajel was rising, but then dropped back down. "I'm sorry if I offended you," he said.

"It's okay," James said. "Just don't do it again. Come on, stand up. It's okay. I'm not here to be worshiped. I'm here to help you."

Fajel stood up and noticed that the others were arriving for the meeting, all of them watching him make a fool of himself. He quickly walked over to a spot on the floor and sat down, embarrassed.

Finally, all of the strike teams were assembled, and the room quieted down to hear Zanth speak. Fajel noticed that there were more occupants to the room than there had been the night before. They must have met separately with the others before bringing everyone together. He even saw a few familiar faces this time, though he didn't dare try to talk to anyone while Zanth spoke.

"Thank you all for returning tonight," Zanth said, standing at the front of the room. "I know how inconvenient it was for some of you. This will be the last time that we'll all be in the same room together. For security purposes, from now on, your strike team leaders will receive orders, and it will be their task to relay that information to their teams." Zanth looked over at James, who stood quietly in a corner of the room, next to where the translating device had been set up. "Before we begin, I want to welcome a very special guest. If you haven't heard of or met them already, James and four other Humans were recruited by the Rajani Elder Rauphangelaa to assist us in our fight for independence from the Krahn. I've asked James to come tonight to speak to you all. James?"

Fajel had thought the room was silent before, but when the Human stepped forward, there was not just silence, but a silent reverence and feeling of awe as James the Human began to speak. Fajel noticed that, while not as tall as most of the Rajani, James the Human was almost as broad. He wore a strange red shirt with a white symbol on the front, a circular object with a wing growing from it. Maybe it was the sign of his clan or species, but Fajel didn't know what it meant.

"Thank you, Zanth," James the Human said. "I haven't had a chance to meet you all, but I know that you are all as dedicated as I am to one purpose, which is defeating the Krahn. If you agree to take part in this mission, your actions will go a long way toward that goal. I don't want to take up a lot of your time here tonight, so I'll be brief and just say thank you, and good luck."

There was much stamping of feet from the Jirina, banging of arms on chests from the Rajani, and hooting from the Sekani when James the Human had finished speaking. Rachal even stood and banged both of his forearms on his chest loudly before sitting back down.

Zanth finally restored order, and everyone was seated again. "Thank you, James," he said. "Now, to follow up on our meeting from last night, I would direct you to the screen set up on the far wall. Mazal?"

Fajel saw Mazal push a few buttons on an interface device, and the oversized screen flickered to life. There was a large map of Melaanse on it, with certain areas marked in various colors and notes, and arrows taking up much of the screen.

"As you can see," Zanth continued, "we know that the main Krahn stronghold is located in lower Melaanse, here." He pointed to a portion of the map with a long staff before continuing. "From intelligence gathered from various captured Krahn, we knew that the main stronghold was somewhere south of our location. Our spies have seen a great deal of activity in and around what was once the House of the Rajani Elder Delataan, who was killed in the first night of the attack. The Krahn have set up barracks in the dwellings of Delataan's servants." He dropped the staff back to his side and paced in front of the group.

"This leads us to believe that they must have access to a landing area somewhere near there," Zanth continued. "Your mission will be to locate the landing area and transmit its location back to us. Once the location has been relayed, we'll inform all the teams, and you will all coordinate an attack on the airfield. You've been split into strike teams because it will be easier to travel through the city undetected in groups of three. You'll attack the airfield as one group, but again, your team will be responsible for stealing or destroying one Krahn ship, if possible," he said, holding up one finger to emphasize his point. "Should the quantity of strike teams outnumber the ships available, your job will be to run interference for those teams that do have a ship. We want you to cause as much damage to the Krahn as possible; there's no such thing as wanton destruction on this mission. Understand?" He waited a moment until a Rajani, his short hair braided in an approximation of a Ralik, stood up to Fajel's left.

"Yes, Welemaan?" Zanth asked.

Fajel almost laughed, hearing Rachal snorting in his mind at the mention of the Rajani Elder's name, but caught himself in time. This wasn't the time for humor, even if the Rajani did look ridiculous with his short, twisted hair.

"As you may know," the Rajani began in a deep voice, "Delataan was my Master before I became an Elder. I spent many years of my life near the area you indicated. If it's true that the Krahn are using his house and grounds for their main base of operations, then there's only one field large enough near it that they could use."

Welamaan practically strutted up to where Zanth stood.

"If I may?" he said, reaching his hand out for the staff that Zanth held.

Zanth gave it to him. "Of course."

Welemaan pointed to an area on the map a ways to the south of the location Zanth had pointed out as being the home of Delataan. "The field is here, and borders this inlet. If the landing area is there, then perhaps we could enter the inlet from the ocean and go undetected." He handed the staff back to Zanth and returned to his seat on the floor.

"Thank you for your knowledge and your suggestion," Zanth said. "We have looked into this, but haven't been able to find any oceangoing vessels that weren't destroyed by the Krahn. I'm afraid our only alternative in this is traveling through the city. Are there any other questions?" He waited another moment, and Fajel saw that no one else stood or raised a hand. "Good," Zanth continued. "Strike team leaders, please wait here. The members of your teams can leave. I would ask that you all please wait to be contacted by your team leaders. As James said, good luck to all of you. May you all return to us safely."

Fajel rose with the rest of the Jirina and Rajani and walked toward the exit. He saw that Mazal and James were standing near the doorway, offering encouragement to the departing teams. As he neared them, Mazal smiled at him and placed a hand on his shoulder.

"Ah, Fajel," Mazal said. "James, have you met my sister's son?"

James smiled at him. "Yes, when he first arrived for the meeting."

"That's right!" Mazal said, clapping his hand on Fajel's shoulder. "I had forgotten. Don't worry, he won't embarrass himself again if I can help it."

Fajel didn't know what to say, so he just smiled shyly and

muttered a goodbye, before catching up with Rachal.

"Well, aren't we all important, talking with The Human?" Rachal said outside the house. "Oh, don't go getting defensive," he said when he saw the look on Fajel's face. "C'mon, I have a bottle of fernta I've been saving. Figure I should drink it now. I might not get another chance."

"Thank you for the offer," Fajel said. "But I'm not yet old enough to drink fernta. My mother would be very upset with me."

"Nonsense," Rachal said, putting an arm around Fajel's shoulders. "If you can die with me, then you can at least drink with me first."

◊

James sat in his room and ate his breakfast while he waited for word on the troops moving into position for the attack on the Northern Krahn base. He was feeling nervous at their chance of success on this mission. This would be the largest test they had faced so far. Before, it had mainly been hit-and-run tactics and the occasional bombing of a small Krahn outpost, just to keep the Krahn guessing at where they would strike next. Now it would be a coordinated attack on a heavily fortified base with a group mostly made up of Sekani and Jirina, with a sprinkling of Rajani, and not many of them were experienced fighters. Or, at least, they weren't used to attacking a large target as part of a coordinated effort.

James, Gianni, and Kieren would be there to help, of course, but this would mainly be the three races from Rajan fighting the Krahn—and for the first time, they would be fighting together as a unified force. It didn't help his mood that they still hadn't heard from David or Yvette. It had been almost three months since they had arrived on Rajan. For all he knew, the two humans, along with Rauph and Bhakat, had not even made it off the ship before it crashed into the ocean.

"James?" a voice said, bringing him out of his reverie. He turned to see Kieren standing in the doorway of his room.

"Are we ready?" he asked, forcing his mind back to the task at hand.

"Not yet," Kieren said. "I was just walking by and saw you. You looked a thousand miles away. Do you want to talk?"

"Oh, you know," he replied, smiling. "Same old stuff. Relations between the juniors, strategy for this battle and the whole war, supplies and food for all of them..."

Gianni, of course, had been the one who had coined the phrase 'juniors' for the three races on Rajan—the Jirina, Rajani, and Sekani, JRS. James had been adamant that he never use the somewhat derogatory term in front of them, but found himself using it instead of having to say all of the species' names over and over again.

"Anything to do with the fact that we haven't heard any word of Yvette yet?" Kieren asked, sitting down on an oversize chair across from him.

He had to admit, she was smarter than he had first given her credit for on the *Tukuli*. He didn't think he would've done as well as he had getting all of the juniors together if it hadn't been for her and her valuable translation power, not to mention her skills as an ambassador and liaison to the Sekani. "Am I that transparent?" he asked, running a hand over his hair. He still wasn't used to its length at times.

"No," she said, smiling. "I just know that if your positions were reversed, she'd probably be going out of her mind worrying about you."

"Yvette?" James asked, surprised. "Nah, she's a pretty cool customer. No, she'd be doing everything in her power to win this fight and go home."

"All I know," Kieren said, "is that she really cares for you. I promised I wouldn't say anything to you, but I figure I'll deal with the consequences after she shows up."

"Well," James said, "then I don't feel so bad about my thoughts of abandoning this whole thing and looking for her."

"If you do," Kieren said, "just know that Gianni and I would understand. And I, for one, would come with you."

"And leave me with this crew?" Gianni said from the doorway. "Not on your life."

"Ha," James replied. "You guys know I would never actually do that, right?"

"It's a good thing," Gianni said. "Because I think this whole damn coalition would fall apart without us. The Rajani and Sekani are arguing about who gets to lead this little party that you've planned."

"I thought we settled this already," James said, standing up and stretching.

"Then it needs to be settled again," Gianni said, smiling mischievously.

"Enjoying yourself?" James asked as he walked out the door.

"Immensely," Gianni said, crossing his arms in front of him and leaning against the doorjamb. Kieren just rolled her eyes at him as she followed James out of the room.

◊

It was two days before Belani finally contacted Fajel. Fajel agreed to meet the other two members of the strike team just after dark. He went and said his goodbyes to his parents. His mother cried, as he knew she would. His father, who up until then had remained stoic and had said nothing about Fajel joining the resistance, had grabbed his son in a fierce hug and told him to be brave, and then he had cried as well, which, in turn, had made Fajel cry. It was an emotional release for the young Jirina, who hadn't known if his parents would look down at him for choosing to fight until that very moment. Now, as he headed to the rendezvous point, he felt that he could at least handle his fear, which had seemed to grow as the time passed since the last meeting at the Elder's house.

Fajel wished that they didn't have to keep meeting after dark. Unlike the Rajani and Sekani—especially the Sekani, who seemed to see just as well in the dark as in the light—the Jirina's eyes were not adapted for night vision. Luckily for him, they were meeting in a particular section of the city that he was very familiar with from before the war. He eventually made it to the corner of a park that he used to help his father maintain. It almost made him cry again to see the furrows in the ground from the landing of Krahn ships and the rubble from destroyed buildings where once there were trees and flowers and a small pond with a fountain. Dead things floated in the water now, and the fountain was just a large chunk of metal sitting among them.

He found Rachal sitting with his back propped against one of the trees that had been knocked over, its roots now sticking out like an outstretched skeletal hand. "'Bout time you got here," the Rajani said, closing his eyes again when he saw who was approaching. "We were beginning to think you weren't coming."

"Where's Belani?" Fajel asked, looking out over the top of the tree trunk before sitting down next to the Rajani. The night was warm, but a cool breeze blew among the dead and dying trees. It would soon be harvesting time, and too soon after that, the harsh winds and rains would descend on the city as the rainy season began.

"I'm right behind you," came Belani's voice from close to his left ear. Fajel jumped and turned to see Belani smiling at him. Rachal chuckled, and Fajel felt his face grow warm in embarrassment. He was really beginning to dislike the Sekani, who seemed to relish pointing out his shortcomings.

"Are you ready to go?" Belani asked. "We need to pick up some supplies before we leave." He led them to a small utility building, and they found two small packs and one large one, as well as two weapons that looked like they had been confiscated from the Krahn at some earlier point.

Rachal and Belani each grabbed a small pack and a weapon, and then helped Fajel heave the large pack onto his broad shoulders. He was disappointed that he didn't get a weapon as well, but Belani explained that there was a shortage, and that each team only received one or two at the most.

"Besides," Belani added, "you wouldn't know what to do with one anyways. It wouldn't do us any good if you accidentally shot yourself or one of us."

Fajel thought this was probably true, but it still didn't make him very happy being treated as a mere beast of burden. They finally set off southward, making their way cautiously amongst the streets and alleyways, always on the lookout for Krahn patrols. Surprisingly, they only saw one small group of Krahn that entire night, where before, there had been large groups in every part of the city.

"The resistance has made them cautious," Rachal said when Fajel had pointed it out to him. "Fearful for their own rotten hides. Good. More scared they are, the less trouble we'll have trying to avoid them."

They'd made their way through most of the northern part of the city when Belani called a halt and they rested in the corner of what used to be a small clothing store. It was getting close to daybreak. Fajel was moving from hungry to starving quickly. He set down his pack and opened it up, hopeful that Belani had packed some food for their trip.

He was alarmed to find that he had been lugging around construction blasting devices.

"What did you think we'd be using to blow up the Krahn ships?" Rachal asked.

Fajel sat down heavily, suddenly weak in the knees at the thought that he'd been carrying a large number of explosives for the last few hours and hadn't even known it. He felt his hunger go away as it was replaced by a sick feeling in his stomach.

"Fajel?" Rachal asked, actually looking concerned.

Fajel didn't answer; he was still running the situation over in his mind. *Maybe I'm not ready for this,* he thought. As if echoing his thoughts, Belani sat down next to him. "Listen," the Sekani said. "If you think you can't handle this mission, we can easily go on without you. We don't need the dead weight."

"Now what kind of talking is that?" Rachal asked, angry now. "We're all afraid, and if you're not, then you're just plain stupid. This is a fool's mission to begin with. We'll probably all die, so whether it's because we're blown up by our own explosives, or because we get caught by the Krahn, it doesn't really matter. What matters is that Fajel had the courage to come along and try to help in this fight, foolish as it is." He snorted and was silent, now checking his weapon.

Belani stood up. "You're right about one thing. We are all fools if we think we can win this war." He walked away, leaving Fajel and Rachal together. By now the sun was breaking over the horizon, and streaks of sunlight were piercing through the gloom inside the building.

"Thank you," Fajel said quietly.

"Was nothing," Rachal replied, placing his gun on the ground beside him. He looked up at Fajel and smiled. "My father always told me that you never really know someone until you drink with them. I never really believed him; always thought it was an excuse for him to get soused on regular occasions." He laughed at this before growing serious again. "But I can see his point now," he continued. "You're a good kid, Fajel. No one can deny your dedication to this fight, which is more than I can say for some others." He pointed the way Belani had walked out and rolled his eyes. "But what I said earlier is the truth," he said, rummaging around now in his pack. "We'll probably all die on this mission, and I would hate to think that we did it for nothing, but there isn't anything I can do about that. I would hate more to see a youngling like yourself die. So if you were to leave now, go back to your family, and live to fight another day, then that's all right. I wouldn't think any less of you."

Fajel sat and thought for a moment. He debated with himself, looking down at the ground around him. He saw all of the various small pieces of rubble and trash that had once been parts of buildings and vehicles and everyday objects that they had all taken for granted, now just strewn about and forgotten. He didn't think he would be able to live with himself if he didn't fight to give others the chance to rebuild those things. He looked up at Rachal, who had pulled a protein bar out of his pack and was chewing on it thoughtfully. "If I stay," he said, smiling, "are you going to share your food with me?"

Rachal snorted and reached into his pack. He threw one of the pre-wrapped bars to Fajel. "Only because you get to share in the misery of eating it," he said.

Just then, Belani walked in. "We stay here for the day. Get some sleep if you can. We should be there by tomorrow morning."

◊

The Krahn struck the house just after daybreak. Their

informant had told them to expect little resistance, and he was correct. There were only a few Sekani and a Jirina in the house, and they were poorly armed. The Krahn numbered twenty, and they easily overpowered the defenders. The lone Jirina was shot and killed outright; the Krahn had no use for him. The Sekani were captured and tied together in a line for transporting. They would be sent to Toruq at Nestbase One for questioning, and then slaughtered for their meat.

The Krahn searched the basement, where their informant had told them he'd met with others for a secret mission, but all they found was a pointing stick and an empty screen.

Chapter 13

Bhakat had grown to respect the Human female named Yvette in the few days that they'd been living at the medical clinic. She was a good fighter; merciless in her dealings with the Krahn, and relentless in her desire to search for the Human male named Dempsey, though Bhakat and David had managed so far to talk her into staying with them, at least until Rauphangelaa was able to walk. He marveled at her skill in dispatching any Krahn they came in contact with as they patrolled around the medical facility, while Rauphangelaa recuperated from his injuries. He had not chosen a mate yet. He was still a Pledge and not yet allowed to breed, but he found it difficult to believe that any Rajani female would be as dedicated to him as Yvette was to James, and the two Humans were not even officially paired.

He knew that depending on how things went, he might never have a chance to pair bond. It was yet another reason to hate the Krahn. He decided that he would add it to his already lengthy list. Bhakat and Yvette sat together most days as she taught him the Earth language called English. He'd been surprised to learn that there were so many different languages on her home planet. Most planets in the Alliance had two or three languages at most. Societies were allowed to have their own languages, but it was Alliance law that all planets taught Talondarian Standard, the official language of the Alliance.

The Human male, David, seemed just the opposite of Yvette. He was becoming more and more distant as the days wore on, with no sign of Janan. Bhakat prayed that his Sekani friend was still alive and well, but he knew the reality of the situation. More than likely, Janan was already dead. *Another item for the list,* he thought. He contemplated his friend's fate as he checked on his Master. Rauphangelaa had been acting differently toward him ever since he'd first woken up and discovered that his Pledge had implanted himself with a Johar Stone. Bhakat didn't blame him. He'd broken the most important law on Rajan. He wouldn't expect Rauphangelaa to just accept it, even if it had saved his life.

Bhakat ran a scanner over Rauphangelaa's broken leg. It was healing well, but he knew that his Master wouldn't be able to walk for at least another few days. His ribs would be sore for even longer, but wouldn't hinder his mobility, at least, though it would hurt him to walk too much for a while longer. He also wasn't experiencing any more concussion symptoms, which was a good sign. Bhakat had feared the worst when he'd woken after the *Tukuli* crashed to see his Master lying on the floor of the bridge, his safety harness broken. Rauphangelaa had been thrown hard into the pilot's control panel during the crash. But it looked like he would make a full recovery, eventually. It was just about time to bring him out of the healing stasis that Bhakat had placed him in when they'd arrived at the facility.

◊

Janan had made up his mind. He hadn't returned to Rajan just to be captured as soon as he got back. He waited patiently, knowing that his daily feeding would occur soon.

Because it was always dark in his cell, he wasn't sure what time they fed him. But his stomach always let him know when it was supposed to be time to eat, despite the fact he was in a perpetual state of hunger. He didn't know what he was going to do yet; he would just have to act if the chance presented itself. It was three more feedings before his Krahn guard came to his cell and told him that Toruq wanted to see him.

"I...don't think I can walk," Janan whispered hoarsely when the guard opened his cell door. In his current state, he felt like he wasn't far from the truth. He felt considerably weakened from the lack of food and clean water, and his throat still hurt most of the time.

"Get up," the guard said in Krannish. "I can't understand what you're saying, you filthy beast."

Janan stayed where he was, sitting on the floor and moaning softly. The guard walked over and grabbed him by the hair on the top of his head.

"I said, get up!" the guard yelled, pulling on his hair and practically lifting him off the ground, painfully.

Janan stood quickly, and as the guard let him go, he jumped up onto the Krahn's chest and used the only weapon he had left. He bit the guard's throat as hard as he could, and felt his mouth fill with the guard's blood and tasted the sickly sweet flavor of it. He felt it overflow the confines of his mouth and spill down his chin. But he didn't let up, not even when the guard raked its claws across his abdomen, opening deep gashes and knocking the wind out of him. He kept chewing, feeling the screaming guard stumbling around the cell and bouncing off the walls. With a last, straining effort, the guard pulled him off. Janan felt the guard's throat part, and a spurt of blood splashed across his face.

Janan landed on the floor of the cell and knelt there,

retching from the taste of the guard's blood and trying to regain his breath. He hardly paid any attention as the guard staggered toward him, blood still spurting from the hole in its neck, and then fell to its knees. He looked at the guard dispassionately. The Krahn was trying to speak, but only accomplished making more blood come out of its mouth. "I'm sorry," Janan said. "I can't understand what you're saying right now, either." He spit a gob of blood in the guard's face.

The guard gave one last gurgle before falling over onto its side into the rapidly congealing puddle of its own blood. Janan knelt there a moment before going to the guard's body. The Krahn wasn't armed. Janan had looked before he attacked the guard, and he hadn't seen a weapon. If the guard had a knife accessible on its belt, Janan wouldn't have taken the chance of attacking it without a real weapon of his own. The guard could have easily stabbed him and ended his bid for freedom quickly. Janan knew that his best chance was surprise and staying away from the Krahn's sharp teeth. As it was, the gashes in his stomach felt like they were on fire, but he didn't think he was losing too much blood from them.

When his breathing had returned to normal, Janan stood and slowly left his cell, listening for the slightest sound that could indicate another guard had heard the first one's screams, however short they had lasted. The only thing he heard was the skittering sounds of the masagas, and the now-familiar sound of water dripping faintly. He walked toward the door, which had been left open by the dead guard. At the doorway, he let his eyes adjust to the brighter light spilling down the set of stairs. He walked out of the basement and quickly made his way up the stairs, stopping once more to listen for the sound of guards. Staying close to the wall, he slowly made his way to what used to be the great room within the former Rajani Elder house. He passed a hallway and walked to a window that had been covered by a large piece of thick cloth. He moved the cloth aside and looked out to see a large yard with smaller buildings surrounding it. He could see dozens of Krahn walking across the yard. He wouldn't be able to escape that way.

Just then, he heard a door open and footsteps. He quickly headed back toward the stairs. The footsteps were growing louder, so Janan turned down the hallway he had passed earlier. He walked by a few doors, checking the handles on each one, but they were all locked. Probably storage rooms or closets, he assumed.

Finally, he reached a large door at the end of the hallway and turned the doorknob. It was unlocked. He quickly opened the door and slipped through, closing the door again behind him as quietly as he could. He found himself in the kitchen. He felt his gorge rise at what he saw. Lying on the floor were the bodies of several Sekani. On a large island in the middle of the kitchen was a dismembered body, a large cleaver sitting next to the skull, which was staring at him with lifeless eyes. Thankfully, he didn't recognize any of them.

He walked over to the island and reached up for the cleaver. He paid no attention to the tears streaming from his eyes. The cleaver was heavy, and he held it in both hands as he walked back out the door he had just entered. He was no longer concerned about being seen anymore. He walked toward the sound of Krahn voices that were coming from the end of the hallway. There were two of them, though neither one was Toruq, unfortunately. Both were armed with knives on their belts. Janan didn't care. All rational thought had left his mind as pictures of butchered Sekani floated in front of his eyes. This wasn't what he'd envisioned at all when he'd dreamed of returning to Rajan.

Janan walked silently down the hall, hiding as best he

could, so that the Krahn facing his direction was blocked by the Krahn facing away. He ran the last few feet and savagely chopped at the first Krahn's leg, feeling the solid, satisfying crunch of connection as the Krahn screamed and fell to the floor. He swung up at the second Krahn's throat, but it jumped back out of reach. He pulled the cleaver back and charged the Krahn, yelling unintelligibly. The Krahn crouched and reached for the knife at its belt. As it was pulling the knife out of the sheath, Janan swung his cleaver, cutting off the Krahn's hand and burying the cleaver deep into its side. The Krahn screamed, its severed stump spraying blood all over Janan. Janan pulled on the cleaver's handle, but it wouldn't come loose. The Krahn fell to its knees.

Janan heard a noise behind him and turned to see the other Krahn struggling to stand. It was bleeding profusely from the deep gash on its leg. Janan gave the cleaver handle one more tug, but it was stuck fast in the Krahn's abdomen. He knelt and grabbed the Krahn's knife, pushing the body to the floor as he did so. He turned back to see the other Krahn was now advancing toward him unsteadily, its own knife in its hand. Janan had never been in a knife fight before. Up until that point, he'd been going on instinct and hatred alone. The limping Krahn hissed at him as it got closer, its hackles extended out straight from its head. It had height and reach advantages on him, but Janan was much more mobile. The Krahn would have a difficult time matching his speed with its wounded leg threatening to buckle under it. At least Janan hoped so.

He thought of throwing the knife at the Krahn in the hopes of getting lucky, but figured that play would only end with him unarmed. That trick might work in the old movies that he and David had watched aboard the *Tukuli*, but he doubted it would work in real life. He was no James Cogburn.

Or was it Cobug? The Krahn hissed again and lunged at him. Janan sidestepped past the knife and brought his own knife up and stabbed the Krahn in the side. He ducked as the Krahn swung its arm back toward him, and then he brought his knife up as hard as he could, stabbing the Krahn through the bottom of its jaw and pushing it until it would go no farther. The Krahn struggled briefly as its legs gave out, but Janan held on and rode it to the ground, landing on top of it. He gave the knife a twist, making sure that the Krahn was dead. He stood slowly, his abdomen on fire from the large furrows inflicted by the guard in his cell.

"Very impressive," a voice said from behind him.

Janan turned wearily and saw that Toruq and four guards armed with projectile weapons had entered the room.

"Drop the knife, snackmeat," Toruq said.

Janan did as he was told. He was exhausted, and knew he wouldn't survive if he tried to attack four armed Krahn. He didn't even flinch when one of the guards stepped forward and hit him in the forehead with the butt of its weapon. The darkness was welcome.

◊

It had taken three years to build his colony ship, and during that period, Ronak had lived on a large freighter that his warriors had captured near the moon of Ivros. That freighter had been cramped and dingy, with little to offer as far as amenities or comforts, which was why Ronak had been so specific in his demands for the colony ship to have a spacious living area for him to share with his bloodmate, Mariqa.

Their private quarters consisted of several comfortably-appointed leisure and exercise rooms, a fully-stocked dining room and kitchen, a computer room, and a large bed chamber. The chamber was filled with plants native to Krahn. When he was banished, Ronak's brother, Maliq, had allowed him to take seeds and animals from Krahn. Ronak's scientists had been able to breed them aboard the ship to ensure that the Horde had a consistent source of food. Ronak chose to believe that this was a further slap in the face by his hated sibling, since all the familiar items did was remind him of all that he'd lost in his failed rebellion.

Candles and incense burned in the bedchamber as Ronak and his bloodmate prepared to sleep for the night. The smoke slowly filtered out through air ducts in the ceiling, purified by the ship's extensive HVAC system. He was lying on large cushions in the middle of the room, appearing as though he was close to falling asleep, though no one could ever tell with him, except Mariqa. He was too unpredictable in his emotions and behavior.

Mariqa was feeding the small, furry creatures that Ronak's warriors had discovered on the planet below to her favorite plant, a species renowned on Krahn for its lethality. This specimen was still young, but it would need to be pruned soon, or it would grow too large to control safely. The creature squealed as it was lowered slowly into the gaping mouthflower of the five-foot plant.

She spoke to the plant like a child, stroking its leaves as the flower closed around the creature. "There, there," she crooned. "Isn't that tasty?" The animal's squealing abruptly stopped as the plant's stamen pierced its body, already beginning to suck out its life juices, while simultaneously injecting it with a chemical compound that would dissolve its tissues. *At least the creatures are plentiful on Rajan,* she thought. She would've been very disappointed if her plants had to starve for lack of a suitable meal. They were so ugly when they went into hibernation.

"The Stones must be found soon, bloodmate," Ronak

said softly. She turned to look at him, aware that although he looked calm, his emotions were barely in check behind his current façade. "These creatures must be found," he continued. "They shouldn't be on Rajan. They've caused more damage to my plans than all of the Rajani combined. They released the Rajani slaves. *My* slaves!" He sat straight up and pounded one hand into the other as his voice got louder.

Mariqa walked over and sat next to him on the cushion. "The fact remains," she said, "they're here. There's nothing that can be done to change this." Ronak rose and began to pace, a familiar sight when he was alone or with her; he never did it in front of anyone else, not wanting to seem indecisive or worried about their current course of action. "You cannot change the past," she said. "You can only look forward to the next battle."

Ronak stopped his pacing. He walked over to where she sat and bent over so that their faces were only inches apart. "Don't you dare quote Xenic's teachings to me, Mariqa," he seethed. "He was a fool and a traitor."

"He merely chose the winning side," Mariqa said calmly, knowing how to stoke Ronak's anger. She was exceedingly good at it by then. It was useful for times when Ronak's resolve seemed close to faltering. She stood and walked over to the small cages located near the wall. "He served your family for many years," she said, pulling another small creature from its cage and tweaking her bloodmate at the same time.

Ronak began to pace again. "He betrayed me! For what? I was his greatest pupil. He handed me over to my brother without a second thought."

Mariqa didn't remember either of the statements being true, but she didn't disagree with him. She'd done enough for the moment. She tossed the last creature to her plant, and then walked over to where Ronak stood. "He'll be the first to be skinned alive when we return. Once we have the Stones, no one will stand before our might."

Ronak stepped closer to her. "Once I have the Stones, all of them will kneel before me, just before I slowly kill them. My brother will be the last to die, and he will be looking into my eyes when the life leaves his."

Mariqa reached out toward him and slowly rubbed his bare chest, not unlike what she'd just been doing to her plant. "Yes, mighty Ronak. You are the slayer of fools. The Prince of the Ebony Night. You are High Vasin of the Qadira Clan. All will fall before you."

"They will all die. All die..." he whispered, almost in a trance-like state now from her calm voice and rhythmic stroking. Mariqa smiled as she helped him to bed.

◊

Rauphangelaa had steadily shown signs of improvement, and soon after he'd awakened from his induced healing sleep, they'd made the decision to leave the medical facility, knowing that the Krahn would only escalate their attacks on the site. They'd easily been able to defend the building, but they knew that, eventually, the Krahn would send too large a force for even them to defeat, and Rauph was still too weak and vulnerable to risk him getting hurt or killed in the middle of an extended fight with the Krahn.

They had relocated in the middle of a mild Rajani night, with Yvette leading the way; her ability to see in the dark a great help as they moved through the abandoned streets of Melaanse. They'd moved northwest, away from the coast, and finally stopped at a transport vehicle factory that David had scouted earlier. After a few weeks of living at the factory, they'd all noticed that they hadn't spotted a Krahn since leaving the medical facility. As Rauph healed, he could walk with only a slight limp, though his healing ribs still ached if he walked too much.

They decided that the time was right to leave in search of any Rajani Elders who might have survived the Krahn attack, over Bhakat's objections. First, though, Bhakat, Yvette, and David went out for one last reconnaissance mission, wanting to find out what had happened to the Krahn. Had the invaders finally left Rajan? It only took a trip back to the medical facility to answer that question with a resounding 'no.'

Krahn bodies littered the ground around the entrance of the facility as the powered-up Humans and Bhakat killed them quickly and efficiently, and, sometimes, in ruthless fashion. They'd come upon the facility to find a dozen Krahn entrenched around the building and camped out in its interior. Now, with all of the warriors except one dead, they were set to question the lone survivor. The Krahn was dressed in better armor and an actual cape, which David had torn off during the battle. The Krahn commander had also been pierced several times by Yvette's spears. Bhakat was holding it by the throat, and Yvette had a band of yellow power around its arms and chest, holding it upright. Blood from one of its wounds poured down the outside of the field, turning it a muddy orange.

"Answer my question," Bhakat said menacingly. "Where was the Sekani prisoner taken? I know he's still alive. *He'd better* still be alive."

"What...matters one less...Sekani?" the Krahn answered before coughing up a gush of blood. Bhakat roared in frustration and pulled back his fist to end the interrogation session for good.

David held up both hands in a warding off gesture to stop

him. "No! No, Bhakat. What'd he say?"

"He claims to know nothing about Janan," Bhakat said, still staring at the Krahn.

"We still need him, Bhakat," David said. "You can't kill him yet. Ask him again."

The Krahn began to laugh as more blood spilled from its mouth. "Hss...sss...sek...will be victory feast...for Ron..." it gurgled before slumping down in Yvette's grip. She dropped her power band and walked away, disgusted by their inability to get an answer from the now-dead Krahn. She was disgusted with herself for having killed it too soon.

Bhakat threw the body against the side of a nearby building. "Garbage!" he yelled, furious that the Krahn had died so easily.

"Well, that's just wonderful," David said, throwing up his hands and walking away.

"They must be coming from somewhere nearby," Bhakat said with his thick Rajani accent.

Yvette turned to look at him. "So, do we keep looking or go back and get Rauph?"

"We keep looking," David said. "Every minute we delay increases the chances that Janan will die." *If he isn't dead already,* he added silently, though they all finished the thought for him in their own minds.

"We've left Rauphangelaa alone for too long already," Bhakat said. "He'll begin to worry if we don't return soon."

They both looked to Yvette. "I think I have to agree with Bhakat," she finally said.

"Shit," David muttered.

"We'll return to the factory and collect Rauph and our stuff," she continued, ignoring David's negative attitude. "Then we'll search for the Elders or the Krahn, whatever comes first. Either way, it's time to leave."

"Yeah, and who put you in charge?" David asked, his hands on his hips.

"James did," Yvette answered. "But if you want to set off on your own, you're welcome to do so."

David didn't answer her, but he followed her and Bhakat when they left the bodies of the Krahn behind.

◊

Ries an na Van, Investigator First Level of Galactic Intelligence, was having a very good day. Not only was he returning to Asnuria in a much different capacity than the last time he'd gone there, but he was no longer shackled by the ASP's petty rules and hierarchies. Now that his training was complete, he was an independent operator, and not subject to the inconvenience that came with the close supervision he'd experienced while a Commander of the ASPs. After waking up in a prison cell on what he later learned was a small space station orbiting around the planet Eddross, he had agreed to become an agent of Galactic Intelligence. GI was the clandestine investigative arm of the Galactic Alliance, and was overseen by the Security General.

Ries had been taken down to the planet's surface and had completed rigorous training that had put his ASP training to shame. Eddross was considered uninhabitable by the Alliance, but GI had built a series of tunnels and underground training centers on the planet. It was where all of its agents were trained before being sent out on their own on assignments. The main drawback of his situation was that he no longer had his own ship. GI didn't have a large enough budget to provide ships to every one of their agents, especially new ones like Ries. He'd been forced to rely on hitching a ride with a Frittelian freighter that was delivering industrial parts to Asnuria. But one of the reasons he'd been recruited by GI in the first place was his ingenuity and resourcefulness, so some small problems were to be expected; and he was expected to overcome them on his own. The minor inconvenience was tempered by the fact that he was still alive to experience it.

As he neared the ASP headquarters building, he checked to make sure he had his credentials with his lower right hand, while simultaneously adjusting the filter mask that he'd placed over the lower half of his face with his upper left hand. The mask had been the first thing he'd purchased when he'd received the order to travel to Asnuria. In the brief time he had lived there, he'd always dreaded going outside, afraid he would run into an Asnurian who wanted to talk. Their odor was a blatant assault on his sense of smell.

He walked up the set of stone steps that led to the enormous façade of the headquarters building. He knew exactly where he needed to go. He had left his weapons in his rental room, except, of course, for his standard issue photon disruptor. The other weapons would cause too much of a problem going through the security checkpoint. He had a license for the gun, and as a GI agent, would be allowed to carry it inside the building. After passing through security, he stepped into the hydro lift and proceeded to the top floor of the massive building. First Admiral Skatala's office occupied an entire half of the floor. Ries had wondered while working there what it would look like. Everyone who worked there talked about the office, but no one he knew had ever visited it. He'd never met the Admiral in person.

Ries stopped at the receptionist desk in the lobby outside the office. The Ingross sitting at the desk looked up at him with a bored expression on her six-eyed face. "Can I help you?" she asked, disinterestedly, moving four of her eyes back to her computer input screen, while a pair stayed on him.

"Yes, tell Admiral Skatala that Agent Van is here to see him," Ries said, his voice muffled through the breathing mask. He'd left it on after passing through security. It was better that not a lot of Officers saw his face. He probably wasn't the most popular former employee.

The receptionist punched a button on her tablet. "Is he expecting you?" she asked, a set of her eyes looking at him, while another set stayed on her tablet, and another watched the screen in front of her.

"Probably not," Ries answered, "but I wouldn't be surprised if he knew I was coming." Ries had passed through security. He knew that the first thing they would do was notify the Admiral that Ries was on his way up. The ASPs and GI did not generally have a good working relationship. This was a delaying tactic, and it was beginning to piss him off.

"I'm not showing an appointment for this morning," the receptionist said, turning all three sets of eyes back to him. "Are you sure you have the correct day?"

Ries had listened to enough. He pulled out his identification and slapped it down on the counter in front of her. "Do you see this?" he asked. "Unless you want to spend the rest of your life in a Tergarian mining pit, I suggest you inform the Admiral that I am growing impatient."

"There's no reason to threaten my secretary," a voice said behind him. Ries turned to see the Admiral standing just outside his office door. The old Sh'kallian was still as stealthy as ever; one of the reasons he had risen to the top post of the Alliance Society for Peace, Ries guessed.

"Then I suggest you stop playing games with me," Ries said. He walked over to the Admiral and presented his identification card.

The admiral took the card in his sizable paw and looked

at it. "Yes, Agent Van. What can I do for you today? We're always happy to help out Galactic Intelligence, of course."

"It concerns Planet A2242," Ries said quietly, taking back his card.

Instantly, Admiral Skatala's demeanor changed. He looked over at his secretary. "Dren, hold my calls for the next hour, would you?" He turned his attention back to Ries. "Come into my office." Ries followed him into his large office, noting that most of it was filled with servers, and not the luxury furnishings and electronic toys that had been rumored. He watched as Skatala punched a code into a tablet sitting next to the door. "There," the Admiral said. "Now that we have a little privacy, just what the blasted slag do you want?"

"A drink would be nice," Ries said, taking off his mask and setting it on a small table near a comfortable-looking chair. He sat in the chair, feeling it instantly conform to his body. "Ah," he said, closing his eyes. "You can't imagine how uncomfortable it is to sleep on an industrial freighter for a week." He opened his eyes to see that the Admiral had not moved from where he stood. His tail was twitching in annoyance as he looked at Ries. Ries thought that he might have pushed things too far. "No drink, then? Fine, let's get down to business. You're planning to pursue a Rajani ship back to Rajan in hopes of bringing its owner in on charges for disabling two ASP ships, are you not?"

"Yes, we are," Skatala replied. "I understand you're to blame for the damage to at least one of those expensive ships."

"Ah," Ries said, smiling. "So you do know who I am."

"We're not totally incompetent here," the Admiral said.

"No, but you are buried in bureaucracy, which does serve our purposes at GI in this instance," Ries said. "Although it has taken months for you to finally give the go-ahead on this mission, I'm afraid I must tell you to cancel it."

"What!" Skatala asked. His tail wasn't just twitching now, it was swinging back and forth behind him.

"Cancel the mission and purge any sign of it from your records," Ries said. "I have an executive order from the Alliance Security General authorizing a shutdown of any and all activities relating to Planet A2242."

Ries pulled out a small tablet from his front pocket and punched in a code. "I have just sent you a copy of the order, which you must promptly delete upon viewing. As part of this order, you must reassign all ASP personnel with knowledge of this mission, including Commander Thydosh Complin. Word must not get out concerning this issue. In other words, Admiral, control your Officers, or GI will do it for you."

"How dare you—" Skatala began.

"Hey, I'm only the messenger," Ries said. "If you have a grievance, you may take it up with the ASG."

The Admiral thought for a moment. Ries knew that he'd have to go along with this if he expected to keep his job. The Alliance Security General was the most powerful bureaucrat in the GA, and any contradiction to his orders would not be looked upon kindly. After a few minutes of silence, the Admiral's tail stopped twitching, and Ries almost jumped out of his chair and danced around the office. He knew he'd won. "Fine," Skatala said softly. "The mission is canceled. Can you at least tell me why?"

"Sorry, Admiral," Ries said, standing and donning his breathing mask once again. "That's a little above your security grade." He turned and walked toward the door, but stopped when he reached it and looked back at the Admiral. "Oh, by the way, may I suggest reassigning Commander Complin to

Finance? I hear you have a couple of openings there. Good day, Admiral."

He left the Admiral still standing in his office and walked back to the receptionist's desk. "Hello, Dren. Anyone ever told you that you have lovely eyes?" he asked. The Ingross smiled at him as he leaned in closer to her. He was on a roll.

Chapter 14

The resistance attacked the northern Krahn base just after sunset. Outside of the Krahn stronghold, James was leading the charge as hundreds of Sekani, Jirina, and Rajani attacked the fortified building. He had weapons in both hands and was powered up. Fighting beside him were Kieren and Gianni, who were also powered up. Gianni was firing bolts of energy from both hands. The structures around the Krahn nest-base were smoking piles of rubble.

A large force of Krahn was entrenched around the building, fighting the invading ground troops. The larger force of Rajani, Sekani, and Jirina were surrounding them. The air was full of weapons' discharge and screams, both of agony, and of fury. Casualties were falling on both sides. James pointed to the right of their position. "Kieren, tell those Sekani to stay back! No hand-to-hand. They don't stand a chance in hell." He turned to look at Mazal, who was behind a blackened vehicle and firing his weapon a couple of feet away from them. "Wait a minute."

He placed his hand on her shoulder and saw the now-familiar flash as her power merged with his. He turned to the Jirina. "Mazal, tell your people to cut around and try to find a weak spot in their defenses. Good luck, my friend." Mazal nodded, and then ran over to a group of Jirina, bending low to avoid fire. James could see him pointing where he wanted them to go.

James still had his hand on Kieren's shoulder. "All right, Kieren," he said. "Tell them to wait for the Rajani to give suppressing fire before they attack the Krahn directly. And be careful."

Kieren looked at Gianni. Their eyes met as she answered James, though neither could see the other's eyes through their power fields. "Always." Gianni watched as she flew off to talk to the Sekani, hoping it was true.

James and Gianni were left to keep fighting. "Okay, hotshot," James said. "Looks like it's you and me, now."

"Let's go do this, old man," Gianni replied, smiling.

They started to move forward. There was firing all around them from both the Krahn and their own allies. James could see projectiles bouncing off of his power field, though he couldn't feel their impact. It was surreal to know that without his powers, he would probably be dead. Suddenly, a squad of three Krahn ships flew over, firing on the resistance fighters below. James pointed toward the sky. "God damn it! Gianni, put up a shield over as many of them as possible."

Gianni was still firing. "No problem! But I won't be able to fire and hold the shield at the same time if it gets too large."

"I don't care," James yelled as he fired at the ships. "Go!"

Gianni ran off as a shield formed about ten feet above him. It expanded, but also grew paler as it grew larger. The ships returned and fired again. The shield held. The resistance troops, mostly Sekani at this point, cheered. They rushed toward the Krahn defenders. Many of each species fell, wounded and dead. Many more made the perimeter and started fighting hand-to-hand with the Krahn. The ships swung around for another pass.

A yellow shaft of energy came up from the ground and

went through one of the ships, which exploded, raining fiery debris down onto Gianni's power shield. A large object sailed up to another of the ships. It was Bhakat. He landed on top of the ship and punched through the top of the cockpit, as well as through the Krahn pilot's head that was inside of it. Bhakat jumped off the ship as it crashed into a group of Krahn defenders.

A blue blur zipped past Gianni. David returned and stopped near Gianni's side. "Gianni! I never thought I'd be happy to see you."

Gianni dropped the force shield above them all. He began firing on the last remaining ship. "Oh, now you show up," he said as he pointed to his left, while still firing with his right hand. "James is over there. Go find out what he wants you to do."

"Fine," David said, turning to go in the direction Gianni had pointed.

"Hey, kid?" Gianni said.

"What?" David answered, turning back toward him.

"Nice to see you didn't do anything stupid," Gianni replied, smiling. "Like get yourself killed."

"You too," David said before he took off in a blur, heading toward James.

The last ship was destroyed by a combination of Gianni's fire and Yvette's spears of energy. Gianni held his hand up to Bhakat as the large Rajani and Yvette approached him. "All right, Bhakat! High five, man."

"Imbecile," Bhakat said, still powered up, his arms crossed in front of him.

Gianni lowered his hand. "Okay. Never mind." He pulled Yvette aside. "Gee, Yvette, is it me, or does he have 'super powers'?"

"It's a long story," Yvette said, smiling. "Don't ask." She

held up an admonishing finger. "And be careful. He's learning English pretty well."

"It's good to see you guys," Gianni said. "I'm sure James will be relieved—"

"If I know James, he has a war to run," Yvette said, interrupting him. "And we have one to fight." She took Gianni's arm in hers, and their suits flashed. "Shall we join in?" Bhakat was about four feet in front of them, leading the way as they headed toward more fighting, arm in arm.

"Imbecile?" Gianni asked, and they both laughed.

◊

James was powered up, fighting a Krahn warrior. It wasn't much of a fight, as he easily broke the Krahn's back over his leg like kindling. For a moment, there were no Krahn at all around him. He stood and watched the fighting, catching his breath. He looked around at the devastation that surrounded him. He couldn't believe there was a time when he wanted to be a soldier for the rest of his life. He'd changed so much since Jenny died, and he hoped it was a change for the better.

Were my eyes truly so blinded by glory and patriotism that I could have fought and killed without caring for anything except waking up the next day to do it again? he thought. The idea surprised him even as he thought it. He'd always looked back somewhat fondly on his time as a Marine. He respected the men and women who could fight for their country, but he was no longer one of them. He looked over at the fighting to see a Krahn pick up a Sekani and bite it savagely on the neck before throwing its body to the ground. Suddenly, the Krahn was swarmed by three Jirina, who took turns hitting it on the head with clubs. It fell, and they hit it a few more times before moving on, leaving it bleeding into the trampled dirt from a crushed skull.

James watched as a Rajani and a Krahn fought hand-to-hand, the Krahn hissing as its nails raked down the chest of the Rajani. It actually looked surprised when its neck was broken by its foe. The Rajani dropped the body and casually stepped over it, looking for his next kill, seemingly unconcerned by his own blood flowing down his chest.

When James thought of what had been unleashed when the Krahn Horde had attacked Rajan, he felt his stomach twist painfully. He hoped he didn't vomit inside his energy field. He could see now why the Rajani were once considered the most dangerous species in the Galactic Alliance. He could just imagine what they'd been like with Johar Stones implanted in them. He took a few deep breaths, and then he was ready to fight again, if only to end the carnage and go home.

◊

Bhakat had broken off from the Humans during the fighting, going to help a group of Jirina who were being hard-pressed to make any headway against the group of Krahn defending the doorway of the largest building in the compound. At first the Jirina had all looked at him with fear in their eyes when he'd approached their position, but then one of them had actually smiled at him. "He's like James the Human," he said to the others.

"Follow behind me," Bhakat told the Jirina. He ran toward the doorway of the building, projectiles bouncing off his power field as he shielded those behind him. When he reached the doorway, he grabbed the nearest Krahn and threw it behind him, knowing that the Jirina would take care of it. He grabbed another Krahn and quickly broke its neck. Soon, the Jirina were involved in the fighting, and the rest of the Krahn in the doorway were killed. When they finally gained entrance to the building, he was surprised to find that it was littered with the bodies of Sekani, some of them half-eaten, and that the Krahn warriors inside the first room they entered looked like they were higher ranking than those who had been fighting outside the building. They were dressed in better armor, and their weapons were of a better quality.

Bhakat and the Jirina fought and quickly overcame the Krahn. He could see that other Rajani, Jirina, and Sekani were entering the building as well, fanning out to check each of the rooms along the corridor and heading up and down various stairwells. He stopped to talk to the Jirina who had spoken before about James. "Where's James?" he asked.

"I don't know," the Jirina said. "He ordered me to come around to this side of the building. He's probably on the other side of the building still. Who are you?"

"My name's Bhakat," he answered simply.

The Jirina's eyes grew wide with surprise before he smiled again. "James told me about you and your Master, Rauphangelaa. He'll be happy that you've finally shown up. I want to thank you for helping us today in this important victory. This is the Krahn's main northern base of operations."

The higher rank of the Krahn made sense when Bhakat learned the importance of the building, and that he'd helped to gain control of it. None of the Krahn had been left alive after the fighting, unfortunately, so they wouldn't be able to ask them any questions. "Please excuse me," Bhakat told the Jirina. "There's someone I need to look for here."

Mazal held out his hand toward Bhakat, and Bhakat clasped it, finding it strange that the Jirina was using a Human custom. The Jirina squeezed his hand once and then let go, already turning to help round up the wounded Rajani fighters near them. Bhakat watched him for a moment before steeling himself for his own task.

He looked at all of the Sekani bodies that littered the floor of the room they were in. He could see that some of them had been alive very recently, and had died from a single shot to the head. The Krahn had killed them all when the attack had begun. He searched all of them, dreading seeing Janan's face, but the little pilot wasn't among the dead. Finally, he finished and was able to leave the room in the hands of the Sekani who had arrived during his search of the bodies. He knew they would take care of their own dead. He left through the front door and took deep breaths of the air outside, though he could still smell death all around him.

◊

Kieren had been glad to hear that the fighting had stopped for the day. They had won the battle, but she was just glad that no one else would get hurt. As she headed back to the headquarters of the resistance, she saw Gianni walking next to Yvette.

"Yvette!" she yelled happily, running over to the two.

"Hey there, stranger," Yvette said, wrapping her in a hug as they both laughed.

"What about David and the others?" Kieren asked. "Have you heard anything about them?"

"I've been living with David, Rauph, and Bhakat since a little while after we arrived," Yvette said. "I'm afraid that Janan was captured by the Krahn shortly after he and David crashed on Rajan."

"Oh no!" Kieren said. She knew what had probably happened to him. "That's horrible."

"David took it pretty hard," Yvette said, looking down at the ground for a moment.

"Just another reason to kill these bastards," Gianni said.

"Gianni!" Kieren exclaimed.

"I know, I know, watch my language," he said.

Yvette looked at the two of them, a question in her eyes for Kieren. Kieren shook her head, smiling sadly, knowing what Yvette meant. She and Gianni were just friends.

Yvette's eyes grew wide for a moment. "Oh, but that's not the biggest news. Bhakat—" Before she could finish her sentence, she was suddenly swept off her feet and into the air. She powered up quickly, her power field curiously flashing as she did so.

"Hey, beautiful, is this dance taken?" a voice said near Yvette. Kieren could tell that it was James. Sure enough, he appeared next to them, holding the still powered-up form of Yvette in his arms. She dropped her field, and he followed suit, then dropped her feet to the ground as he embraced her.

Kieren didn't know why tears came to her eyes. Part of it was from happiness at seeing James and Yvette reunited, she supposed, but another part, way deep down in her mind was saying 'what about me?' She quickly squelched the thought, feeling like she was being selfish for thinking that way. She looked over to see Gianni looking at her intently. He saw her gaze and quickly turned away. Kieren wiped away a tear and smiled, watching James and Yvette kiss. A blue blur came sweeping by them, and she knew that David had arrived as well. He came around and stopped near them, a large smile on his face as he dropped his power field.

Kieren threw her arms around his neck, happy to see him alive still. He returned her embrace and laughed. "Well, at least someone's happy to see me," he said, jokingly.

"Ha-ha," James said. "Just because I didn't give you a big, mushy kiss doesn't mean I'm not happy to see you."

"I think this calls for a celebration," Yvette said. She still had an arm around James. Kieren didn't think they would be separated for a long time.

"I agree," James said. "I think we can take a break for tonight. The fighting is over for now. I'll get everyone's debriefing later. Let's have a party."

"Fernta for everyone," David said, and everyone groaned. Kieren laughed, happy to have almost everyone back together and safe.

◊

Rauph had been left by Bhakat in a relatively safe place when they had come upon the fighting. Yvette, David, and Bhakat had chosen to join the fight, so Rauph had taken refuge in a burned-out building as he waited for them to return. He still wasn't happy about the fact that Bhakat had forsaken the Kha in his bid to free Rajan, but he could live with it, he supposed.

Bhakat is his own Master now, he thought. By choosing to abandon the Kha, he was no longer Rauph's Pledge. It made Rauph sad to think that he'd wasted so many years teaching Bhakat. *No,* he thought, *they weren't really wasted.* Bhakat had been placed in a terrible situation, both by the Krahn invasion, and by the crash of the *Tukuli* that had forced him to choose between implantation and death. He was sure, though, that his voice would be a minority among the Elders if he tried to commute Bhakat's sentence for breaking the law concerning the Johar Stones. It was unfortunate, to be sure. He would just have to hope that the extenuating circumstances would help Bhakat's case, if and when he ever went to trial.

Rauph sat down on the ground, his side aching from the walk so far. He leaned back his head and was almost asleep when a noise came from outside the building. He sat up, adrenaline kicking into his system. He wasn't so tired anymore, suddenly. If it was the Krahn, he was in trouble. He stood slowly, and walked over to an opening in the wall. He looked out and saw wounded Sekani and Rajani sitting down next to the building. Relieved, he left the shelter and walked out to them.

"Rauphangelaa?" a voice said from his left.

He looked over to see a Rajani he didn't recognize. He was surprised to see that the Rajani had short hair, only a few inches long. He also had a patch over one eye, further disguising him. Rauph walked over to the Rajani for a closer look. "Yes," he said, uncertain. Then he saw who it was. "Volaan?" he asked.

"It's Kedar now, actually," the Rajani said, standing up. "I'm happy to see you're well."

"It was a close thing," Rauph said.

"Well, your Human friends have told us what happened to you," Kedar said. "I'm not surprised."

"What about you?" Rauph asked, looking at the other Rajani. "What happened to you?"

"Oh," Kedar said, running a hand over his head. "All courtesy of the Krahn, I'm afraid. I assume you'll want to talk to the other Elders. I'm sure Tumaani will be happy to welcome you back."

"Tumaani still lives?" Rauph asked, smiling.

"Yes," Kedar said. "Although I'm afraid we now share the same haircut. Ah, here comes your Pledge, if I'm not mistaken."

Rauph turned to see Bhakat approaching from down the street. He was not powered up. *Good,* Rauph thought. *We'll get to that later.* Better for now that he kept his new powers a secret, at least out in public. "Yes," he said.

Bhakat walked up to the group and nodded to Kedar. He bent to check on the wounded. None of them seemed too badly off, to Rauph, but he was no expert. "Bhakat can take care of the wounded, if you'd like to escort me to where Tumaani can be found," he said. "I assure you, they're in safe hands with him."

"Wonderful," Kedar said. "I leave them in your capable care, then, Bhakat."

"Be safe, Bhakat," Rauph said to his former Pledge. "We'll speak again later."

"Be safe, Rauphangelaa," Bhakat said, bowing slightly. He turned his attention back to a Sekani with a bullet hole in his shoulder.

"Lead the way," Rauph said to Kedar. He followed the other Rajani slowly along a narrow street. His ribs would not allow him to move too quickly.

"You brought back help," Kedar said as he walked. "I must tell you that I was surprised when I first saw the Human named James in the prison camp. When he first appeared, I thought he was a Rajani out of legend, wielding the powers of the Johar Stones, here to strike down all the enemies of Rajan. It wasn't until after he let his façade drop that I realized he was from off-world."

"Yes, well, I found that I didn't really have much of a choice in the matter," Rauph said. "It was all I could do at the time. They were our only option."

"I understand," Kedar said. "I just don't know if any of the Elders will."

"You talk of the Elders as if you are no longer a part of us," Rauph said, stopping to look at Kedar. "What happened?"

"The Krahn," Kedar began. "They took away everything. My mate. My youngling. Even my Ralik, as you can see. Which I suppose was symbolic. I've lost my faith in the Kha, as well. I don't consider myself an Elder anymore, so I went back to my birth name. It seemed better this way."

"I'm truly sorry, Kedar," Rauph said, looking at the other Rajani's scarred face. "I hope that when all of this has passed, that you'll regain at least a little of your faith."

"We shall have to see if that time comes to pass," Kedar said. "And if we both live to see it."

◊

James had left the after-battle debriefings as soon as he could, to return to his room, where Yvette had been waiting for him. They had embraced and just held each other for a long while, but then he had leaned down and kissed her gently on the lips. After that, there had been an urgency to their lovemaking that he hadn't felt since the first time aboard the *Tukuli*. It had been a few months since they had seen each other, but to him, it felt like much longer. As they lay next to each other on his bed, he wrapped his arms around her, determined that they wouldn't be separated for so long again.

Later that night, James lay on his cot, exhausted from the fighting earlier in the day, and his own private reunion celebration with Yvette earlier that night. Still, he was unable to fall asleep. He listened to her breathing as she slept beside him. They had defeated the Krahn and captured the northern base, a strategic win before they pressed on to the south of Melaanse and the main Krahn stronghold. He knew that it would be a much larger fight than the one they had just gone through.

The days had started to run together; a blurry tapestry of fighting and strategy sessions that seemed never-ending. He'd been surprised when Bhakat had informed him earlier that day that they had left Earth's solar system almost six months earlier. *Was it truly that long ago?* he thought, amazed that the time had gone by so quickly.

He knew for sure now that there was no going back to his life the way he remembered it. Things had changed too much for that. He had changed too much as well, to settle for returning to his life as a cop. He'd been thinking about retiring for years, but it had taken an alien abduction to finally set events in motion. He would miss some aspects of the job, but more often than not, he'd been either miserable or frustrated, or both, as he'd gone through the day-to-day tribulations of being a big city police officer. He remembered how he'd felt the day of the abduction—knowing that he'd have to go to the autopsy of the young girl who had been pushed from the top of her hotel, and also knowing that her killer was still no closer to being brought to justice. James tried, but he couldn't remember her name. But her face sprang easily to mind. No, he would never forget her face. He remembered all of them, even after all the killing he'd witnessed on Rajan.

Damn it, what was her name? he thought. But he lost his train of thought, knowing that it didn't really matter. She'd been dead a while now. Hopefully her killer had been arrested or killed by now too. If he ever got back to Earth, he would at least check on the case somehow.

He lay on his cot next to the sleeping form of Yvette and knew he was no longer a cop. He smiled as he fell asleep. He was no longer a cop.

Chapter 15

Ries an na Van was returning to the planet Eddross to meet up with his GI superior, Odorey T'van. He'd completed his mission on Asnuria, having been assured that the Alliance Society for Peace wouldn't follow up with the Rajani, or more specifically, with the starship called the *Tukuli* and its registered owner, Rauphangelaa tuc Nebraani. He was ready now for his next assignment. T'van didn't trust meeting over a communications link, so they would have their meeting face-to-face on the Eddross space station. Eddross was an obscure little planet far away from the main space lanes, so it had taken Ries a while to find passage there on a slow-moving ore trawler.

Ries had been surprised when he'd first met his new boss. T'van wasn't what he'd expected when he'd first heard his voice coming through the speaker of a Galactic Intelligence holding cell. But he knew why he hadn't seen anything when he'd looked out the window on the door of the cell. T'van was only about four Standard feet tall.

Once the space trawler he was traveling on docked at the space port, Ries made his way to the private wing that T'van was using as a base of operations. He walked the maze-like route of corridors that led to his boss, and wondered how his life had changed so much is so short a time. It really was miraculous, in a sense. He'd never believed in any set religion growing up, but he could almost believe that his life was being overseen by some higher power. When he reached the outer door, he punched in a security code on the pad next to the door, and it opened just long enough for him to walk through. Once inside, he waited while a scanner ran over his body, making sure he was unarmed and not carrying anything that could pose a threat.

Ries had thought his boss was overly paranoid about security when he'd been let out of his holding cell and been allowed to walk free once more, but after meeting him, he could sympathize with the high-ranking agent. He'd feel vulnerable too, if he was that small, and he'd quickly learned that being paranoid could save your life in his line of work. The inner doors of the chamber opened, and Ries walked in to find T'van reclining in a comfortable chair in front of a roaring faux fireplace. He was drinking a dark liquid and smiling at Ries, his small, sharp teeth reflecting the light of the fire.

Ries sat down in the chair opposite his boss. His antennae were beginning to twitch, which was never a good sign. Something didn't feel right. And it wasn't just that T'van seemed happy for the first time since Ries had met him.

"From what I've heard so far," T'van said, "everything went well on Asnuria."

"What have you heard?" Ries asked, feeling defensive but not knowing why.

"The ASPs are in a tizzy," T'van responded. "But they'll stay away from Rajan, at least. Their admiral has already put in a formal protest to GI, but it should blow over quickly. The Security General will make a few minor concessions, and things will be back to normal soon enough."

Ries reclined in his chair before speaking again. "I've been thinking," he said tentatively. "What exactly is there to gain by having the Krahn Horde attack the Rajani?"

"Gain?" T'van asked. "Freedom for not one, but two repressed species on Rajan, and hopefully, the annihilation of the Rajani menace that has lingered for far too long. Isn't that enough?"

"But why does GI care about the Rajani?" Ries asked. "Why upset the status quo now, when the Rajani haven't been a threat for thousands of years?"

"My dear Agent Van," T'van said, taking a drink from his glass. "Who ever said that Galactic Intelligence knows anything about the Krahn Horde attacking Rajan?"

Ries's antennae weren't just twitching now; they were in full spasms. "What?"

"Yes, I am a senior agent of Galactic Intelligence," T'van said. "But this is my own little...side project, if you will. This one is personal. Don't worry, GI will never find out. I've given express orders to my Krahn contact that the Rajani are to be exterminated, quickly and quietly, once they've obtained their objective."

"Which is what?" Ries asked.

"Mere baubles," T'van answered. "I doubt they even exist anymore. But I promised the Krahn that they could search Rajan to their hearts' content once they arrived. A promise is a promise. And while their attention is solely on the Planet Rajan, they're no longer a menace to the space lanes. It's a win-win scenario all around."

"So, what about me?" Ries asked. All sorts of scenarios were playing through his mind, and none of them were good.

"What about you?" T'van asked. "You are an agent of Galactic Intelligence who has finished his task for the time being. Enjoy your downtime on this station, until I give you your next mission." He held out his glass toward Ries. "Would you like some fernta?"

◊

Rauph and Tumaani had known each other a long time. They had pledged the same House together when they were young. They had been friendly rivals for as long as they had known each other. In that time, they had gotten into some major arguments over the leadership of their species, and while the Kha forbade any type of physical confrontation, they had learned long ago that words could be just as powerful as a blow when used correctly. Their differences were always based more in their moral outlooks than the fact that they competed in everything from their first mate to Rajani contact with other worlds. Rauph believed there was nothing wrong with using the latest technologies and keeping up diplomatic relations with other Galactic Alliance worlds, while Tumaani believed that the Rajani should stay secluded from other worlds, and had gone so far as to suggest seceding from the Galactic Alliance altogether.

Their current argument threatened to make the others pale in comparison. They had met privately to discuss the state of the Rajani, and any possibility of things going back to the way they were before the Krahn had attacked them. So many things had changed that Rauph doubted they could ever go back to being the quiet society of scholars and priests that had existed prior to the invasion. He was trying to explain this to Tumaani, with little success. The warmth of their first meeting since the Krahn invasion was long forgotten by the second meeting.

He calmed his thoughts a moment and began again. "Tumaani, I don't wish to fight with you. I've had enough fighting for two lifetimes. But you must see that Rajan will come out of this war a changed society. We cannot go back to the way things were, even if we wanted to. Our males have fought and died, and you yourself have said that you haven't even been able to find where the Krahn are keeping our females and offspring prisoner. Besides that, do you really believe the Sekani and Jirina will go back to being second-class beings willingly?"

"No," Tumaani replied softly, slumping in his chair. "We should've seen this possibility years ago. The Sekani were always a proud race, even after the Rajani conquered them all those years ago. The yoke of our oppression must have been so heavy that they were willing to invite monsters as liberators. But I tell you this, Rauphangelaa: I would rather that we all live in mud huts than go back to the way things were before the Kha."

"We may not have a choice in the matter," Rauph said. They both sat a moment, pondering what Rauph had said. "This fight is testing our species' resolve in more than one way. The teachings of Ruvedalin may not be enough to keep them in control. I've already seen Rajani turn away from the Kha."

They sat for a moment, both thinking about Volaan, who now preferred to be known as Kedar. His exodus from the Priests of the Kha and as an Elder had done more to recruit fellow Rajani to his Vaderren than anything else.

"There is one other matter we must discuss," Tumaani said, breaking the silence that surrounded them.

"And what's that?" Rauph asked, dreading his peer's answer, but already sure what he was going to say.

"You know as well as I why the Krahn came here," Tumaani said.

"Yes," Rauph replied, sighing. "The Johar Stones."

"As Keeper of the Stones, it was your duty to keep them safe and out of the hands of any beings other than the

Rajani," Tumaani said, straightening up again in his chair. "And the first thing you did was implant five aliens from some backwater mud ball of a planet. A violent species that doesn't even have nulldrive technology yet. What exactly were you thinking?"

"We were in a desperate situation," Rauph said. "And really, the Humans have proven to be quite an interesting discovery." *In more ways than one,* he thought.

"A curiosity, maybe," Tumaani said. "But I think you overestimate their ability to help us. I mean, even with the aid of the Johar Stones, they are only five in number."

"Yes," Rauph agreed. "But have you seen the powers they display? Amazing. There are no descriptions of anything similar in all of Rajani history."

"And unpredictable as the beings who wield them," Tumaani replied. "What do we really know about these Humans? It could be years before they're even ready to be included in the Galactic Alliance, let alone be vetted and accepted. And we're just supposed to let these five leave Rajan after all is said and done?"

"What is it that you are suggesting, Tumaani?" Rauph asked. The conversation had just taken an unexpected and dangerous turn.

"I'm not suggesting anything," Tumaani replied, scowling. "Other than being cautious when it comes to the Johar Stones. How are you supposed to guard them if they are light years away on this Earth planet?"

Rauph hesitated a moment. Not even all of the Elders knew the true nature of the Stones. He decided that now was not the time to divulge it. "All I can tell you," he said, standing up and moving toward the door, "is that the Johar Stones are safe, whether the Humans are here or on their own planet."

"And what of the remaining Stones?" Tumaani asked.

"Who says there are any?" Rauph replied, and walked out the door.

◊

Kieren was surprised at how quickly she and Gianni had been accepted by the Sekani. She no longer felt like an outsider, at least. No longer was their every word or action looked on with distrust or suspicion. It helped that she and the other humans had done their best to improve the lives of the Sekani. A lot of progress had been made since that first realization that she and Gianni had made when they were brought to the Sekanis' home; the Sekani were no longer dying of hunger, lack of clean water, and unsanitary conditions. Zanth was organizing them into a real society. After so many years of being separated by the various Rajani Elder Houses that they had worked for, they were no longer servants. He was attempting to make them into a sovereign nation on Rajan, independent of their former Rajani masters. It was a difficult undertaking; she knew how little sleep Zanth was getting every night.

She had agreed to stay with the Sekani after James had mentioned how badly they would need them in the coming fight against the Krahn. She seemed to have been caught in the role of liaison to them, and Gianni was just part of the package deal. James had also implied that she was better at keeping him in check, which wasn't a bad thing, either. The only thing was, she wasn't really keeping Gianni in check. He was doing that himself. James wasn't around enough to see that Gianni had changed, and he had changed on his own. It seemed to have been his choice, at least. He still had his moments, but he was no longer the insufferable jerk that he'd been on the Tukuli.

She just wished that she had at least something to do with his turnaround. She hardly saw him on a day-to-day basis anymore. He'd taken to going out on patrols with the Sekani, trying to secure the areas around the Sekani base and weeding out the Krahn security checkpoints that had been set up after the invasion. At times she was happy to see Gianni contributing to the effort, but at other times she was sad, thinking that he'd left her behind. She had plenty on her own plate dealing with Zanth and the Rajani Elders, but that didn't mean she wasn't lonely.

Then Yvette and David had shown up. She was happy to see Yvette was okay, and see her and James reunited. She was surprised, though, at how happy she'd been to see David, and how that same sentiment was reflected by him. It was confusing, and a little bit scary. Did she have feelings for him, outside of friendship? They hadn't spent a lot of time together on the trip from Earth, but she had enjoyed running with him and hanging out with him in the common room, along with the others. But they had rarely spent time alone together outside of that, and he'd never shown any interest in her, other than as a running partner.

She was getting ready for bed as she thought about her feelings for both men, when there was a knock on her door. She actually thought about not answering it, not wanting to deal with the latest Sekani crisis, but then thought better of it. If they needed her, then she would help. It was the sole reason she'd come to Rajan. As she neared the door, though, she had a feeling it wouldn't be the Sekani. She realized that she hoped it was Gianni, and was surprised at the feeling of anticipation she felt at the prospect.

It wasn't.

"Hey," David said when she opened the door.

"Hey," she replied, not knowing what else to say at the moment. She hoped that her disappointment hadn't shown on her face when she'd opened the door. It wasn't his fault he wasn't who she wanted to see.

"Can I come in and talk to you?" David asked, smiling.

She had to admit, he had a nice smile. And he was cute, in a boy-band sort of way. She noticed that his hair had grown longer in their time apart. Instead of a boy band member, he looked more like one of the Bee Gees. They were one of her brother's favorite bands, but she couldn't stand them. "Sure," she said, standing to the side. "C'mon in."

"You weren't sleeping, were you?" David asked, looking around her room. "I can come back later, if you want."

"No, it's all right," she said. "I was getting ready to go to bed, but I'm not really that tired." She sat down on her bed, which was the only piece of furniture in the cramped space. He sat down on the bed as well, only about a foot away from her.

"I can't sleep, either," he said, looking down at the floor. Kieren was suddenly aware of how close he was. She could smell his breath when he spoke. She could tell that he'd been drinking fernta.

He looked up at her, their faces only a few inches apart now. "I can't sleep because of you," he said. "I...can't stop thinking about you, for some reason." He smiled briefly, and then grew serious again, looking unsure of himself.

Kieren was surprised as well. This was happening too fast. She didn't know what she wanted anymore. Gianni didn't seem that interested in her. But did that mean she should just go to David as a fallback option? That wouldn't be very fair to him. Suddenly, he leaned forward and kissed her. His lips were warm and soft, and, for a moment, she closed her eyes and allowed him to kiss her. The taste of fernta was not unpleasant on his lips. Then she pulled away, her eyes wide, realizing what she was doing.

"I'm sorry," he said, standing up. "I shouldn't have—"

"No, it's okay," she said. "I'm sorry. I shouldn't have let that happen." She saw the look of disappointment on his face for a brief moment, before it cleared away. "No, that's not what I meant," she said. What had she meant to say? "David, I like you. A lot. But I don't know if I like you in that way."

"I'm sorry," he said. "I shouldn't have come here." He walked toward the door of her room. She couldn't help but notice the change in his voice. He seemed...colder, suddenly.

"David, wait, we should talk—" she began, standing up.

He turned to her, and she could see his eyes. They reflected the coldness of his voice. "No, there's nothing to talk about." He turned and left, closing the door behind him.

She stood there a moment, shocked at what had just happened, and the change in David at the end. It was like he had turned into a different person than the one who had entered her dwelling. It was a long time before she could fall asleep.

◊

Ries sat in his room and wondered how he kept finding himself in such dangerous situations. Everything had been going so well in his new job, and now he found out that his superior at Galactic Intelligence was acting on his own to carry out some sort of personal vendetta, and had used Ries to help in his quest to overthrow, and possibly exterminate, the Rajani.

Ries had been so angry at first, he'd thought of just killing the little Sekani and trying to disappear somewhere where GI couldn't find him. But after seriously contemplating the scenario, he knew that there was nowhere in Alliance space that he could go. He thought about trying to escape to space controlled by the Supreme Consortium, but relations between the Alliance and the Consortium were not exactly amicable. He could be shot just trying to enter SC space.

No, he had to get out of the mess the old-fashioned way, by using his wits. He turned the attention of both of his brains to the problem at hand, knowing that if he was going to escape this latest mess, he would have to be at the top of his game. He needed to implicate T'van anonymously, so that none of the Sekani's stench stuck to him. He poured himself another glass of kolan, knowing it was going to be a long night of scheming, but then, scheming was what he did best.

He finally decided that the Security General himself should learn about T'van's plotting, not just whatever lies T'van had told him so he'd agree to strong-arm the ASPs into abandoning their quest for the Rajani ship. The only question was how he was going to get word to him. He couldn't just hop the next ship to Sh'kall, the seat of Galactic Intelligence. T'van had an elaborate system of agents and informants, and he would know what Ries was planning.

◊

The Sekani were celebrating their victory; their first major triumph over the Krahn. The victory over the Krahn at their northern base had cost the lives of hundreds of Sekani, but it was a sacrifice they were willing to make. They had set up one of the large warehouse buildings near the shore of the ocean to have a victory feast. Gianni was the guest of honor, his standing among the young male Sekani at an all-time high. After the third large glass of fernta, he had stopped drinking, feeling lightheaded and much too warm. His small group of warriors had tried to get him to stay and drink more with them, calling out his Sekani name, Sedan'ka, and generally acting like he would offend them if he left.

He had begged off anyway, telling them that he needed to get some sleep. In reality, he wanted to see Kieren. Call it liquid courage, but he felt ready to finally talk to her. He was tired of pretending he didn't care about her. She needed to know the truth, if only so that he could stop carrying the load of feelings around like an anchor on his heart. He walked, somewhat unsteadily, over to where her room was located. He had to stop for a minute, feeling like he was going to be sick. *Never should have drank that third glass,* he thought, grimacing.

After the wave of nausea had passed, he continued walking. At first, he thought he was seeing things when he saw Kieren inviting David into her room. His legs felt weak, and he had to sit down. He was too late. She'd moved on. He scoffed at the thought. How could she move on when they'd never been together in the first place? There was nothing to move on from. He sat there a few minutes wallowing in self-pity. He was just about to stand up and head back to the celebration, perhaps to drown out the sight of David going into her room, when the door suddenly opened up and David emerged. He slammed the door and seemed upset. Good, Gianni thought, smiling.

He closed his eyes. *Good,* he thought again. *I'll get up and talk to her as soon as I rest a little.* When he woke up a few hours later, his head pounding and a thick coat on his tongue, he decided that maybe it wasn't such a good time to talk to her after all.

◊

David had not been able to sleep after leaving Kieren's room at the Sekani compound. He'd returned to his own room, but had stayed up until he saw the first light of dawn coming over the eastern horizon. He should have known that he would be rebuffed by Kieren. Women were all the same. They acted nice to you, but they weren't really. His father had tried to tell him, but he hadn't listened. He had fought against him, fought against the truth his entire life. But no more. He knew now that they were all unworthy of him.

He left his room and went in search of Krahn. He'd discovered that he enjoyed hunting the Krahn on his own. He felt free to take out his pent-up anger on the creatures, and it also gave him time to think. His thoughts, always seemingly going too fast, seemed to slow down as he concentrated on searching for his next prey. It was close to the way he had felt back on Earth before agreeing to leave with the Rajani. He found his first Krahn warrior a little while later, squatting next to a large piece of stone that had once been a corner of a building. It held its gun casually, as if it were taking a break.

David didn't feel like doing anything extensive, so he just ran to the Krahn, picked it up, and ran it straight into another large piece of stone some twenty feet away. He ran it headfirst into the stone; its struggles were inconsequential. The Krahn exploded between the stone and David's power field, covering him from head to foot in gore, which slowly slid down the field toward the ground. He looked down at himself, surprised at the mess he'd made. *Maybe that wasn't such a good idea,* he thought. He began to run as fast as he could, watching the blood and other bits of Krahn slide off his field. When most of it was gone, he slowed down and dropped his field briefly, allowing the rest to fall away before powering up again. *Good as new,* he thought, grimly.

He smiled when he caught sight of another Krahn. Better just do this the old-fashioned way. He raced up to the Krahn and picked it up before it knew he was even there. He then raced for the nearby coastline. He'd found that most of the city of Melaanse was bordered on its eastern side by a sandy beach, but the northern area of coast rose in height to tall cliffs that overlooked a small bay. This was where he took the Krahn warrior. When he reached a point where he knew there were jagged rocks far below, he hurled the Krahn off, watching as the body bounced down the cliff face and came to rest at the bottom.

He stood there a moment, looking down at the body of the Krahn where it rested. There were four other bodies lying next to it, where he'd also dropped them. They were all in various stages of decomposition. Satisfied, he took off once again, heading back to the city of Melaanse, and another hunt.

Chapter 16

Ries an na Van was meeting with his new boss, Agent Fourth Level Kamran Ne. His former boss, Odorey T'van, who had initially recruited him to Galactic Intelligence, had been labeled as a rogue agent and discharged from the agency. T'van was to be apprehended with extreme prejudice by whoever saw him, whether ASP officer or GI agent, or whatever bounty hunter got lucky enough to collect the reward money. The Security General had not taken the news well when he'd learned about the machinations of the rogue agent. Ries had been careful to remain anonymous, but had used communication channels that were available to all agents of GI.

Ries didn't know what the ASG's anger meant for his own standing in GI. How was he supposed to have known that he'd been working for someone who had been operating outside of GI protocol? Now he just needed to do everything possible to stay alive. He walked into Ne's office, unsure what to expect. It was a simple, unadorned workspace, much different than the luxury preferred by T'van. There was a desk with a small computer screen on it. There was no chair behind the desk, though there was one in front of the desk for visitors. There were no pictures on the walls. He would not have thought that anyone was using it, if not for the large glass of water that had been set on the corner of the desk. He stood there, looking around the office and wondering if he should sit. He decided he'd better just stand and wait.

It was a few minutes before Ne entered. Ries was surprised to see that he was a Mling-don, an aquatic species that traveled around in mechanical bodies. Ries had to stop a smile that threatened to split his face. His small Sekani superior had been replaced by one even smaller, and possibly more vulnerable.

Ne walked over to the desk without a word and placed a file he'd been carrying on the desktop. When he reached the area behind the desk, he stood there a moment, his circular tank just at the level of the top of the desk. Suddenly, the top half of his mechanical body bent backwards, extending its arms toward the floor. When its arms had set down on the floor and stabilized, the top of the tank sat just below the level of the desk. Ries heard the sound of machinery working, and the tank began to rise. It finally stopped when it sat a full standard foot above the desktop. Ries could see Ne turning around in the tank, the wires leading from his head to the mechanical body floating around it in the water. Ne stopped when he was facing in Ries's direction. "Please, have a seat," Ne said through a translator built into his mechanical body, his small arm pointing toward the chair. Ries sat down. "Water?" Ne asked.

"No, thank you," Ries answered.

"Suit yourself," Ne said. A small hose slid out from the mechanical body and dipped into the glass of water sitting on the desktop. The water level in the glass slowly decreased. When the water had all been vacuumed into the mechanical body, the hose slid back to its original position. "Ah, much better," Ne said. "My filters work well enough, but there's nothing like some fresh water to get the blood pumping."

Ries just sat there, wondering if he was going to be killed by someone who swam around in his own waste. It didn't seem fair.

"Now," Ne said. "I suppose you've heard about my predecessor's undoing?"

"Yes," Ries answered glumly.

"Then you know why I've called you in," Ne said. "We can't have our agents performing unsanctioned missions, especially when those missions involve the toppling of sovereign and Alliance-recognized governments."

Ries almost laughed. Toppling governments was what Galactic Intelligence specialized in. He kept his face emotionless, though. No need to unduly tempt fate.

"Agent T'van chose to operate outside of GI control," Ne continued. "Even going so far as enlisting his own agents, such as yourself, Agent Van. It's a practice that is frowned upon by Galactic Intelligence, though not without precedence." He paused a moment, his unblinking eyes studying Ries from behind his clear orb. "I'm willing to overlook the impropriety in this instance. I've read over your records, and if you're willing to work for me, and more importantly, work within GI's stated legal limits, then you still have a job, as far as I'm concerned. Do you choose to do so?"

Ries was still digesting everything that he had just heard, and the fact that he had survived yet again. It took a moment for him to answer. "Of course," he said. "Yes. Whatever you'd like me to do."

"Good answer," Ne said. "First things first. We need to clean up T'van's mess."

"Planet A2242?" Ries asked, already knowing the answer.

"Of course Planet A2242," Ne said. "I tell you, I don't know what T'van was thinking when he agreed to help the

Krahn Horde. But I want to emphasize the fact that he was working alone in this instance. Is that understood?"

"Of course," Ries answered, wondering if it was actually the truth. He supposed it didn't really matter.

"We can't be dragging the Alliance into this," Ne said. "Very touchy matter, and all that."

"I understand," Ries said.

"So, what I want you to do," Ne said, "is immediately break off all communication with your Krahn contact—what's his name?" he asked himself, looking down at his notes, which he'd laid out on the desk before him. "Oh, yes, Ronak. Fancies himself the leader in exile of the entire Krahn planet. Looney as can be, from what I've heard. Immediately break off communications with this Ronak. From now on, he's on his own."

Ries sat there a moment, perplexed. He hadn't been aware that T'van had a contact within the Krahn Horde, let alone that it was Ronak himself. All he'd known was that T'van had recruited a Sekani on Rajan and had been working with him to overthrow the Rajani Elders, and possibly destroy the Rajani completely. Every time he thought he knew what was happening, there was another layer to uncover. He had survived twice now. He didn't know if he'd live to see another layer uncovered.

"Of course, this issue would take the talents of someone performing above your pay grade," Ne said, breaking into Ries's contemplation. "So you are promoted to Agent Level Two, effective immediately. Is this acceptable to you?"

Ries almost fell out of his chair. "Yes," he barely squeaked out, amazed once again by the turn of events.

"Now," Ne said, looking at Ries intently. "About this Sekani saboteur on Rajan. He must be silenced for the good of Galactic Intelligence. If word ever got out of GI's part in all of this, it could turn into a real public relations nightmare."

Ries once again felt his emotions take a complete turn, knowing where the conversation was headed. His amazement was again turned to dread.

"It's your task," Ne said, "to go to Rajan and find this Sekani contact, and make sure he is either captured or killed. Doesn't really matter which, since he'll be dead soon enough. Unfortunately, T'van never wrote down the contact's real name. All we've been able to find was a code name. Also, you must determine what the Rajani know about the plot, if anything. I don't have to tell you what would happen if they discovered that they are not on their original home planet. Can't have them looking for a planet that's under strict Alliance quarantine. Do you understand your mission?" Before Ries could answer, Ne broke in once again. "Oh, and if you happen to run into T'van on your journey, be sure to kill him. And make sure it's painful."

"Yes, sir," Ries said.

"I've put in a request for a ship, and it should be waiting for you at the docking station. You are to leave immediately. That is all," Ne said. "You're dismissed. I expect a full report of your success when your mission is complete."

Ries stood. "I understand," he said, though he couldn't tell at that point if Ne was even listening anymore. He slowly walked from the room, wondering how he was going to find one single Sekani in the middle of a war zone.

◊

Kieren had just returned from sitting in on school for the young Sekani males. She'd been surprised to find that male and female Sekani were taught separately. While the males were taught how to be pilots and work in various other industries, the females were mostly taught to perform more menial jobs, like cooking and cleaning. At first Kieren was shocked at the inequality, but then she learned more about the Sekani culture. Because of the social nature of the family units, the females were expected to work half of the time watching and teaching the young, and cooking for the whole unit. They would take turns working at the Sekani dwellings and working for the Rajani.

While it might not look ideal to a modern American woman, the system had worked fine for the Sekani. Now, though, Zanth had been attempting to change the culture. Since they were no longer beholden to the Rajani, he was trying to open up the possibilities for females, even going so far as to suggest that male and female young should be taught the same subjects together. This, of course, had been met with some resistance from both male and females of the species, from what Zanth had told her. Kieren knew that if change was to happen, it would probably happen slowly, but she was encouraged to see it happening at all.

She had just sat down in her room with a protein bar and a bottle of water when there was a knock on her door. She looked longingly at the protein bar before sighing and standing up. She had a feeling she wouldn't be eating anytime soon. She opened her door to find a young Sekani female whom she hadn't met before.

"The Rajani Elder Rauphangelaa is at the front gate," the Sekani said quickly, almost tripping over her words in her haste to get them out of her mouth. "He said he needs to speak to you."

Kieren smiled at her. "Thank you. What's your name?" she asked as she closed her door behind her.

"My name is Kalen," the Sekani answered, smiling shyly up at her.

"I'm glad to meet you, Kalen," Kieren said.

"I'm happy to meet you, too," Kalen said. "Is it true you

can fly?" she blurted out excitedly.

"Yes," Kieren said. "Maybe I can take you up for a flight sometime, if this war ever ends."

The young Sekani's eyes grew wide, and she smiled for a moment before the smile disappeared and was replaced by a sad look. "I don't think my father would let me," she finally said.

"What's your father's name?" Kieren asked. "Maybe I can talk to him about it."

"Golena," Kalen answered. "But he's not here right now." She looked around dramatically and then whispered. "He was sent on a mission for Zanth."

"Well, when he comes back, I'll definitely talk to him about it," Kieren said. They had almost made it to the gate by then.

"Really?" Kalen said, looking up at her with wide eyes.

"Promise," Kieren said.

Kalen smiled wide and waved as she ran off, probably to tell her friends, Kieren assumed. She smiled as she finally arrived at the gate. She could see Rauph standing patiently on the other side, his arms crossed in front of him as he surveyed the Sekani compound.

"Hello, Rauphangelaa," she said, walking through the now-open iron gate and past the Sekani guards.

"Hello, Miss Grey," he said, smiling at her. "How have you been?"

"Busy," she said. "The Sekani were in pretty rough shape when we arrived. But they're doing much better now."

"So I've heard," he said. "This is part of the reason I'm here, actually."

"Oh?" she asked, wondering what he was getting at.

"Yes," he said, folding his hands before him nervously. "I was wondering. That is, I was wondering if you could do me a favor?"

◊

James wasn't sure what to expect when he went to visit Mazal in what had essentially become the Jirina district of Melaanse. The three species on Rajan had been separated by the Krahn and by necessity. The Krahn had no interest in the Jirina, knowing that they had neither the will nor the power to threaten them. He hadn't been back since first arriving on Rajan. He thought back to that time; it felt like it had been so long, though he realized that he and the others had only been on Rajan for a little over three months.

The first thing he noticed was that the streets were still full of debris, and in some cases, there were transport vehicles with the bodies still inside of them. Most of the Jirina were still too scared to leave their dwellings. James would have to speak to Mazal about it. They had better take care of the burned-out transport vehicles that had dead in them, at least. There was too great a chance of disease breaking out if the corpses were just left to rot. As James walked down the street that led to Mazal's place, he passed buildings and could see Jirina peeking out of the windows or from doors that were open just a few inches. And everywhere he walked, the Jirina smiled and waved at him.

He'd gathered a crowd by the time he reached Mazal's building. They began to chant his name, "James the Human! James the Human!" James wondered if he shouldn't have been a little more discreet. Although the Krahn had been pushed back from the northern part of the city, there was still a chance that a Krahn patrol could hear the commotion and come to see what it was. Maybe he should have come in his invisible mode. But then he thought about it a little while longer. Like it or not, he was a hero to them. They needed to *see* him. He gave them hope, and they would need all the hope they could get in the war that was coming. It was the reason he was paying a visit to Mazal. He needed to make sure that they were prepared for what was going to happen when they attacked the Krahn's southern stronghold. If things went against them, then the Krahn could retaliate, which meant that they all would be in danger, not just those engaged in the fighting.

James turned and waved at them all and waited for their chanting and feet stomping to stop. Once it did, he smiled. "Thank you for that welcome to your homes." He waited again for another round of chanting, feeling almost embarrassed now. "Thank you so much for your support, but the real hero here is Mazal. His courage and leadership is what is going to help you through this difficult time. I hope that you will extend to him the same faith."

There was another round of stamping of feet, which James had come to know was the equivalent of clapping on Earth, and the crowd began to dissipate, most of the Jirina returning to their buildings. Soon the street was clear once again. James hoped that it wouldn't stay that way for long. The Jirina needed to come out of hiding.

He turned toward the building and opened the front door, remembering where Mazal's room was located. He walked up to the door and, not seeing a doorbell, knocked. The door was opened and Mazal peeked around, looking nervous. His expression changed to joy when he saw who it was.

"James!" he said, smiling widely. He opened the door wider. "Come in, please."

James walked through the doorway and saw that there was an older-looking male and female Jirina sitting in the small room. "If I came at a bad time, I can return later," he said.

"Don't be dense," Mazal said. "You know my home is always open to you. I'd like you to meet Ternel and Dulen. There son is Fajel, whom you met at the strike teams meeting."

"Oh, yes," James said, smiling at the two Jirina. They didn't return the smile. "Very nice to meet you," James said, unsure if they were scared or just not very happy to see him.

They both stood and walked toward him. The female, Dulen, if he remembered correctly, spoke to him. "James the Human, I cannot say I am pleased that my son has volunteered to fight. I worry for his safety."

"So do I," James said, truthfully. "But he is fighting for something he believes in, and something that is essential if this planet is ever to be free again. I'm sorry that I cannot guarantee his safety to you. I truly wish I could."

"I pray that he returns safely to us," Ternel said, putting an arm around his mate. "But I dread losing both of my sons to the Krahn. It just doesn't seem fair."

"Both?" James asked, looking at Mazal.

"Yes," Mazal said, quietly. "Tenel, their oldest, was killed on the night of the first invasion. I think it's one of the reasons why Fajel volunteered."

"I'm sorry," James said, looking at both of them. "I did not know. I could contact Zanth and have him pull back Fajel's strike team—"

"No," Ternel said. "Fajel is no longer a youngling. He has made his own choice, and we're proud of him for doing this. We'll just worry until he is back safely to us."

"Then I will, as well," James said.

"Thank you for your words with us," Dulen said. She turned to Mazal. "We'll speak with you later, Mazal. I'm sure you have much to speak about with James the Human."

James cringed inwardly. He had told Mazal over and over

that his name was just James. Adding 'the Human' after it seemed too much like an honorific title. He waited for the two Jirina to leave, smiling and nodding to them one last time, and then turned to Mazal. "Why didn't you tell me when I met Fajel that he was the only son they had left?"

"Because I knew what your reaction would be," Mazal said. "Exactly what you are doing now, James. Like they said, Fajel has his horns. He is old enough to make his own choices, and we must honor that. I'm proud of him."

"I am as well," James said. "Hopefully he'll return safely from his mission."

Mazal motioned toward the chairs. "Please sit. I think I have some fernta around—"

James held his hand out toward the Jirina. "No, thanks. I don't know that I want to drink any right now. I have too much on my mind."

Mazal looked at him blankly, and James thought he might have offended him. "Well, one small glass wouldn't hurt," he said.

Mazal smiled and walked through a doorway that led to his kitchen. James shook his head and smiled. He walked over and sat on the chair that had been recently vacated by Fajel's parents.

Mazal soon appeared with a bottle of Fernta and two huge bowls. He filled up both and handed one to James. James took a small sip of the liquid for appearances and set the bowl down on the floor. "Thank you," he said, feeling the now familiar burn of the liquid in his throat.

"Now, I'm sure you didn't come here only to drink with me," Mazal said. "What can I do for you?"

"I was just wondering about the state of the Jirina," James replied. "I know that you are a peaceful species by nature. I wanted to make sure that the strain of the fighting was not becoming too much to handle."

"Do you doubt our heart?" Mazal asked after taking a large drink of his fernta.

"No, it's not that at all," James said. "I just know how difficult it must be for the Jirina to be involved in the fighting."

"I assure you, James," Mazal said, "we'll be there until the end, whatever that may turn out to be."

"I know you will, Mazal," James said. "I hope you don't think that I presumed it would be otherwise. I'm still not completely comfortable speaking Talondarian Standard. Sometimes my true meaning gets lost in the translation." He took a larger drink of his fernta. "I'm not worried about your heart," he began again. "I worry about your spirit. I don't want to win this war only for you to lose your customs. I've seen the effects of war on my own people. I don't want to see it happen to yours."

"I appreciate your concerns," Mazal said, putting his empty bowl on the floor. "They reflect my own. But there's really nothing that can be done about it now. We must prevail in the coming fight, or the state of our willpower won't matter. If we're to be broken, then let it be in our fight for freedom, and not as a species hiding from our own destiny."

James smiled, somehow not surprised by the Jirina's words. He had found out long before that the Rajani had underestimated their servants. He would never do it in the future.

◊

Dreben was on patrol around the farm, a weapon from the creatures that had attacked them strapped to his back. The creatures had returned twice since that first night. The second visit, Dreben and some of his farmhands had been able to ambush them within the Sekani and Jirina bunkhouse, where Dreben had set up a trap. He'd set up the door to the building to lock after it closed. It was held slightly ajar by a small piece of wood that fell away when they opened the door. Once the four creatures were locked in the building, Dreben had rammed their ship with a harvesting machine, knocking it from its landing gear and then rolling it onto its side to make sure it couldn't take off again.

Luckily, the ship had landed next to the rows of now knee-high plants, so no more of the harvest had been affected. After that, it was just a matter of waiting for the creatures to become desperate enough because of lack of food, water, and sleep to agree to surrender. It had taken almost two weeks before the pilot had opened the hatch on the ship. The creatures in the building had taken a week longer. They'd attempted everything, from shooting out the windows and trying to shoot out the handle on the only door, but to no avail. There were always a few of Dreben's farmhands waiting for them to come out, sharp farm instruments ready to jab at the creatures who may have tried to escape.

When they had finally opened the door of the building, Dreben found one of the creatures was dead and half-eaten by the others. In their desperation, they had turned to cannibalism. One of the creatures had attacked a Sekani farmhand and had been beaten and stabbed to death by the other Sekani and Jirina. That left two from the building and the pilot from the ship. Dreben had forced them to relinquish everything but their clothing and had sent them walking out toward the Desert of Ambraa.

Two days after they had left, another ship had appeared above the farm. By then, Dreben had made all of his farmhands set up a shelter beneath the cover of the orchard. They had even dragged the captured ship under the trees and were using it to store supplies. No farmhands were in the two bunkhouse buildings when the ship demolished them from the air, not even bothering to land afterward. Dreben and his workers had already removed anything valuable or usable from the buildings before the attack, so it wasn't a huge loss. The buildings could be rebuilt.

So now they worked the fields, knowing that the harvest would provide the only food they would have during the long cold and rainy season to come. But they also had armed lookouts always keeping an eye on the sky, which was why, when Dreben saw the object flying over the farm, all of the farmhands took cover in the orchard soon after that. He had four armed hands stay close to the orchard to protect the rest of the workers, and he ventured close to the burned-out remains of his former bunkhouse.

As the object got larger in his vision, it became more difficult to understand what it was. At first he'd believed it was another ship returning to investigate the scene, but as it came closer, he could see that it was no ship; at least not one he had ever seen before. To him it looked like a flying rock. Then he thought he saw what looked like two pairs of legs sticking out of the back of it, covered in the same stony substance.

Finally, the object touched down on the road leading to the farm, about five hundred yards away from where he crouched next to the still-smoldering timber that had once been his house. Then something happened that he never would have expected. The stony exterior disappeared as if it had never been there, exposing two individuals. One was much larger than the other, and Dreben could see that it was a fellow Rajani. The other was not anything he'd ever seen before. But his attention was on the Rajani, who was speaking in hushed whispers, lamenting the state of his farm.

"Rauphangelaa?" Dreben yelled, not believing what he was seeing at first. He slowly stepped out from his shelter.

The stony exterior suddenly appeared again around the creature that was with his boss as it stood in front of him, sheltering him from any threats.

"It's all right, Kieren," Rauphangelaa said, placing a hand on its shoulder. The exterior disappeared again, and as Dreben came closer, he could now see that it was actually a she, though he had no idea what species she was.

"Dreben," his boss said, a worried look on his face, "what happened here? Are you all right?"

"We've been attacked three times now from hideous creatures in ships," Dreben said. "The last time, they just came and destroyed the bunkhouses. We're all living out in the orchard now."

Rauphangelaa walked toward him slowly. As he reached his employee, he threw his arms around him, and Dreben returned the embrace for a moment. Then he stepped back and looked at his boss, smiling. "I didn't think you'd ever return."

"Forgive me," Rauphangelaa said. "I was away for a while. I went to get help." He turned to the female beside him. "This is Kieren. She is a Human, from a planet called Earth."

"Nice to meet you, Dreben," the one called Kieren said.

"Same to you," Dreben said, bowing slightly.

"Now that we've made our introductions," Rauphangelaa said, looking over Dreben's shoulder, "we need to get down to the reason I'm here." He began to walk toward the fields of plants. "You can't imagine the food shortage we're experiencing back in Melaanse. I'm pleased to see that you haven't abandoned the farm."

"I know my duty, Rauphangelaa," Dreben said. "Besides, there was nowhere else to go. We didn't know what these creatures were that were attacking us, or where'd they'd come from. We were just awaiting word."

"They are known as the Krahn Horde," Kieren said.

"Krahn, eh?" Dreben said. "We killed one that was trying his best to eat one of my farmhands, and they killed one of their own and ate him while we had them trapped in the bunkhouse over there." He pointed at one of the burning piles of rubble.

"If my calculations of the height of the plants are correct," Rauphangelaa said. "The harvest should be on schedule. The jubka should be ready to pick in four standard weeks, and the guardo trees should be ready to pick in about five."

"That's correct," Dreben said.

"I can only say that I'm thankful that we'll have anything at all," Rauphangelaa said. "I don't know the state of the other farms. I don't know yet if this is all we'll have to feed thousands. I hope not. All I can say is that, the Krahn attacks notwithstanding, this is still a much safer place for all of you than the city. I would be most grateful if you and your workers could stay on until the harvest is complete."

"Of course," Dreben said. "Like I said, we don't have anywhere else to go." He looked back toward the orchard and saw Terin approaching, followed by some of the other farmhands. "But I do have one request to make before you leave again," he said.

"If I can fulfill it, I will," Rauphangelaa said.

"I want one large bunkhouse built after all of this is over," he said, turning to his boss.

"Yes, I can make that happen," Rauphangelaa said. "Do you need anything right now?"

"We could use some food supplies ourselves, if you can spare them," Dreben answered. "I don't want my hands turning on each other like the Krahn did." He smiled at his boss, letting him know it had been a joke on his part, but also to let him know how truly happy he was to see him.

"I'll have Kieren return with what we can spare," Rauphangelaa said. "As you can see, she can get around a little better than me."

"Yes, your entrance was quite impressive," Terin said, finally reaching where the three of them stood.

"Thank you," Kieren said, smiling at them.

"Then it's settled," Rauphangelaa announced. "I'll go now, but Kieren will bring back supplies for all of you." He was speaking to the entire gathered group of farmhands now, his voice raised so that they could all hear him. "As I told Dreben, I'm very grateful to have such dedicated workers in my employ. After this war is over, no matter the outcome, I promise that you shall have updated quarters and amenities, as well as the thanks of all who live on Rajan. Kieren, if you would?"

The female, a Human, he thought she was called, walked up behind Rauphangelaa and placed her arms under his and clasped her hands around his chest. Suddenly, they were once again surrounded by the stony exterior and began to slowly rise off the ground.

"Be careful," Rauphangelaa called down to them as they built up more speed and moved away from where Dreben and his workers all stood, watching them become smaller and smaller in the sky. He hoped that she would return quickly.

◊

James waited patiently in the meeting room inside the Sekani compound. The meeting place had been an acknowledgment to the Sekani and their leader, Zanth, of the importance that they had played in the attack on the northern Krahn base. James needed to keep the Sekani involved, or he feared he might lose them in the ever-changing political relations and maneuverings between the Rajani and Sekani. He'd asked the leaders of the three species to meet and talk about plans for the future. Yes, they had won a great victory over the Krahn, but there was still much more that needed to be done. It was difficult enough trying to win a war without having the two species arguing over every part of the strategy.

When he had arrived at the Sekani compound, he'd been politely ushered to a small room and left to sit, wondering where the others were. *Late, as usual,* he thought. He was beginning to think that each of them needed a personal assistant to help them keep their appointments. He was interrupted in his musings by the door opening. Mazal entered, led by the same Sekani female who had shown James to the room. Mazal bowed to her briefly and then turned to James, smiling. "James! How are you?"

"Doing well," James replied. "And you?"

"Busy," Mazal said, sitting in a chair across from James at the table. "Very busy, as usual. I apologize for being late."

"Well, as you can see," James said, "you're not the only one. I know this meeting was a bit last-minute, but I was hoping for a better showing."

Just then, the door opened once again, and Zanth and Kedar entered behind the Sekani female. They were in the middle of an argument, and both of them only nodded to James as they sat down at the table, continuing their discussion about whether to wait on attacking the southern Krahn headquarters or doing it as fast as possible to maximize the element of surprise.

James sat and listened for a moment before clearing his throat. Both Zanth and Kedar looked at him. "And here I thought you two were late to the meeting. I see you actually started it before you arrived."

Both Kedar and Zanth were polite enough to look somewhat chagrined by James's words. "I apologize," Kedar said. "We ran into each other in the hall, and I guess we were too impatient in our haste to work out our differences."

"It's understandable," James said. "I know that you both want what is best for your species."

"Then you see why it is imperative that we attack the Krahn now, while they are still caught off-guard by our most recent victory," Zanth said.

"I'm afraid that I have to agree with Kedar on this," James said. "To surge headlong into another fight so quickly after the last could prove disastrous."

"We have the momentum. We must continue on the present course," Zanth said.

"I thought this meeting was to decide what the present course was," Mazal protested.

James, Zanth, and Kedar all looked at the Jirina, surprised that he had spoken up. "That's correct, Mazal," James said, smiling inside, though he kept a serious exterior. His Jirina friend had changed quite a bit from the first time they'd met.

"Then what would you propose?" Kedar asked Mazal.

"I think we need to wait at least until we hear from the strike teams and their level of success in stealing or destroying Krahn ships," Mazal answered, looking at each of them in turn. "I think we were very lucky that we were only attacked by three Krahn ships in our last battle. If more had come, we may not have been as successful as we were."

"I agree on that point," Kedar said.

"Besides," Mazal said, "the Jirina need time to recover. I don't think they would do very well if they were thrust into another fight so soon after this last one."

"Are you saying that we wouldn't have the Jirinas' support if we went now?" Zanth asked, a note of anger entering his voice.

"No," Mazal said. "I'm only saying that the support may not be as strong as it could be once the Jirina have had a chance to rest and recuperate from fighting. We're not like the Sekani or the Rajani, I'm afraid. We fight because we must, but we find no solace in knowing it's the right thing to do. I'm afraid that we may never recover if forced to fight for too long a span."

"I would have to agree with Mazal," James said, thinking about the conversation he and the Jirina had earlier that day. "Our troops need a break between fighting, or their morale will be shot. Let them savor their victory for a few days. I say we wait to hear from the strike teams, but we give ourselves a deadline also, just in case. If we haven't heard anything in say, seven standard days, then we attack the Krahn base in the south of Melaanse."

"I second that motion," Kedar said, looking over at Zanth. James knew that the two spent a lot of time together and had grown to respect each other. He hoped that it would help keep their alliance strong.

"I can see that I've been outvoted," Zanth said with a sigh, looking around at the others. "Seven standard days it is. But I also propose we meet again within three to talk about our strategy in the attack. And I say we bring more than just those present now. The more voices that can contribute, the better, I think."

"Then it's agreed," James said, standing up. "I thank you all for coming today, and look forward to speaking with you again soon."

"As always," Kedar said, standing also and smiling, "we appreciate your willingness to assist us with our petty squabbles."

After Kedar and Zanth had walked out of the door to the room, leaving James and Mazal alone, James turned to his friend. "I'm impressed at your newfound negotiating acumen," he said.

Mazal smiled shyly up at him. "I only said what I said to support your argument, James. I have no ego, and neither do my species, when it comes to this sort of thing, really. Yes, my species does have pride in ourselves, but that is a different thing altogether."

"Well, I'm just happy that you're on my side," James said, returning the smile. "I will talk to you soon, my friend," he said, shaking the Jirina's hand.

Chapter 17

Kieren was heading out to have lunch with Yvette. She had just returned from ferrying food and supplies out to Rauph's farm outside the city. After that, she had a short meeting with Zanth, where he'd informed her of the outcome of his meeting with James, Kedar, and Mazal. He had not seemed happy about what was decided, so she'd done her best to placate him. She and Yvette hadn't had the chance to talk since the *Tukuli* crashed. They had a lot of catching up to do. Yvette had said that James would be in meetings all day, so they had agreed to meet at the gateway of the Sekani compound.

Kieren had shown up early, after the meeting with Zanth had ended earlier than she thought it would. He wanted to start sending out scavenging parties north of Melaanse, to find whatever they could that would be usable. He wanted a better idea of where they should go, so he'd asked her if she would scout the territory from the air first. He'd been thrilled by her report of Rauph's farm and the promise of fresh fruit and vegetables at harvest time. Kieren had willingly agreed. Any chance to be able to fly, no matter what the mission, she'd take it.

She was standing with her back against a stone pillar

at the entrance to the Sekani compound when she noticed Gianni and his little band of Sekani warriors approaching. They had a Krahn tied up and gagged, and were leading it toward the compound.

"I don't think Zanth would appreciate you bringing a Krahn this close to the compound," she said, smiling at Gianni.

He didn't return her smile. "That's what I tried to tell them," he said.

One of the Sekani—Botran, she thought he was named— went ahead into the compound. "I think they brought him back to interrogate him," Gianni said. "So, are you waiting here for your boyfriend, or what?"

Kieren froze for a second. Had David said something about what had happened the other night? "What do you mean?" she asked.

"Oh, c'mon. Don't give me that Miss Innocent routine," Gianni said. "I saw him go into your room. You must have really missed him while he was gone."

"That's really none of your business, Gianni," she said. "What, were you spying on me?"

"No," he answered defensively. "I was just walking past, and I happened to see you throw your doors open wide for him."

"How dare you," Kieren said, seeing the obvious sexual connotation he was making. She'd meant to explain that David had left shortly afterward, but she wouldn't give him the satisfaction of making some kind of crude joke about David's sexual stamina. He could keep guessing. "What I do with my time is none of your concern. I'll spend it with whoever I want." She could feel tears in her eyes, and that just made her even angrier. Yvette walked up to the compound. "Hey, guys, what's going on?" she asked, smiling at them.

"Nice catch," she said in Talondarian Standard to the Sekani, looking at the Krahn warrior.

"Nothing," Kieren answered, wiping her eyes. "Nothing's going on." She looked at Gianni. "We're done here." She grabbed Yvette's arm and led her away from the compound. She'd tried to work things out with him on too many occasions, and she could see now that he'd never change. She was finished trying. She hoped she could just be far enough away from him before she started crying in earnest.

◊

Ronak sometimes woke up in the night wondering where he was. Other times he just pondered how it had come to this; banished, light years from home and now losing a war he had started with such confidence that losing hadn't even entered his mind. He would only admit the fact that they were losing to his bloodmate, and only when they were alone in their private chambers.

No matter how much he yelled; railed against counselors and his warriors alike, it wasn't enough. He'd believed that the fact that the Rajani were now a bunch of spiritual hermits would mean they could walk right in and take over. And since no one would come to their aid; his contact at Galactic Intelligence had assured him of that. They were safe to search for the Stones no matter how long it took. If not for the one ship that had escaped, the plan would have worked perfectly. And then, to top it all off, Krahn ships had arrived with food and aid supplies. His cursed brother had tried to help his enemies. He added it to his list of grievances against Maliq.

He'd had no choice but to board the three ships and kill all aboard before they could make planet fall. One of his captains—his own nephew (one of hundreds, at least)—had questioned his orders to kill his brother's followers. He'd then had the temerity to suggest that Ronak had made a mistake by attacking the Rajani now and not waiting until their own numbers were stronger. He'd taken great pleasure in watching the captain slowly skinned alive and fed his own flesh before Ronak personally cut off his head. The denuded skull now adorned the steps to his throne, a warning to others of what happened to traitors.

Ronak now sat upon that throne and waited for word that his lander was prepped and ready. He and his bloodmate would oversee the war from the planet's surface. The loss of his largest nestbase in the north of the city had sent him into rants; it had taken him days to calm down. When he could finally think past the red fury in his mind, he had known that he had to personally go down to the planet, or else all would be lost. His troops were already running short on fuel and supplies. Soon it would be too late for all of his warriors to even leave the planet. They must crush the rebellion and find the Stones, or he would never be able to challenge his brother and claim the Krahnish throne. And if it meant killing every inhabitant of the planet below, then so be it. His GI contact, T'van, had all but sanctioned it.

Just then, one of his counselors, Martek, entered the throne room and bowed to Ronak. "Mighty Qadira," he said, still bowing. "You have a communication on the private channel."

"Is it my idiot cousin Toruq on Rajan?" Ronak asked.

"No, Mighty Qadira," Martek answered. "The caller claims to be from Galactic Intelligence."

"I'll take it in my private chambers," Ronak said, standing up. He was surprised. He hadn't talked to the agent named T'van in weeks. The last time they'd talked, T'van had assured him that all Alliance concerns had been taken care of, and he wouldn't have to worry about any surprises while on Rajan. No matter, Ronak thought. *He probably just wants a progress report.* He would lie, of course, but then, he didn't think T'van was being entirely truthful with him, either.

He made his way to his chambers and found the computer room empty. He looked at the computer screen and saw the words 'communication open' blinking on it. Unfortunately, the distances were too great between stars to use voice communication. But the Alliance had found a way to attach text information to cosmic rays, essentially allowing them to travel to any point in the galaxy almost instantaneously. He pressed the screen where it read 'acknowledge.' A line of text appeared on the screen.

Eyes Only: Ronak, High Vasin of the Krahn Horde.

What do you want, T'van? he typed.

T'van is no longer assigned to this case, the line back stated.

What? Ronak typed. *Who is this?*

Not important, came the immediate reply. *This is to inform you that you will no longer receive aid from usual sources.*

Ronak knew what that meant. Whoever it was didn't want to state that GI had anything to do with his little invasion.

This is last communiqué, a line on the screen read. *Wish you luck in your endeavors.*

"They can't do this," Ronak said, under his breath. He typed. *When I need your help, I will ask for it, you piece of pond filth.* He was so angry that he raked his nails across the top of the desk he was sitting at, creating long grooves in the wood. He waited a moment for a reply, but it seemed the conversation was at an end. He picked up the screen and threw it across the room. It shattered as it struck the wall. He let out an inarticulate scream. After a moment, he calmed down enough for rational thought. He didn't need their help, anyways. He would win this war on his own, if he needed to.

Kalik, his main counselor, entered his chambers. "Mighty Qadira, are you all right? Did the computer malfunction?"

Ronak turned to him, his eyes still wide with anger. "Yes, of course, I'm fine. Inform Mariqa that I want to speak with her as soon as possible."

Kalik bowed and left the chamber. Ronak looked down at the jagged pieces of glass from the computer screen, each one reflecting a different portion of his face back to him. It seemed he really was alone in this fight, but it was a fight he was resolved to win, no matter the cost.

◊

Gianni was sitting on the ground outside of his room in the Sekani compound, drinking fernta from a bottle. He and some of the Sekani males that he knew had just returned from another patrol, where they hadn't even seen a single Krahn. *Typical,* he thought. The one time he really wanted to take his anger out on someone, and even that didn't work out for him. What was more disappointing was that he'd been stupid enough to lose Kieren to David, of all people. Of course, her choices were limited, but that wasn't the point.

He wondered if he did it to himself on purpose, unwilling to let anyone past his defenses. At first, he'd done his best to keep all of the others away, unsure of his situation and knowing that if they found out what he'd done for a living, it would be all they thought of him from then on. Especially after he found out that James was the cop that lived in his building. He'd managed to act like a jerk to all of them at one time or another on the ship, but after a while it had just been easier to play the part than show them who he really was. Or at least who he thought he was. He wasn't sure anymore.

When he'd arrived on Rajan and began helping the Sekani, he'd been able to change the way he viewed others. They didn't care about his former life. They needed his help now. And he was happy to be needed, and to be able to make a difference in their lives. But he'd neglected his relationship with Kieren, and she'd moved on. He took a long swig of fernta and winced. He just needed to go to bed and sleep it off, he knew. Then he saw David. He was walking a few hundred yards away, looking like he was heading toward Kieren's room again. Gianni stood up, unsteady from drinking fernta on an empty stomach. He began walking toward the other man.

◊

David wasn't sure what he was going to do when he got to Kieren's place. Apologize for storming out earlier? Ask her if she wanted to give them another try? Maybe he'd moved too quickly the first time. He'd let the situation get away from him, he knew that now. And if she still rebuffed him, then what? His thoughts had been dark since he'd woken up in the Rajani medical facility and learned that Janan had been taken by the Krahn. He'd been able to curb his more violent tendencies aboard the Tukuli, but once on Rajan, and especially after the loss of his friend, he'd fallen into the same black hole of despair that he'd been in back on Earth. He was unloved. He was unwanted by those that he loved. And in his despondency, he was lashing out once again. The Krahn were easy targets, though a bit too simple to kill for his tastes. He was broken out of his reverie by the sound of a bottle dropping to the ground and breaking close behind him. He turned and just managed to duck a haymaker from Gianni.

"You sonuvabitch," Gianni said, a slight slurring to his words. He'd been drinking, David could see—and smell. Gianni took another swing at him, and he instantly powered up and ran around behind the other man before he'd even completed the punch. He dropped his power field and put

Gianni in a full-nelson, wrapping both of his arms under Gianni's and interlocking his fingers behind the other man's neck.

"What the hell is your problem?" he asked.

"No powers, you little shit," Gianni said. "Just you and me. No powers."

"Fine," David said, unlocking his fingers and pushing the other man forward, away from him. This had been a long time coming. It was time to finally end it. He curled his hands into fists and brought them up in front of him. Gianni was taller and probably outweighed him by twenty pounds, but he was also drunk and uncoordinated at the moment, if his first two punches were any indication. David hadn't been in a fight since his freshman year in high school, and even then, it had been more of a pushing match than anything else. He ducked a roundhouse swing and brought his right fist up into Gianni's gut. He heard a satisfying *woof* of expelled air, and Gianni dropped to the ground on all fours, heaving for breath.

"You're pitiful," David said. "You act like an ass to everyone around you, and I'm sick of it." He swung his fist and connected with Gianni's left cheek, knocking the other man on his back. He thought about kicking him in the ribs for good measure, but then he looked up and noticed that they had begun to draw a crowd of Sekani to their little bout. "I don't know why you even bothered coming with us. You're worthless." He stopped a moment, shocked to hear his father's words coming out of his own mouth. A swirl of emotions rose up inside of him.

Just then, he heard Kieren yell, "Stop!" He turned and saw her running toward them. When she got closer, he could see that her eyes were puffy from crying. He could also see Yvette trailing along behind her. He'd have to wait to talk to her. Now was not the time. There were too many other people around, and he felt...confused. As she approached, all he mumbled was, "He started it," knowing how lame it sounded. He turned and walked away, hating that he heard her asking Gianni if he was all right. He needed to get away. He quickly powered up and ran toward the coast, to think.

◊

Kieren and Yvette had talked for a while, and Kieren had cried, but felt better for it. It was nice to have another woman around to talk to about her problems. She'd determined that she was better off without Gianni. He was too difficult to deal with, and had truly hurt her by what he'd said when they'd argued earlier. She was heading back to show Yvette her room at the Sekani compound when they'd both seen the commotion. She stopped a passing Sekani female. "What's going on?"

The Sekani female, Setanni, smiled. "I think there's a fight in the courtyard. The Human males are having an argument."

"Thank you," Kieren said, smiling back at her and hurriedly moving toward the gathering groups of hooting Sekani males. She picked up her pace even more when she saw Gianni kneeling on the ground in front of David. Then David punched him in the face. As he tumbled to the ground, her heart felt like it stopped for a moment in her chest.

She finally reached them, and David mumbled something, but she didn't hear what he said. She knelt down next to Gianni, smelling the fernta on his ragged breath. "Are you all right?" she asked. He didn't answer for a moment, and she thought at first that he'd been knocked unconscious.

Then he opened his eyes slowly, his left cheek and eye already starting to swell. "Ow," he said quietly, and smiled at her. She smiled back at him, glad to see that he seemed okay.

She looked up to see that David had disappeared somewhere. Gianni began to sit up slowly. She reached out to help him, but he gently pushed her hand away. "No, I'm okay," he said. "I deserved it. Started it."

"What a surprise," Yvette said, walking up to them. "At least you got it out of your system now. A good ass-kicking will tend to do that."

"Why did you start it?" Kieren asked, although she thought that she already knew the answer.

"Doesn't matter anymore," Gianni said, staggering to his feet. "Too late. You...made your choice." He walked away, leaving her kneeling on the ground.

She stood quickly and followed him, ignoring the Sekani who were still gathered in the courtyard, watching them. She came around in front of him and stood there with her hand pushed out at his chest. "Yes, I did make a choice. It was you, you asshole. And you blew it." She was beginning to cry again, and she stopped talking to wipe her eyes. "Why do you always blow it?" she asked softly, looking up at him.

He stopped and finally looked her in the eye. "I'm sorry," he said after a moment. "It's complicated. I-I think I'm going to be sick." He staggered over to a building and threw up, bending over and then going to his knees as the spasms racked his body.

"Typical man," Yvette said, though she softened the words with a gentle hand on Kieren's shoulder. "C'mon, I think he needs to be alone for a while."

"Yeah," Kieren said, turning away from him. "So do I."

◊

Yvette was exhausted from her day. Who knew that hanging out with Kieren and Gianni would be so difficult? She returned to her house to find James already in bed, sleeping. She knew that he had a lot on his mind, and was busy in meetings for most of the day, but she was still disappointed that he wasn't awake to talk to her about her day with the dysfunctional love triangle. She slowly got undressed and slipped into bed next to him. She wasn't too concerned about waking him. He didn't stir as she climbed in beside him and pulled the covers up over her. She sighed. There was only one thing to do. She stuck both of her bare feet on his legs. He jumped, as she knew he would. Her feet were always cold.

Without turning, James spoke. "I hope that's you, Yvette."

She poked him in the side. "Who else would it be?"

He turned toward her, smiling. "In this place, who knows?"

She could smell the fernta on his breath. She knew that the custom on Rajan was to drink it as a show of friendship, but it didn't mean she wanted him drinking it all of the time. "You didn't brush your teeth," she said, scrunching up her nose.

He stopped smiling. "Yeah, I know. I was just so tired when I finally got home. And the fernta didn't help, either. I was talking to Mazal about the plans for the coming battle, and he wouldn't let me even start without drinking a glass of the stuff. And that was after sitting and drinking with him this morning too."

"I could tell," she said. "So..."

"So I'm going, I'm going," he said, sitting up. He went into the bathroom, and she could hear him spitting after a few minutes. They didn't have running water, nor did they have the nifty little contraptions that they'd used on the *Tukuli,* so they'd been forced to improvise toothbrushes and use water from bottles. It was better than nothing.

When he returned to bed, she snuggled up against him,

glad that he was there. "Much better," she said, softly.

"Tough day?" he asked, returning her embrace.

"Not so much for me," she said. "I was Kieren's shoulder to cry on. Twice."

"Oh," he said. "Gianni?"

"And David," she said.

"Really?" he asked, arching his brows.

"We have our very own soap opera," she said.

"As the Alien Worlds Turn," he said dryly.

She looked up at his face, seeing that he was smiling. "You have no idea," she said, smiling back at him. "I'm so glad that I picked you."

"Me too," he said. "More than you know."

She kissed him on the lips, and then turned away from him, feeling his strong arms slip around her as she drifted off to sleep.

Chapter 18

Fajel didn't sleep well that day. Whether it was because he was worried about the mission, or the simple fact that the sun had lit the room they were in and was telling his body that it was time to be waking and not sleeping, he couldn't say. He spent the day changing his position on the floor and trying to get comfortable as the shadows changed around the room. Finally, as the sun began to sink behind the horizon, he sat up, disgusted that he'd managed to sleep for only three hours the entire day. But at least he felt somewhat rested, if a little stiff from lying on the floor. His stomach, however, told him that he wouldn't last very long without something to eat. Protein bars didn't go a long way on filling him up.

Rachal was snoring softly in the corner, and Belani was taking his turn at watch at the door of the building. Fajel had spent his time on watch thinking about his parents and watching a pair of masagas, which seemed to be everywhere in the ruined city, chase each other amongst the rubble. *They really are disgusting creatures,* he thought.

As the day grew darker, Belani entered and kicked Rachal's foot, startling the Rajani awake. "Get up, it's time to go," the Sekani said, sounding like he wished he'd been able to kick the Rajani harder but didn't have a good enough excuse to do it. Fajel thought the Sekani had been acting strange from the moment they'd set out. He was belligerent, even angry at times, and for no detectable reason. And most of his anger seemed directed at Fajel.

Guess we all handle our fear differently, he thought as Rachal sputtered awake. Fajel threw the Rajani the last of their protein bars, and they sat, eating silently together while Belani dithered with his pack, seeming to look through its contents but not really paying attention to what was there.

None of them spoke as the room grew dark, signaling that it was time to leave. Fajel said a silent prayer and hefted his pack to his shoulders, feeling the soreness in his back and shoulders return immediately. Belani scanned the area outside their temporary refuge and they left. Only the masagas watched them leave, and when the Krahn arrived shortly afterward, they scattered.

◊

Welemaan tuc Xenaani had grown up on the ocean of Rajan. His father owned a fleet of ocean-going vessels and took pride in knowing how to operate all of them, even if he wasn't the day-to-day pilot of any of the ships. As an Elder, Xenaani's time had been consumed with more important duties. But he had loved the ocean, and had imparted that love upon his son, taking him out with him on many occasions and teaching him how to handle just about any sized ship.

When Welemaan had agreed to become a member of a strike team that would be heading to the south of Melaanse to find the Krahn's main airbase, he hadn't known at the time that he wouldn't be in charge of it. The announcement at the meeting had been a surprise, and not a pleasant one. On top of that, he had tried to impart his knowledge of the area to Zanth, the leader of the Sekani, and had been treated with nothing but condescension from the Sekani. Even his friend

Volaan had sided with the Sekani leader.

No, he's Kedar now, Welemaan thought. Kedar might be willing to give up his Elder name, but Welemaan would keep his. The name was not just a ritualistic change; it was a title that said he should be respected. Kedar meant well, he was sure, but Welemaan believed that his friend and the new Sekani leader were wrong. There was too much risk approaching the airfield from the north, and Welemaan, for one, was not going to take the chance of being caught before his mission was completed.

As soon as he and the two other members of the strike team left for the airfield, he began to work on Y'tan, the Sekani who had been placed in charge of the trio. Finally Y'tan had relented and agreed to sail down the coast of the continent, and the three of them headed east toward the coast to search for a ship that was still serviceable. When they arrived at the coast, they found that most of the larger ships had been destroyed in the initial Krahn attack, but they finally managed to find a small ship that was in dry-dock, but turned out to be oceanworthy, at least, though it would need to be constantly bailed out. Welemaan wasn't going to be picky. They would stay close to the coastline, anyway, and would arrive in good time to complete their mission.

◊

Ronak, Mariqa, and Ronak's counselors arrived on Rajan in the middle of the night. Ronak's plan was to use the cover of darkness to mask the fact that he was there. That plan went straight into the defecation chute when they exited the lander to find a full military formation waiting for them, with his cousin Toruq at its head.

"I see now why things are going so badly down here," Ronak said when he made his way to his cousin. "You are still as stupid as ever, Toruq."

"I assumed you'd need an escort from the airfield—" Toruq began.

"What I *need* is someone who will follow my orders," Ronak said, his plumage raised in dominance.

"B-but—" Toruq said, sputtering when he saw the expression on his cousin's face. He'd seen it directed at soon-to-be dead Krahn warriors plenty of times before.

"But *nothing*," Ronak said. "Because of your incompetence, the Rajani are sure to know now that I've come down to their accursed planet. But no matter, I'm here to put us back on track. Our mission will succeed despite your utter lack of intelligence. You're relieved of your command." Ronak and Mariqa walked past him, followed by his counselors. Toruq was left standing in disbelief.

"Are our forces in position?" Ronak asked, turning to Kalik.

"Yes, Vasin," Kalik responded. "The Rajani 'strike teams,' as they call themselves, should all be approaching our airfield from the north. Our Sekani contact has provided us with an approximation of their locations."

"The information had better be correct," Ronak said. "The airfield is of vital importance. We've already lost Nestbase Two because of my cousin. We cannot afford to lose the airfield. Is that understood?"

"Yes, Mighty Vasin," Kalik responded, bowing. He turned and hurriedly walked away from the procession.

Ronak turned to look at his bloodmate. "So, what should I do with Toruq? I grow tired of killing incompetent warriors."

"I don't think you should kill him quite yet," Mariqa said. "He could still prove to be valuable to us."

"But where to keep him," Ronak said absent-mindedly as he climbed aboard a transport vehicle that would take them to Nestbase One.

"I've thought of the perfect place," Mariqa said, climbing in next to him on the seat of the vehicle. "And he won't even have to go very far."

◊

The night passed uneventfully for Fajel and his companions as they made their way through the heart of the city. They had not seen a Krahn patrol in hours. The night was warm, and Fajel found himself plodding along, falling into a semi-trance at the rhythmic sound of his own footfalls. He kept his eyes on the ground, no longer wanting to see the devastation around him. The center of the city seemed to have been the hardest hit in the initial Krahn attack. There were hardly any standing structures left, though there were still enough large pieces of rubble to hide their passage. Soon the buildings grew recognizable again, though most were still damaged. They also began to spread out more as the three reached the southern edge of the city. Fajel could see a large compound in the distance to his left, which stood out in the predawn light.

"That would have to be the Krahn base," Rachal said softly, pointing toward the group of buildings. Fajel was definitely awake now. They were near their destination, and the danger of being discovered was at its greatest. He could feel his mouth grow dry at the thought.

"We head southwest," Belani said, pointing out the direction. He had an edge to his voice that made Fajel pause.

Is he going to crack under the pressure of the mission? Fajel wondered as he looked at Belani's pinched face. They were all under a lot of stress, but Belani's anxiety had seemed to become worse the farther south they had traveled. They walked on for a short time before Rachal, who was on point, suddenly crouched down, motioning for the others to do the same. Fajel knelt down uncomfortably, his pack threatening to topple him over, and wondered what Rachal had seen. He soon heard the sound of footsteps approaching. He saw that both Rachal and Belani were clutching their weapons tightly.

Fajel was surprised when Belani suddenly smiled and said something softly in a language that he'd never heard before. The sound of footsteps stopped abruptly, and there was only silence for a moment. Then someone answered back in the same language as three figures emerged from the gloom. It was another strike team.

There were quiet but happy greetings all around as the two teams came together. Fajel had never met the Rajani named Velden nor the Sekani named Golena, but the Jirina named Ardel had been a friend of his brother. Ardel embraced him warmly when he saw who it was. "Tenel would be proud of you, Fajel," he said.

"Don't hug him too hard," Rachal said, smiling. "He's liable to go off." Even Fajel had to laugh.

"We did a preliminary reconnaissance of the airfield," Velden said. He was a young Rajani, and seemed very excitable to Fajel. "There was no ground cover on the western side, so we backtracked to go around east. There are some trees that are close enough on that side that should provide what we need."

"We can't go that way," Belani said sternly. "It takes us too close to the Krahn base. We're liable to get trapped between the Krahn on the airfield and those at the base."

"But there's nothing on the western side of the airfield except a very small grove of trees," Golena said. "We saw for ourselves."

"You go east if you want," Belani said, "but my team is going west. I won't risk their safety or the success of this mission."

"You always were a stubborn fool," Golena said. Fajel

guessed that the two Sekanis had known each other a while. It was hard to guess their ages, but he thought that Golena seemed the older of the two.

"Be that as it may," Belani said, moving closer to look straight into Golena's eyes, "no one is telling me how to run my strike team. If you're heading east, then go." Belani turned and began walking the way he had initially pointed before they had joined up with the others.

Golena looked like he might have pursued Belani to continue the discussion, but Velden placed a hand on his shoulder. Golena finally shrugged off the hand and turned away from the direction that Belani had departed. He didn't say another word.

"Well," Ardel said, "I guess this is where we part ways." He gave Fajel one more quick embrace and whispered "good luck," and then the two parties set off in their separate directions.

Fajel carried his pack in his arms, still uneasy about its contents. Rachal shook his head and muttered quietly, but Fajel couldn't make out any of the words. His own joy at seeing his brother's friend had been dampened by Belani's attitude. Finally, they caught up to the grumpy Sekani.

"Hope you know what you're doing," was all Rachal said. Belani didn't reply.

They walked a moment in silence. Fajel was beginning to wonder if they were doing the right thing, or if Belani's stubbornness would cause their entire mission to fail.

They walked nearly to the top of a low knoll when Belani motioned for them to stop. He took off his pack and crawled to the crest. "The airfield is just over the hill," he said quietly. Fajel gratefully placed his pack on the ground and stood up straight.

"Now, how would you—" Rachal began, before the sound

of gunfire rang out, silencing the dran that had been singing out, welcoming the early morning. Fajel thought Rachal had punched him in the middle of the back. He turned slowly to ask why the Rajani had hit him and saw that Rachal was now lying on the ground, a look of surprise on his face and a large puddle of blood growing next to him.

"No!" he heard Belani cry out.

"What?" was all Fajel could say, confused still. His legs felt heavy. He looked down to see his own blood running down his legs from a gaping wound in his abdomen. Just then, his knees gave out, and he tumbled to the ground, his pack forcing him to his side on the soft grass.

"You said they wouldn't be harmed," he heard Belani say.

Fajel's legs felt cold now. Belani stepped into his field of vision. Fajel could see a group of Krahn warriors now behind the Sekani. Belani came closer and bent over him.

"Stupid youngling," Belani whispered. "I don't care about the Rajani oppressor, but I tried to save your life on more than one occasion."

Fajel was still confused.

"I did what you told me," Belani said. He had stood back up and was talking to the Krahn. "Where are my siblings?"

The last thing that Fajel saw before the world went dark was one of the Krahn warriors raising its weapon and pointing it at Belani's head.

The End - Resistance

Look for

The Rajani Chronicles III: War
by Brian S. Converse

Coming in early 2019!

Updates on

www.BrianSConverse.com

www.ingramcontent.com/pod-product-compliance
Lightning Source LLC
Chambersburg PA
CBHW021000120726
47905CB00009B/2784

* 9 7 8 0 9 9 8 7 9 6 4 5 1 *